Game of Scones: The Cana Island Lighthouse Mystery

Kathryn Buchen

1

For all the Kindred Spirits

The meaning of life is to find your gift. The purpose of life is to give it away.

--- William Shakespeare

Kindred spirits are not so scarce as I used to think. It's splendid to find out there are so many of them in the world.

--- L.M. Montgomery, *Anne of Green Gables*

Chapter One: Scone with the Wind

Gather ye rosebuds while ye may,

Old time is still a-flying;

And this same flower that smiles today

Tomorrow will be dying.

--From *To the Virgins, to Make Much of Time*, by Robert Herrick

It was high summer in Door County. The jeweled colors of the season shone in the golden fields of corn and wheat, the scarlet cherry trees, the ruby red, cerise, jade, violet, lavender, magenta, sapphire, purple, and saffron of the gardens. I gazed out the window in a daydream until Krystal rudely interrupted my thoughts.

"Everybody is in bed with everybody. All these old people in their thirties and forties are climbing into bed all over the place. It's disgusting! There is so much moral turpentine in this town I can't stand it!" said Krystal.

"Don't you mean moral turpitude?" I asked.

"Yes, exactly. A lot of immoral people drowning in their own turp and tude. Especially my part time gig boss, Pilar Lightfoot."

"Right," I said. "Something like that."

"You know why all these men fall for Pilar, don't you?" asked Krystal.

"Why?" I asked. "Because she is married and doesn't want them to divorce their wives and marry her. She is also beautiful, filthy rich, without moral judgment, and a total nympho."

"All that, but mainly because she knows how to do hooker sex," said Krystal.

"What do you mean?" I asked.

"Do I have to explain everything to you, Sister Tabitha of the Convent of the Virgin Martyr? With all the lovers Pilar has had, I'll bet my employee of the month parking space that she lures them in with experienced call girl sex. How many marriages has she broken up and destroyed?"

5

"Your guess is as good as mine," I said. "At least three, maybe four. She is getting to be a real cougar. She likes them young. Of course, I heard that her husband Nick is a runaround male slut, so I guess that works both ways. Yes, I heard that he is a sidewinder, a rapscallion runaround. This is still a small town, you know, and word gets around."

"Yup, Nick is a real devil. There is a reason that the devil is always portrayed as a man. Men are evil. Yup, they're devils, alright, especially our Mr. Nick. Did you know that the devil is sometimes referred to as Old Nick? As for Pilar, she could be a high-class call girl. She has the experience and the attitude. She would make a great call girl if she weren't a rich heiress," said Krystal. "I'll bet you lunch at the Screaming Seagull that she was in bed with at least fifty men by the time she was twenty-four years old. My age, my precise age. I've only been in bed with…well, let me think. A very few."

"I'm sure you're right," I said. Krystal glanced through the Sunday supplement of the newspaper. She likes to drink her Starbucks coffee and read the paper on Sunday morning. Lately, Krystal has taken a deep dive into

6

astrology and studies everybody's sun and moon signs assiduously. She gets their charts done for free on a website she swears by. She tells me that I am a Scorpio with a large amount of Libra in my chart, so much so that I am a double sign person. I am split between Libra and Scorpio. That means I waver between being a charming people pleasing peacekeeper who desires harmony and equanimity and a psychotic deep and dirty schemer who will slaughter anyone to get what I want. I guess my boyfriend Brook doesn't call me Spooky for nothing. My mother is a Libra, and I can tell you they are only charming and sweet half the time when their scales are balanced. The other half of the time they are Genghis Kahn on a mission. She has three personalities, sweet and cheerful, silent mysterious sphinx, and wicked witch of the west. Pray she shakes that third one off before you get hit by the flying monkeys.

Librans are funny. Like my mom, they make excellent lawyers. Sometimes they play nice-nice while they calculate your weaknesses and develop strategy. That's just before they annihilate you. They are always nagging you to do better and be a better version of yourself. That is their way of saying they love you. If they stop nagging, they have probably stopped loving you. They talk a lot too. It's when they stop talking that you need to start worrying. It means they are about to go for the jugular, but they always do it in the nicest way and are so sorry that they are about to destroy you, because after all, wouldn't it be a better world if everyone would just be nice to each other?

"Omigod! Tabby do not do anything today! I'm not leaving the house. I just read our periscopes in the Sunday paper," said Krystal. She loves to read the daily horoscopes.

"Periscopes?" I asked.

"Yes, it says that Scorpios, meaning you, are in danger all week. Taurus the bull, meaning me, will go through a transitional phase filled with tumult. We are supposed to have a metamorphosis resulting in a whole new stage, like a larva becomes a caterpillar and then a butterfly."

"So?"

"So? So? What do you mean with that offhand so?" insisted Krystal. "I don't want a whole new stage. I don't like tumult. I like the stage I'm in. I'm not into being a larva and a caterpillar. I don't like bugs anyway. I am already a beautiful butterfly, and I don't need to change anything. You know I hate change."

"No, you are perfect the way you are. Never change, my friend."

"I don't plan on it," said Krystal firmly. "I just hope that the planets aren't crossed or retro or star-crossed and I will be forced into some new stage. I especially dread the Saturn return. Nothing is going to happen to us, is it Tabby?"

"I certainly hope not," I said. "I don't think so. I don't feel any tidal wave of change coming, do you?" Krystal looked at me with that look she has when she gets an intuition.

"Oh, no," I said sincerely. Famous last words. That was our last lazy summer Sunday before things started up again just like they did last summer. By things, read on and see what I mean.

"Don't you just hate it when someone says, "I told you so?" I do, especially when they wait to say I told you so until the whole thing is over and then they want to take credit for knowing what you should have seen, known, and done to begin with. Know-it-alls! After my last adventure, certain people, i.e., my older sister Jen the psychologist who thinks she is the Delphic Oracle, said that I should have seen the whole thing immediately. A lot she knows. Jen and her psychologist boyfriend Calvin love to lecture people, especially me. Can you feel my gag reflex working? Jen is almost as obnoxious as my older brother Matt the super star athlete and defensive football coach who also knows everything. Matt and his girlfriend Kelly live in a kinetic world of the here and now. They know all about how to maximize your athletic performance and what your financial plan for life should be, and they are more than happy to tell you about it. Mom does not give advice or words of wisdom anymore. At least, not too much. I think she gave up trying to talk some sense into my head about five years ago when I reached the ripe old age of twenty.

Into every life some rain must fall. Isn't that what they say? I just wish mine wouldn't be a deluge. An occasional sprinkle would be just fine with me. I don't relish contemplating how to build an arc. I ask you, what would Dr. Phil say about the flood of human foibles that make up my latest story? My guess is that it would give him something to ponder for quite a while.

This latest caper of ours is one for the books. More than once I thanked God for my guardian angel who kept me safe through it all. I think she works overtime. In fact, I think she brings in extra help sometimes to double team me. I suspect that my guardian angel has worked overtime for years. She has probably begged God, "No, please don't kill her off. Let me work on her some more! She is salvageable."

By saying this caper of ours, I refer to myself and my Kindred Spirit and BFF Krystal Morales. We have been inseparable since my family moved north from the state capitol of Madison, Wisconsin to the small town of New Belgium, LaFollette County, population 365, when I was fifteen. The town is made up of a motley crew of Shakespearian characters worthy of a sixteenth century comedy at the Globe theater. My lawyer mother Rhiannon Nolan, her BFF Didi Spencer, Didi's English Baronet husband Charles, and my stepfather Stan are numbered among them. My mom has had four husbands. The first two marriages were mercifully brief, forgettable, and regrettable. Then came my super cool dad, Mick Nolan, who was killed in a plane crash over Lake Michigan.

Rhiannon is now married to Stan the super mechanic and obsessive-compulsive walleye fisherman. Even though Stan likes to eat a predatory diet which includes things like bratwurst, sausage, and beef, he is a pretty good stepfather. He is an expert at fixing cars, which is good because Mom destroys them at an alarming rate. He never gives earnest lectures, and all I have to put up with are the fish lessons in life, such as, "Some days you catch some, some days you don't," or, "Drive safe and live to fish another day." His other favorite is, "Live smart, live wily, keep your scales on, live long like the old trout in the deep weedy pond, and may the fish be with you." Cool, Stan.

Krystal's mom is an ER nurse and has been widowed many years. Krystal's dad was killed serving in Iraq on his third tour of duty. Krystal comes from a long line of warriors who served with distinction in every conflict dating back to the Revolutionary War. I have seen the warrior in her DNA, and all I can say is, I'm glad she is on my side.

Now Krystal and I are grown up and have careers as clinic nurses in Sturgeon Bay, Door County, to the north of New Belgium. We work together and we are also roommates. We are into classic punk rock and bands such as the Clash and the Ramones. We are into classic films with stars like Audrey Hepburn, Bette Davis, Maureen O'Hara, and Jimmy Stewart.

We love living and working in God's country here in the Door. The Door is home to cherry orchards, artists and art galleries, quaint shops, cows, corn, cheese, vacation homes, tourism, shipbuilders, state parks, and glorious autumn color worthy of a Michelangelo or a Botticelli. By the way, we could do with a few less tourists. Chicago people, please take note. We don't get any reprieve from the busloads of tourists who swarm the county until the dead of winter.

Door County is the thumblike peninsula which sticks out into Lake Michigan and draws tourists from all over the world. The population enjoys a wholesome lifestyle and three short idyllic seasons followed by six months of winter. Or perhaps it only seems that way when we are waiting for spring and long to see the colorful tulips and the golden daffodils. "Yes, yes, yes, it's finally here," they whisper as they nod on their long green stems.

Our latest conundrum started when Krystal, the former punk rocker who used to be known as Constance, in addition to her nursing job, took a part time gig as a maid in the home of Pilar Lightfoot. Pilar is a wealthy socialite and businesswoman who is just slumming with all of us local yokels here in Sturgeon Bay.

In addition to the usual duties such as cleaning, scrubbing, polishing the silver, and walking the dog, Krystal, on her breaks and for her own amusement, busies herself with snooping, gossiping with the help, and listening at doors. This is probably a good thing, as she has been known to break a lot of glass and crystal when she is dusting. In our house, I do most of the cleaning. It's safer that way.

14

Krystal fills me in on all the juicy scandal in the Lightfoot house. While moonlighting as a maid at Pilar Lightfoot's mansion, she overhears a lot. The work is easy; mostly just light housework and running errands for Gina, the head housemaid. Krystal must also walk Pilar's obnoxious dog Truffles. Truffles is a psychotic purebred Pekinese. Krystal finds that walking Truffles around the mansion and the grounds gives her a chance to do a lot of snooping and eavesdropping.

Pilar pays in cash and Krystal is saving up to buy a condo, so she has an ideal situation for snooping. She infiltrates by playing like she doesn't understand English all that well. Si, senorita! Besides, as a maid and Hispanic female, she is all but invisible to Pilar and her upper-class friends. They trust Krystal implicitly because they think she can't understand English, so they talk freely in front of her.

Pilar hired her through Gina. Pilar likes to hire Hispanic women and Gina prefers to work with Hispanic people. Gina hires everyone who works on the grounds, in the house, and in the gardens. Gina is Latina and an illegal alien, but nobody needs to know that. That is why Gina is so loyal to Pilar. Gina needs to remain in the states and send money back home to Mexico to help support her sister and nieces.

Gina tells Krystal what really goes on in that house between Pilar and her husband Nick, and I'm telling you, Dr. Phil would have a field day. In fact, I think Nick and Pilar would make perfect candidates for Dr. Phil's show. Nick sails, swims, bikes, and invests in art. He brings home young girls he picks up at bars in Green Bay and entertains them in the carriage house over the garage. Nick also has a lover in Bailey's Harbor named Skylar. She is a financial advisor. Personally, I would not ask her to advise me how to get to the nearest Quick Store, but to each her own.

As for Pilar, you will hear lots more about her. She is surely a case for the couch and would give Dr. Phil enough material for several shows. Gina has heard Pilar and Nick fighting and so has Krystal. It goes something like this.

"You better leave the girls alone Nicky baby, or I'm going to divorce you and leave you without a cent to your name. You did sign a prenuptial agreement, you know. In addition, that gambling habit of yours has got to go and go now."

"You wouldn't dare divorce me, Pilar darling, and besides, prenups can be broken in court. The little money I lose gambling is nothing compared to the amount you spend. As for the girls, I don't hear you complaining when you're running around under my nose with that pathetic lapdog you call a lover. What is his name again? Charlie the gardener and pool boy? Isn't it a bit like *Lady Chatterley's Lover*? Really, darling, you could have picked someone a bit classier than Charlie. Taking advantage of the help is so over. It's so twentieth century. Isn't there a law against that? Does he even have a green card? How old is he? There should be a law."

"There should be a law against being married to a lying, cheating scum like you, darling. Now get out and go see one of your little girlfriends. I have adult things to do. I'm busy keeping this menagerie afloat while you have your minions do your supervisory duties and amuse yourself gambling, buying art with my money, and running around with the riff raff of the county. Just like a man. You act like the last tycoon but really, how hard do you work? How about that little financial planner or whatever she purports to be in Bailey's Harbor? Skylar, isn't it? Speaking of age differences, how old is she? Does she still play with Barbie dolls? Why don't you get out and go have your dissipated idea of fun?"

"Gladly, darling, and I'll be late, so don't wait up. You older women need your beauty sleep. Botox can't hide your sins forever."

"Older? Me? You should talk. I believe you are two years older than me, nearing forty, past your prime, and fading fast. You better enjoy what is left of your virility before it starts to slip. Hate to tell you darling, but you're not the stud you used to be."

That is just the beginning. It gets worse from there. There are many others besides Nick who love to hate Pilar Lightfoot. The list of people who carry a grudge against Pilar is as long as a time share condo salesman's nose.

Pilar has just dumped her stockbroker again and he hates her for it. His name is Hadley Radcliffe. Hadley was in the clinic just the other day where I work as a nurse.

While I was taking his blood pressure, Hadley confided in me.

"Did you know that Pilar just fired me for the fourth time in three months?" he asked morosely. "I have a lot of difficult clients, but she takes the cake."

"No, but I know that you better calm down. Doctor Murphy is going to be upset with the state of your blood pressure."

"Forget it," said Hadley. "I'll be lucky if I live another year without having a stroke. I should have been a lawyer like my mother told me to do. People like Pilar have me drinking Maalox out of the bottle. Between her and my other clients and the stock market, I'll be dead of ulcers in another year."

"It isn't that bad, is it?" I asked.

"Worse," sniffed Hadley. "Are you kidding? Pilar is a monster. She is just a spoiled brat who happened to inherit a multi-million-dollar empire. She acts more like a painted white trash hooker who should be living in a trailer court, working as a waitress, and selling weed on the side to make a few bucks. You think she knows anything about finance? She knows nothing. If it weren't for me Pilar and that dick of a husband of hers would have squandered her entire fortune ten years ago when they first married. They both have a huge problem called ego. The only good thing about them is that they didn't pass on their narcissistic personality disorder genes to the next generation. Luckily, they have no children."

"Maybe you should take a vacation," I offered. "Listen to classical music. Take a yoga class. Try golf."

"I've tried golf. That drove me to drink. After the disaster that is my putting, I went into the clubhouse and drank myself into oblivion each time I went golfing. I go on vacation and get constant calls from my clients. I tried yoga and ripped out my Achilles tendon doing the stretches. I tried jogging but I couldn't stop throwing up. Classical music gives me a headache. So does opera. So does jazz, pop, and country. The only kind of music I like is elevator music."

"Maybe you should try swimming at the YMCA," I suggested.

"Are you kidding? I can't even float. The smell of that chlorine simply makes me reel," said Hadley.

"Perhaps try reading some nice, peaceful novels that act as a soporific in the evening. Doctor Murphy will be in soon," I said, and made a quick getaway. Old people. Yikes!

I ran into Krystal in the break room and told her about Hadley.

"It seems that Nick isn't the only person who hates Pilar," I said. "You should have heard what Hadley Radcliffe, that stockbroker, had to say about her while I took his blood pressure."

"Yeah, I heard about their latest feud from Gina. Oh, there's more," said Krystal. "Just this morning while I was bringing little Truffles the brat Dr. Jekyll Mr. Hyde Peke doggie in from his walk, I heard Pilar in her office screaming at Franky Perri."

"What was that about?" I inquired. "Franky used to work for Pilar, didn't he? I thought he was the head of one of Pilar's companies, wasn't he?"

"Yes. Apparently, Don Derrick bought Kerry Industries from Pilar and closed the company, consolidated the assets, and fired all the employees. The problem is that they all blame Pilar for the whole debacle. They say she knew Don Derrick would turn them out on the street, but she didn't care because she made a tidy profit on the deal."

"What did you hear? Were you listening at the door?" I asked.

"I didn't have to listen at the door. The whole place heard her screaming at Franky right in front of all his friends. She said, 'What do I look like, a charity? Just get another job! You people have been living off me for too long in your cushy little jobs. After all, it's just a marketing company. You can get a job in any big city, and the secretaries and assistants can get a job anywhere. Get off my case, will you? It is not my fault if Don Derrick decided to downsize the company, consolidate the assets, and pour them into his Alston companies.'"

"She is such a harridan," I said.

"No kidding," said Krystal. "Franky Perri threatened to kill her in front of about ten witnesses standing there with him in the office. All those friends he brought into the office, the former employees of Kerry Industries, heard him. Franky said he could just kill Pilar and he probably should. Then he said it would be worth it. That was just before they all stomped out swearing and cursing. They cursed her all the way down the drive and into their cars."

"She isn't exactly the flavor of the month, is she?"

"Tabby, she isn't even close," said Krystal. "If she were a flavor, it would be rotten apple cider vinegar with a touch of arsenic. I looked up her chart. She is a Leo with a moon in Capricorn and overloaded with her big planets in Aries."

"What does that mean?" I asked.

"It means a scary diva with a heart like ice and a serious case of me first and the rest of you proles wait in line. You might as well say she has a moon in mental, Mars in mean, Mercury in mercurial, Neptune in nefarious, Venus in vicious, and Saturn in sick. Her flavor of the month is poisonous rattler, and her color is puce. Speaking of the flavor of the month, do you want to stop at Minty's for ice cream on the way home?"

"Before supper?"

"Yes, before supper, silly. All we have in the fridge is leftover cold pizza. How does that sound?"

"Pretty pukey," I said. "I guess a small ice cream cone wouldn't hurt."

"Or an icy mound of M&M Minty shake, or maybe a Minty bar." Krystal pulled a small plastic bag from her purse. "Have to eat my gummies. I've been waiting for this for an hour."

"Krystal, seriously? Gummy Bears for break? Why don't you have an apple or some carrots? I asked.

"Why don't you take a long walk off a short plank? Why don't *you* eat an apple or an orange? Maybe a plum or a pear?"

"I don't like apples. I would rather eat nothing. I don't like fruit except for blueberries or raspberries."

"Exactly. If I am going to put up with Doctor Diva Darlene Dalhousie all morning, I am eating these Gummy Bears. It's either that or stick a knife in her neck. Take your pick. I suppose I could drug myself up with valium, but my mother takes a dim view of that and since she is the senior emergency room nurse at the hospital, I suppose I should try to emulate her. Hey! Did you hear what I just said about Doctor Diva Darlene? Isn't that altercation?"

"I think you mean alliteration," I said.

"I think your break is over," said Krystal. "Get lost and go babysit our Dear Doctor Murphy. Keep his files in order and keep him from walking into walls like a blind man, would you? It's a miracle he finds his way to the exam rooms. I'm going to buy him a white cane for Christmas. At least his argyle socks match today, and his scrubs aren't on inside out. Maybe his wife dressed him. Talk about a hopeless case. How did he ever get through med school?"

"I'm not sure. Hey, how is your mom doing on her guided tour of Italy?"

"Tammy is good. She is in love with all things Italian. She can't get enough of all that Catholic history and Roman drama. She goes on and on every night on the phone about how beautiful it all is. If I didn't know her better, I would say she is in love. She seems thirty years younger." Krystal frowned. "I hope that isn't a bad sign. Do you think she is having a mid-life crisis? Is she going to become a cougar and buy a Maserati?"

"Isn't she too old for a mid-life crisis?" I asked.

"I think so, but you know Tammy. She thinks young. Thank God for Gummy Bears. Now I can face Doctor Diva Darlene without sticking a needle in her jugular. See you later."

I got the chance to witness the effect Pilar had on people that evening as Krystal and I sat outside at Minty's eating our ice cream; a small vanilla cone for me, a Super Icy Blast M&M Minty shake for Krystal. We just happened to be sitting under the striped umbrella at our table discussing Dr. Evans's spectacularly bad bedside manner, when along came the queen herself.

Pilar and a pal waltzed up to the takeout window for chocolate shakes. I should say that Pilar got ice water and the pal got a super thick large chocolate shake. Krystal informed me that Pilar's pal was Bristol Taggart, her longtime publicist, assistant, marketer, and general factotum.

They sat down at the next table. Bristol started slurping his milkshake while Pilar took tiny sips of her ice water, which was about the same temperature as the blood in her veins. Pilar looked at Bristol with disgust. I should say that she almost looked disgusted. It was hard to tell because it looks to me like she has had an eyelift, frowny, eyebrows threaded, lips plumped, Botox, and possibly a nose job. Any facial expressions are clearly muted. She weighs about nothing and has a beautiful figure if your goal is to look like a Vogue model, Amazon tall and Hollywood bony. She has unusual eyes. One eye is green, and one eye is hazel, and her hair is a perfect shade of flowing golden color with champagne highlights.

"I'm sorry Bristol, but you are getting too old and too fat," said Pilar. "This is why I came here with you tonight. You are getting disgustingly fat and that ice cream habit of yours is not helping. You need a makeover, a weight loss program, and new ideas if you want to be my publicist and market my companies. Since I highly doubt that will happen, I have decided to replace you with a younger, trendier man with loads of moxie. I'm bringing in someone new. In fact, I'm thinking of hiring Brendan

O'Hara." Krystal sipped her shake and rolled her eyes at me.

"See what I mean?" she asked *sotto voce.*

Bristol almost choked on his milkshake. There was a loaded pause before the deluge of his indignation found its voice.

"What?" he barked. "Brendan O'Hara? Pilar, you can't be serious! Come on, Pilar. After all these years? I'm too old? I never dreamed you would throw me over for a younger man, especially that simpering little milquetoast. I can guarantee you he will not be able to satisfy your, shall we say, extreme requirements and extracurricular demands. Brendan O'Hara? Don't make me laugh! Is this some sick joke?"

"I'm not laughing. Do you see me laughing?" she asked archly. "He is on trend, ambitious, and raring to go. You, my darling, are getting just a wee bit old and tired."

"Don't be stupid, Pilar. Haven't I been your loyal Joe Friday for years? Haven't I gone beyond the pale for you and given you everything you wanted and been a faithful servant?"

"Yes, but it is now time to move on, for both of us," she said.

"No way. I'm not moving on to some little corporate job and starting at the bottom of the ladder. I have no intention of being passed over for another man. I love you. I would do anything for you and have, many times over. Don't you understand?"

"Your mistake," said the Snow Queen. Bristol looked like the ice cream in his mouth had just turned to lava.

"You must be insane!" yelled Bristol. "I think when you say I'm getting old, you mean that you are afraid you are getting old! Now that you have reached that watershed year of thirty-five, you seem to want a total life makeover. It's you and your pool boy. I guess the rumors are all true. It's Charlie, isn't it? You've been fooling around with Charlie the gardener. I didn't believe it but now I see that the rumors must be true. How disgusting can you get?" he said on a rising note of rage. "Are you seriously thinking of replacing me with Brendan O'Hara? Why don't you add insult to injury? Charlie and Brendan? Brendan couldn't write his way out of a paper bag."

"Let me put it to you this way," said Pilar. "Brendan is young, handsome, and trendy. You are getting old. As for Charlie, my groundskeeper, gardener, and pool boy, that is neither here nor there, and it is none of your business."

"Oh, I get it. You need both men to keep you happy. Is that what you're saying? You need two trophy toy boys to show off to the world? You're nothing but a nymphomaniac! I'm getting dumped and replaced by two young toy boys? You disgust me! Honestly, you take this moment to play the insatiable old cougar? This is what I think of your plan, you disgusting cougar!"

Bristol tore the cover off his shake, stood up, and dumped the entire thing directly over Pilar's head, right onto her expensively highlighted, gloriously tinted champagne and café au lait hair. Then he got right into her chocolate milkshake covered gasping face and screamed at her.

"I'm not the only one who is getting old! You better start thinking about more Botox, babe! Your looks are going! Let me be the first to let you know! Looks don't last forever, Pilar, even with the help of the plastic surgeons. Where are you going to be when you lose all your adoring acolytes? I hope your stinking fortune goes up in smoke and the stock market crashes! You're going to pay for this, Pilar! You have friends you haven't even used yet, I guess. Looks and money don't last forever. There will come a day when you can't beg, borrow, or steal a friend, and that day is fast arriving!"

Pilar spit milkshake at him, which only added fuel to the fire. Bristol roared like a wounded lion. He seemed to puff up and the hair stood up on his head. He turned red and then purple with rage.

"To think I gave up three great girlfriends to devote myself to you. I could have been married with a devoted wife and a couple kids by now. How stupid could I be? You were just using me all along, weren't you? Is that the idea? I have news for you, you lousy witch! One day very soon someone, namely me, is going to get you and pay you back for all your evil deeds! You better watch your back! Your karma is on its way!"

With that last insult, Bristol crushed his Styrofoam cup right onto her head. The chocolate ice cream mess and tiny bits of Styrofoam ran and dripped down her perfectly made-up face, ruining what was left of her makeup.

Pilar sat gasping and sputtering as Bristol stomped away, hurled himself into his Porsche 911, and roared off, leaving Pilar ignominiously dripping ice cream. Krystal and I sat there staring with our mouths wide open. Even Krystal, seldom at a loss for words, was speechless.

We watched as Pilar slowly stood up, gasping and sobbing, and walked away, not even bothering to wipe off her hair, face, and clothing. We watched her limp off, half crying, half choking. Eventually, she found her voice and started screaming and swearing. Expletives deleted here as Pilar swore her way down the drive. Finally, she thought to pull out her cell phone and scream orders into it. Presumably, she commanded one of the underlings to come and get her immediately at Minty's.

"Wow! What a scene! I'm thinking Oscar worthy," I said. "She gets the Oscar for best performance as a despicable witch in daytime drama. And the Tony, and the Emmy too. She is thicker than double stuffed Oreos, and a major league drama queen to boot. I think this case is Dr. Phil worthy."

"Definitely! I am truly impressed," said Krystal. "Now that's entertainment. I'm talking Emmy. What a drama! I really thought Bristol might kill her."

"Did Pilar see you sitting here?" I asked. "I'm surprised she didn't order you to take her home," I said.

"Tabby, please. She probably doesn't even know that I work in her employ as a temporary maid," said Krystal. "She isn't used to seeing me outside of my maid role, so I'm sure she didn't recognize me. She looks straight at me and doesn't see me. Pilar doesn't speak to peons like me. Are you nuts?"

"Probably," I said, and took a lick of my ice cream cone. "Wow! I sure am glad we came here tonight. Ice cream and drama. How much better does it get? This is almost as good as a Bette Davis movie on the Turner

Classic Movie channel. Maybe even Jimmy Stewart or Maureen O'Hara."

"You're such a classic movie nerd," said Krystal.

"You should talk. Who was watching *Breakfast at Tiffany's* this morning?"

"I had to watch an Audrey Hepburn clip. She is so skinny that she inspires me to diet," said Krystal. I eyed her super milkshake.

"Doesn't look like it's working so far," I said.

"Oh, shut up, bony girl."

#Emmyworthy

Chapter Two: The Beautiful and Groomed

All the world's a stage,
And all the men and women merely players;
They have their exits and their entrances,

And one man in his time plays many parts,

His acts being seven ages.

--From *All the world's a stage*, by William Shakespeare

When Krystal and I got home from Minty's, our kitten Cuckoo demanded that we pet her and play with her since we had both been gone all day. Krystal was thrilled to find that she had forgotten that she bought four scones at Tasty Pastry, raspberry orange, almond, lemon, and chocolate dream. She had hidden them on top of the refrigerator so she wouldn't eat them all at once. We had tea and scones for supper. Krystal slathered her two scones with butter and sprinkled sugar on them. I liked mine plain. So yum. My raspberry orange was gone in a trice, though I did save a few bites for Cuckoo. She likes scones too.

"Mew, meow, mirr!" she said, and promptly ate her share.

"Cuckoo, you wouldn't believe what we just witnessed," said Krystal as she took a bite of her favorite, chocolate dream.

"I don't think my baby should be witness to violence and fighting. It could affect her adversely. She is at a vulnerable stage," I said, and cuddled Cuckoo in my arms.

"Poor baby," said Krystal. "She is the most pampered kitten I have ever seen."

"Pilar better be careful," I said. "This is a very small town. I'm sure she enjoys being a big fish in a small pond, but there is a limit to what people will put up with."

"Mew, meow, mirr," said Cuckoo. She always agrees with everything we say. We rescued Cuckoo in our last case, which you can read about in *Marriage is Murder: The Door County Special*. After that adventure, I acquired Cuckoo and my boyfriend Brook, or Brook Trout, as we sometimes call him. Not only did Krystal and I solve the murder, but I managed to take Brook away from Bridezilla Horrible Holly on their wedding day, a feat of which I am inordinately proud. But that is another story.

In fact, at that moment I felt that I just had to call Brook and tell him the entire story of the Pilar brouhaha. He laughed himself silly, and then drew the obvious comparison between Pilar and his late, great, unlamented love, Horrible Holly the Bridezilla of Egg Harbor.

"Yes," I agreed. "I'll have to ask my sister Jennifer the psychologist about classification of nutcases. I don't know if she would say that both Pilar and Nick are narcissists with borderline personality disorder, bipolar, or simply antisocial, but I think they both classify as socially inadequate at the very least. As for Holly, I would say criminally insane and a nympho."

"How about labelling all three of them as terminally selfish and in need of a conscience makeover," said Brook.

"What would Dr. Phil say?" asked Krystal. She always listened in on our conversations.

"I think he would pronounce both Nick and Pilar in need of a great deal of counseling, and possibly beyond help," I said. "I think that he would recommend a brain scan."

"I think he would say that they are a shrink's paradise and a shrink's field day," said Brook. "They could give any shrink a busman's holiday."

"I think they are psycho brain fodder," said Krystal. "They are the type that drives the shrink crazy, so crazy that the shrink must get help. They give shrinks nightmares and keep them up at night staring at the ceiling murmuring, 'Where did I go wrong? Why didn't I become a hairdresser? I need Prozac and I need it now.'"

The next day was Saturday. I was in the middle of a riveting novel and thinking about how I should be cleaning the apartment when Krystal called me.

"Hello?"

"Tabby! Emergency here. I'm at Pilar's cleaning the house. Correction. I was cleaning the house. Right now, I'm hiding in Charlie the gardener's tool and pool shed calling you." I sat up straight and tossed the book onto the coffee table.

"What happened?" I asked.

"I told you about Tiggy Butterfield, right?" said Krystal. "Pilar has two new best friends. One is that snooty English girl, Bunty Essex Jones. Bunty amuses herself by working as a golf pro at the country club. It isn't like she needs the money. She is some upper crust aristocrat from Yorkshire, England. What she is doing here I really don't know but there is something slimy about her that I don't like. The other new best bud is Tiggy Butterfield. Do you remember me mentioning her?"

"Right. She is Pilar's new best friend, confidante, and shopping partner. She replaced Piper the childhood friend as the new gal pal when Pilar had an affair with Piper's husband and caused them to divorce, resulting in a lot of bitter accusation. Tiggy is the one who is the tennis pro at Pilar's country club. Did I get that right?"

"Right. Go to the head of the class. Tiggy and Pilar play tennis every Saturday afternoon all afternoon here on the estate and Pilar gets a free lesson. Then they have a glass of wine upstairs in Pilar's bedroom suite. Guess what I just discovered."

"What?" I asked.

"They have the wine and then Pilar takes a shower and changes. While she is showering, Tiggy lifts another piece of her jewelry."

"What?" I asked, incredulous.

"That's right. Pilar has a bad habit of leaving her jewelry lying around. I'm telling you if I were a thief I would be in heaven in this place. There are treasures and jewelry everywhere, not to mention Nicky baby's priceless art collection. Tiggy is apparently quite an accomplished jewel thief. I caught her in the act and figured out what is going on. She is lifting it alright. Guess where Tiggy hides the stolen treasure."

"Where?"

"She hides it in the hollowed-out handle of her extra tennis racket that she carries with her in case she needs a second racket. The handle is plugged up with putty. Apparently, this is how she finances her fancy lifestyle. Let's face it. Being a tennis pro doesn't pay all that well, and Tiggy has very expensive tastes. She keeps pace with Pilar on the spending habits. The sky is the limit for those two from what I can see."

"Holy man. That is unreal," I said.

"Yeah, Tiggy Butterfingers Butterfield, or should I call her Light Fingers Louie, sure knows how to work a racket. Ha! A racket, get it?"

"Yes, Krystal. I get it."

"What an operator! She lifts the goods and then replaces the piece with a paste copy and fences the original to her contacts, whoever and wherever they are. Do ya think?"

"I think you are perceptive, my dear friend. How in the world did you stumble on this conclusion?"

"Here is how I solved it. Gina told me to dust all the upstairs rooms, so I was upstairs dusting. You know how I am with dusting. I won't touch anything valuable for fear that I'll break it, so that is somewhat limiting. I moved the tennis racket because I was dusting one of the dressers. I felt a rattle in the grip. I poked around and realized the grip was filled with putty. I pulled it out and right there in the handle of the tennis racket was a ruby necklace. I'm talking major stones here."

"Geez!"

"I can't say that I wasn't suspicious to start with. I spied on Tiggy one Saturday from around the corner in the hallway when Pilar was in the shower. At first, I thought that Tiggy was just tightening the handle of the racket. Then I realized she might be hiding something in there. When she went downstairs today, I decided to investigate. It is true that I was dusting, but I decided that Pilar's dressers needed special attention. I slipped into the bedroom. I could hear the shower running so I knew that Pilar was still in the shower."

"I'm surprised you had the nerve to nose around with both of them so close."

"Hey, I'm just cleaning and dusting. It's not my fault if Gina told me to go dust the upstairs bedrooms. I'm just following orders."

"Right!"

"I followed up and twisted the putty off and sure enough, just as I had suspected, there was a nice set of ruby red stones there."

"Weren't you scared?"

"Not until I heard Tiggy's feet pounding up the stairs. I shoved the putty back in, replaced the racket on the dresser just as I found it, and got real busy polishing the armoire. Tiggy burst in and didn't even see me, until she pivoted towards me and screamed at me for sneaking up on her and started swearing at me for being in the room."

"Oh, cripes! What did you do?"

"I played dumb of course. I apologized and acted like I didn't know much English."

"Seriously?" I laughed.

"Hey, they think I'm probably an illegal alien who doesn't even know English."

"What did you say?"

"Si senorita. Hola! Adios amiga! Bye-bye!" Then I smiled and looked dumb.

"That is what you said? Seriously? You acted like you didn't know English? You just played dumb and got away with it? Did she fall for it?"

"I acted like I didn't know much of anything, English or Spanish. Yes, I guess she did fall for it, because she stopped looking worried and angry and waved me out of the room. So, I waltzed out. I didn't know what else to do. I acted like I didn't know what was going on. This time it was a ruby necklace. Last week when I spied on her, I swear I distinctly heard the rattle and watched her open it up. I saw the bright sparkles. I think it was diamonds. That's why I was so anxious to get in here and follow up this week."

"Let's just repeat to confirm. You mean that Tiggy is stealing Pilar's jewelry and hiding it in the handle of the secondary spare tennis racket she always carries around with her? Then she smuggles it out and fences it?"

"Yes, she has a real racket going." Krystal started to giggle uncontrollably.

"Yes, Krystal, I get it. A racket. Tiggy must fence the real stuff and replace it with a copy. She replaces the real jewelry with a replica, also carried in the racket and smuggled back in when Pilar is in the shower. Then she throws the paste copy on the dresser or wherever she found the original while Pilar is in the shower. Wow! Tiggy is an honest to goodness professional jewel thief. Pilar makes it all so easy for her."

"You betcha! You should have seen me playing the dumb bunny. The hilarious part about all of it is that it's Spanish I don't know much of, not English. I'm glad Tiggy didn't start quizzing me in Spanish to see if I knew anything. Thank God she must not know any Spanish. Tabby, I'm telling you, I would have been sunk if she did. I just put this dumb look on my face and acted confused, as if I had just stumbled into a Buddhist temple and I didn't know if I should kneel, bow, or stand on my head."

I laughed uproariously. "You have got nerve, girl," I said. "I'll say that much for you."

"Hey, I'm just the part time maid. No comprenez, babe. Go on stealing right under my nose. I see nothing. I hear nothing. I say nothing. Everyone thinks that if you are Hispanic, you should be able to speak Spanish. Not necessarily so, folks. By the way, I think that Tiggy was the one who stole that diamond necklace and hid it in the toilet tank. Remember how Maria got fired and Pilar blamed the theft of the diamonds on her?"

"But why would Tiggy hide the necklace in the toilet tank instead of in her racket?" I asked.

"Possibly to deflect attention from herself. Possibly to get Maria accused of jewelry theft in case Pilar discovered other jewels missing. That way Maria could be blamed for all the thefts in case Tiggy needed a patsy."

"Good thinking. Good detective work. You have got nerves of steel, girl. Krystal, you are too much," I said.

"I am, aren't I?" asked Krystal. "I am just too blasted much. I scooted out of there pronto, amiga, before old Light Fingers Louie Tiggy Butterfingers Butterfield could start to suspect that I am not quite as dumb as I look. Now here I am in the shed talking to you."

"Incredible, my friend."

"I thought you would be entertained. Anyway, about Tiggy. I think that Tiggy has a face like a ferret, you know, one of those foxy faces. She is a type I cannot stand," observed Krystal.

"Yes, she does have a face like a ferret or a fox," I said.

"Or maybe a guinea pig," said Krystal. "With that tanned skin, that short boy cut blonde hair, and that long skinny body, she thinks she is the cutest little thing in town. She is so vain, almost as vain as Pilar," said Krystal.

"It seems to me that Pilar and all her friends are vain, and that vanity arises from all their artificial beauty aids."

"Such as?" asked Krystal. "Inquiring minds want to know."

"Namely Botox, tummy tucks, facelifts, frownies, fillers, plumpers, breast implants, and I don't know what other things," I said. "I don't want to know, and God preserve me from ever thinking that I need it."

"Really? Do you think that they have all had work done? Aren't they a little young for all that?" asked Krystal.

"No, not since the whole country became California-ized. Now everyone over thirty thinks they should get the entire array of plasticized California face and body," I observed. "So ugly, not to mention expensive."

"I am never getting work done," said Krystal. "I don't care if I get old and wrinkled. Those fake faces make me want to puke."

"You and me both," I agreed. "When can you come home?"

"I'm due to spit and polish for another hour. Then I walk the psycho Peke Truffles. Then I nose around for a while pretending I'm working. Then I come home, and we go out for ice cream so we can have a good laugh about this."

"Sounds good to me. But what happens when Pilar discovers that most of her jewelry is now paste copies of the real thing?" I asked.

"I don't know, but I don't want to be around. There will be hell to pay. My guess is that Pilar will blame the Latina help, namely Gina and me. Just the thought of that puts a sick feeling in the pit of my stomach. I bet she will have Gina arrested by ICE and she'll be deported, or worse, jailed."

"Too bad you can't make a video of Tiggy stealing the jewels. Perhaps you should do that in case someday you need proof of your own innocence and her guilt."

"That is a spectacular idea my friend," said Krystal. "I just might do that. I could hide around the corner and video Tiggy on my phone as she lifts the pearls or whatever the jewel of the day is. Then I can film her stuffing the jewels in the hollow handle of the racket. In fact, I think I will. Oh, I think I hear Charlie the gardener tromping through the garden. I better slip out of here and get busy dusting and polishing before he finds me in here and reports me to Pilar the Princess. He is her lover, you know."

"Poor him."

"Some people will make any sacrifice to keep their job. Gotta run," said Krystal, and rang off.

#ChannelingLadyChatterley'slover

Chapter Three: A Broom of One's Own

All the world's a stage, but some of the players have been very badly miscast.

--Oscar Wilde

A late model silver Audi roared into the long drive at Pilar's mansion as Krystal and I were walking Pilar's dog Truffles the psycho Pekinese. Little Truffles had been acting particularly psycho that day, so Krystal phoned and asked me to help take the little fur baby for his Saturday morning walk around Pilar's upscale neighborhood. Truffles likes to nip and claw if he doesn't get exactly what he wants when he wants it, rather like his owner. That morning, Gina the head maid had run out of Truffles' favorite treats and Truffles was not happy. In fact, he was downright annoyed, grouchy, and generally growly.

Truffles' owner Pilar the Princess of all Pills was jogging her way up and down the driveway. She was dressed in something I would have worn to a party, and she had on full makeup, right down to the false eyelashes. She looked better and more stylishly dressed to jog up and down her own driveway than I looked to go to church, when I went to church that is. The Audi screeched to a stop in front of us. Piper Cannon, Pilar's heretofore so-called best friend and lifelong buddy, school mate, travelling partner, and gal pal jumped out of the Audi, stalked up the drive, stomped up to Pilar, and shook her fist in Pilar's face.

"Are you insane?" screeched Piper. "Did you send a policeman to my house to interrogate me because you fell off your scooter? Do you have some delusional idea that I caused you to fall? Have you developed Alzheimer's? Do you have hardening of the arteries?"

"I swear you tried to kill me!" screamed Pilar.

"No, I didn't try to kill you!" yelled Piper. "You are delusional! As much as I hate you, I wouldn't try to kill you! So many people would love to kill you, Pilar. But don't think I would do something so stupid!"

"Admit it! You sprayed my scooter tires, didn't you? It was cooking spray, wasn't it?" demanded Pilar. "I know it was cooking spray! I just know it! Are you going to deny it?"

"What makes you think that dope?" asked Piper with scorn. "You are a class A paranoid psychotic delusional egotist with a persecution complex!"

"The reason that I think that you tried to kill me, little Miss Pseudo-intellectual, is because I turned a corner with the scooter, slipped, and went down," said Pilar. "I scraped my knee in the process, and it could have been so much worse! I know you were nosing around the garage when you were at the house a few days ago. Charlie told me that he saw you skulking around the garage the other day. When he asked you if you needed anything, you looked startled and acted evasive. He said that you made up some lame excuse about leaving a gardening tool there."

"What if I did? I did leave my favorite gardening tool in the garage months ago," said Piper. "I just remembered that it was there and went back to look for it."

"Don't make me laugh!" said Pilar. "You never gardened in your life. You don't like getting your hands dirty. That's why you have Marcos do your lawn and garden. If there are any flowers in your yard, it certainly isn't due to your pitiful efforts at gardening. You probably don't know a rose from a hibiscus. You were there to spray my scooter tires with cooking spray! It's a good thing for you that I slowed down for that corner on the scooter. Lucky for you I didn't take it at full speed. I could have killed myself. I checked the tires and they felt sticky, as if someone had sprayed them with an oil."

"You were probably drunk and roaring around on the back roads on the scooter like you love to do. You put the scooter down and you want to blame it on me," Piper flung at her. "It won't stick, psycho witch from hell! It won't fly, Lucretia Borgia in diamonds! How many more men are you going to need? How many have you already gone through? How many of us have you used and unceremoniously dumped? Do you have any friends left? I doubt it!"

"It was you, jealous freak!" insisted Pilar. "You were in the garage. You know that no one rides that scooter but me. You were trying to kill me!"

"You have no proof of that! If the tires were indeed sprayed, anyone could have done it. How many people have you antagonized lately? Anyone could have been in that garage. You are a complete bipolar psycho narcissist from hell! Prove it, adulterer!" screamed Piper.

"I knew it! We're back on that, are we? It wasn't my fault that your wandering husband just chanced to look my way. Face it! I'm simply more attractive than you are, and he couldn't resist me!" asserted Pilar.

"Isn't that just like you?" sneered Piper. "You think no one can resist you. You think that you are so irresistible to every man you see. You flirt shamelessly with everything in pants, don't you? Anything between thirteen and ninety is a likely victim for you. Tell the truth. You tried to seduce my husband for years. Your best friend's husband was fair game for you. Your lifelong best friend isn't even sacred to you. Every man is fair game for you. You feel the need to prove a point, don't you? You're nothing but a nymphomaniac!" screamed Piper. "You are a deeply disturbed psychopath! You are a bottomless pit of need for applause, for admiration, for attention, and for sex! You can never get enough! You are the perfect narcissist!"

"Sour grapes!" yelled Pilar. "Just because I easily seduced your stray dog of a husband you try and kill me by sabotaging my scooter. You wanted to kill me, and you could have succeeded! What kind of a friend are you, anyway?" sneered Pilar.

"I'll show you what kind of a friend I am, nympho! With friends like you, who needs enemies?" yelled the distraught Piper.

She launched herself into the air directly at Pilar, who dodged adroitly. Piper fell to the ground screaming with rage. She jumped up and sprang onto Pilar and the two started a caterwauling, bellowing, snarling cat fight complete with scratching, kicking, hairpulling, and biting.

"Holy guacamole!" breathed Krystal. "Don't watch this, Truffles."

I stood there with my jaw hanging open. Krystal and I, and everyone for a block east and west heard Pilar and Piper fighting like two juvenile delinquents on the playground. Even Truffles stopped in his tracks and stared at his mistress as if he didn't know what to make of this charade.

"Should we get in there and pull them apart?" I whispered.

"Are you kidding? This is too good to interrupt," said Krystal. "I want to see them slaughter each other!" The fight seemed to be equal for a few minutes, but then Pilar dominated until Piper jumped to her feet, trying to shield her face against Pilar's gouging claws.

"I'll get you for this you witch!" screamed Piper as she ran for the safety of her Audi and roared away. Pilar stomped up the drive to the house, cursing all the way.

"I'll just bet Piper will get the witch," said Krystal and whistled. "Tabby, you should have been here a few hours ago. Today is Pilar's day to garner more enemies. Guess what else happened with Pilar and her staff."

"After all that I've heard about her, I don't think I will be shocked," I said.

"I don't know. This one is a doozy. Listen to this," said Krystal.

"What is it about?" I asked. Truffles the psycho Pekinese snorted and growled. He flopped down on the green, just mown manicured lawn and refused to move. Krystal urged him on with kissy noises. Truffles grudgingly got up and started to amble down the sidewalk. He liked Krystal. No one else could manage him.

"I'm surprised I didn't tell you before," said Krystal. "This is about Martha, Pilar's long-term secretary. Pilar fired Marty this morning, and very cruelly. Gina told me the whole background story after it happened."

"Of course," I said. "Gina knows everything."

"First, I'll tell you the background story and then I'll tell you what happened this morning. Fifty years ago, old spinster Martha, or Marty as everyone calls her, Pilar's secretary, killed the lover who spurned her in her youth."

"What? No!"

"Yup, Martha fixed him a cocktail drink filled with digitalis. She used his heart meds. This older man was a big playboy who was just toying with Marty when she was a beautiful young girl of only eighteen, but she didn't know that. She was head over heels in love with him. Marty was just an innocent young girl whom he seduced and then jilted. Marty found out that he had women all over town and that marked his death knell. Everyone thought that it was an accidental overdose at the time, and indeed, it might well have been."

"Oh, brother."

"No kidding. The terrible thing is, Marty doesn't know if she gave him enough to cause an overdose or if he accidentally took too much, but she has always felt guilty about it. In fact, she never went out with another man because of it. She felt so hurt and guilty that she might as well have been a nun. She is a lonely spinster. She had various secretarial jobs at different companies and then fifteen years ago, she started working for Pilar."

"Lucky her," I quipped. Truffles balked and dug his nose into the grass. We stopped to wait for him, and Krystal continued the story.

"Martha's job is the only thing that she has, or I should say had, because she doesn't have it anymore, thanks to Pilar. In a weak moment long ago, Marty somehow confided her story to Pilar after they had a glass of wine together. Pilar promised to keep it a secret. Yeah, right. She told the whole staff. She held it over Marty's head ever since."

"I hate Pilar even more than I used to," I said.

"Listen to this. When Marty started to show her age after working for Pilar for the last fifteen years, Pilar decided to fire her. You know how Pilar has been steadily getting rid of everybody. Early this morning, she decided to get rid of Marty too. Marty is sixty-eight, but her Social Security won't be enough for her to live on, so she keeps working. Marty pleaded with Pilar to keep her as her secretary. They were in the morning room, and we were all listening at the door."

"Who was listening?" I asked.

"Me, Gina, and Charlie," said Krystal. "Marty pleaded to keep her job, but Pilar wasn't having any of it. She was merciless. It was pitiful. Pilar's answer was that Marty was too old and she should get out. Pilar said that she was cleaning house, and all the old employees must go."

"No, say it isn't so," I said. "To do that to an old lady? That is disgusting."

"I'm afraid it is. 'You must go too, Marty! You're too old! Just go on Social Security and leave me alone! If you bother me, Marty the martyr, I'll spill your secret all over this town! Wouldn't everyone like to know how you fed your old goat lover his own digitalis meds and watched him die? Martha the martyr isn't so holy after all. Wouldn't your priest love to know you are a murderess? Did you ever confess it or are you content to die with that mortal sin on your soul and go straight to hell? Was his death an accidental overdose, or was it murder? They would throw you in jail for murder in the first degree! I need something young and attractive sitting in my front office, and you are not it!' Yup, that is just what Pilar said."

"What did Marty say when Pilar fired her so cruelly?" I asked.

"Let me give it to you verbatim. Marty said, 'You wouldn't! Not after all these years!'"

"Try me!' said Pilar the wicked witch."

"After all the favors I've done for you, now you are going to dump me?' asked Marty. 'After all the lies I have told for you to cover up your money laundering, cheating on your taxes, and the way you screwed your employees? I was loyal to you for all those years and now you dump me like yesterday's newspaper. No! Not happening! You do this to me, and I'll get you, Pilar!' Marty said to her. Pilar, being her usual evil self, started yelling at Marty and getting abusive," said Krystal.

"No, you won't! Now go away to your old age home or the senior center and play cards with the old people! Go volunteer to tutor math in the schools to a bunch of snot nosed brats! Just get out! Write yourself your last paycheck and leave! Get out!' Pilar just screamed it at her."

"That's terrible," I said.

"Marty got out alright. She wrote herself a check for triple her month's salary and slammed out of that office vowing revenge. Knowing Marty, she will get it, too," said Krystal. "She vowed she would get her revenge, and I believe it. After all, she did get her revenge on that old goat who seduced her."

"Did Marty tell Gina that she was going to go after Pilar?" I queried.

"Marty told us both! Charlie was so disgusted with Pilar that he went out to the pool. He couldn't take listening to her anymore. Marty said, 'I'll get that rotten witch for this! Just see if I don't! Pilar has fired all her best staff, loyal employees, and advisors like Franky Perri. She keeps threatening to divorce Nick who has put up with her cheating and her fishwife screaming just because he cheats on her with young women. So what? Don't all men cheat anyway? Pilar will get rid of Nick. She got rid of her personal assistant Bristol Taggart after ten years. She got rid of her stockbroker Hadley Radcliffe after as many years. She took a new much younger lover when she hired Brendan O'Hara, and she already had Charlie the gardener and pool boy in her tentacles.'"

"I guess Marty really knew what was going on, huh?" I asked.

"You bet. She might seem like a dotty old lady, but she is with it, believe me."

"What else did she say about Pilar?" I asked.

"Marty told Gina and me how she wants revenge on Pilar. She said, 'Now Pilar is getting rid of me, her most trusted and oldest employee of fifteen years. What am I going to do at my age? I can't live on Social Security alone, and at age sixty-eight, no one is going to hire me. What should I do? Work at McDonald's? Do you want fries with that? Pilar is going to pay for this!' That is exactly what Marty said to Gina and me. Then she slammed the front door for the last time and left. That was it."

"Sounds like another case for Dr. Phil. Too bad he isn't here to negotiate a truce and advocate on Marty's behalf. But then, I doubt that even Dr. Phil could fix Pilar enough to satisfy any of her employees, friends, or family," I said. "I think she is the devil incarnate, and who wants to deal with the devil?"

"El diablo, yes indeed," said Krystal. "Guess who else Pilar fired today."

"You're kidding," I said. "She is on a real spree, isn't she?"

"She fired Maria this morning because she suspected her of stealing a diamond necklace off her dresser and hiding it in the toilet tank in a plastic baggie."

"What?" I inquired. "That's crazy. A diamond necklace in a plastic baggie in the toilet tank? Wacko."

"The point being, why did Pilar immediately charge Maria with it? It could have been anyone who took that necklace. Pilar leaves her jewelry lying around all over her bedroom. We all have access to it. But she picks on Maria. I think it's because Maria doesn't speak English, and everyone knows she is an illegal. In addition to that, Maria has been cleaning for Piper as well as working for Pilar. Since Pilar and Piper are having a big feud over Pilar having an affair with Piper's husband, there is a war going on between the two of them."

"Sounds like Peyton Place," I said.

"Exactly, and not a nice Peyton Place episode," said Krystal.

"Poor Maria. I bet she didn't do it," I said.

"I highly doubt it," said Krystal. "Maria is the sweetest, nicest girl in the world. She is also highly and strictly Catholic. I would bet my Gucci watch that Mom gave me for my twenty-first birthday that Maria didn't steal that diamond necklace. I'll bet you anything that Tiggy did it and deliberately planted that diamond necklace inside the toilet tank so she could accuse Maria of the theft. That would set up Maria to also take the fall for all the other thefts that Tiggy committed if it ever became necessary. Maria is innocent and I'll bet my Gucci watch and my Prada bag. I mean it."

Krystal loved expensive name brands that she couldn't afford, so on her May twelfth birthday, her mom bought her Coach purses, Prada bags, and Hermes scarves.

"So now Maria will work only for Piper as a maid and no one else," continued Krystal. "Pilar screamed at Maria when she fired her that she isn't getting a reference. I hope Piper gives Maria more work and a raise. So sad that Pilar is such a mean old witch."

Just at this point, Truffles the psycho Peke again plopped down and refused to move. He had many strategies. One was lying in tall grass surveying his kingdom and refusing to move. He would stealth pull on the long leash until he had pulled us at least ten feet into the field and then throw himself down like a dead weight and refuse to move. He lengthened his average walk by up to a half hour with this little trick.

Krystal gazed at Truffles and frowned. "He is crabby today. His favorite treats are gone, and he won't settle for the fake tasty bones. Do you think Pilar has enough enemies?" She yanked on the leash. "Come on psycho dog. Time to end this walk."

"Enough enemies and then some," I said as we sauntered toward the front door. "Come on, Truffles, go!" I urged our little charge as he snuffled and shuffled his way toward the door, where he knew there were none of his favorite treats waiting for him after his walk. Life is hard when you want your favorite treats, you expect your favorite treats, and you don't get your favorite treats. No wonder the poor little fellow was so crabby and growly.

#gimmetreats

Chapter Four: Clotted Cream

Blow, blow, thou winter wind, Thou are not so unkind
As man's ingratitude; Thy tooth is not so keen,
Because thou art not seen, Although thy breath be rude,
Heigh-ho! Sing, heigh-ho! Unto the green holly;
Most friendship is feigning, most loving mere folly;
Then, heigh-ho, the holly! This life is most jolly.
--From *Blow, blow, thou winter wind*, by William
Shakespeare

Gina and Charlie the gardener brought Pilar into the clinic a few days later. Pilar manifested symptoms of some type of allergic reaction. She was suffering from headache, blurred vision, dizziness, ringing in the ears, nausea, diarrhea, flushing, tingly feeling, and vomiting. As she could barely speak, Gina spoke for her.

Gina, between her sobbing and crying, managed to choke out that she thought Pilar might have an allergic reaction and she believed that Pilar had somehow swallowed some tonic water. Pilar was allergic to quinine. But Gina just couldn't understand how Pilar would have gotten any quinine into her system because Gina made sure it was never in the house and never stocked the refrigerator with tonic water.

Pilar had not eaten anything with peanuts in it and said she hadn't eaten anything at all that morning. Peanuts and quinine were her only known allergies. She had a drink of her usual iced chocolate at ten o'clock that morning, but nothing else that she could recall. She knew quinine had a bitter taste and couldn't remember drinking tonic water, but she was sure that she was suffering from an allergic reaction.

Dr. Thompson agreed. He admitted her to the hospital immediately and they treated her for quinine poisoning. As severe as her symptoms were, they apparently were not enough to kill her.

Krystal and I had a quick whispered conference in the corridor at the clinic.

"Who knew that Pilar was allergic to quinine?" I asked Krystal.

"No clue," said Krystal. "I don't think it could have been too many people though. It certainly wasn't common knowledge among the staff. Gina knew. Nick must know. I suppose Marty could have known, or Pilar's very best friends."

"Friends such as Piper?" I asked.

"I would think Piper would know. They have been best friends since childhood."

"I think Martha, or Marty as most people call her, would know since she has been Pilar's personal assistant for the last fifteen years. She vowed vengeance on Pilar for the way Pilar treated her and that would be a good way to get it. Piper also vowed vengeance on Pilar, for that matter," I said. "Piper might be the perpetrator."

"Then there is always the lovely Nick to consider," said Krystal. "I don't think he is above trying to kill her.

He gets nothing if he divorces her because of the prenuptial agreement."

"So true. What about Franky Perri?" I asked.

"I doubt if Franky would know what Pilar is allergic to," said Krystal. "Or how to plant the tonic water so she would drink it. Quinine tastes awfully bitter."

"Unless you have a very small amount of tonic water in some other strong drink or sugary drink such as Pilar's daily ten o'clock iced chocolate to cover up the bitter taste," I said. "I think we are looking at a recently discarded and close friend such as Piper or Marty. Either one of them could have easily slipped into and out of the house this morning without being seen."

"Or Hadley Radcliffe her scorned stockbroker, or Bristol Taggart her discarded lover, publicist, marketer, and chief right hand man. Bristol might have known about her allergy."

"Who knows? There are so many people who would do her dirt," I said and sighed.

"I'll talk to Gina later," said Krystal. "I'll bet Pilar will blame it on Gina and insist that Gina's carelessness led to Pilar being poisoned with the quinine in a glass of tonic water."

That evening after work, Krystal and I took a walk over Sturgeon Bay bridge. We looked out over the water, and admired the burnished orange, pink, and lavender sunset just beginning to tinge the river with a golden glow. We leaned on the railing and looked out over the water.

"I talked to Gina about the quinine incident, and I was right," said Krystal. "Pilar did blame Gina and she screamed down the house when she got home from the hospital. She insisted that Gina's carelessness was to blame, and Gina was responsible for not keeping tonic water out of the house. She threatened to report Gina to ICE and have her deported."

"That's ridiculous," I said.

"Everything about Pilar's household is ridiculous," said Krystal. "Pilar is like the Red Queen in *Alice in Wonderland*. She might as well run around the house screaming, 'Off with her head!' She is irrational and ridiculous. Especially ridiculous is the fact that there are so few treats in that house that I can barely scrounge a snack when I'm there. Honestly, I think Pilar is anorexic. I have never seen her eat."

"If I were married to Nasty Nick, I would probably never eat either," I said. "I would be so nauseated that I would never eat a bite."

We walked on, admiring the view from the apex of the bridge.

"Guess what," I said.

"What?" said Krystal.

"Guess what Didi found out about our friend Bunty Essex Jones. Remember, I asked her to consult her husband Baronet Charles Huntington-Gore about Bunty. Mom and Stan, Didi and Charles ran into Bunty at a charity gala. She tried to give them the lady of the manor act and they thought she was all wet. Charles knew right away that she was a fake.

Bunty claims that she is the daughter of an English baronet who is a recluse and has a manor house in

Yorkshire. That is what she told Pilar and she has been telling everyone in this little town. You know that Charles is a real English baronet and a Peer of the Realm. He owns a haunted castle in Yorkshire which has been in his family for generations, so I asked Didi and Charles to do a little research. Didi called me today and gave me the scoop on our Bunty."

"What did they find out?" asked Krystal.

"She and Charles found that there are no Essex Joneses in Yorkshire. There is no manor house owned by a recluse named Nigel Essex Jones whom Bunty claims is her father. They are not listed in the book of the English peerage. There is no Bunty Essex Jones. It is all lies. Everything about Bunty is fake, right down to her fake English accent, which Charles detected within about twenty seconds. After all, he is the real English scone with Devonshire clotted cream, and Bunty is not even a biscuit, much less high tea."

"Could have seen that one coming!" exclaimed Krystal. "I thought she was a fake from the minute I saw her gushing and mushing all over Pilar and Nick. 'Oh,

Pilar, you're such a saint!' If Pilar is a saint, I'm Mother Theresa. Bunty sure knows how to feed their egomaniacal needs. She's all full of charm. I cannot stand charming people. I never trust them."

"The next logical question is who exactly is Bunty and why is she hanging around?" I asked. "Didi and Charles did a little digging. Boy, did they come up with some juicy news. Bunty is no aristocrat. She is just flashy trashy, honey. I put the bloodhound Didi to work, and she got the goods on Bunty. Bunty's real name is simply Jane Jones. She is nothing but down home southern white trash.

It turns out that Bunty is wanted in Texas for attempted murder of an ex-boyfriend. She drugged him with opiates and set his house on fire after he dumped her for a twenty-year-old Texas beauty queen. He barely got out alive. On Jane's way out the door she stole all the jewelry from the safe and took a suitcase containing fifty grand in cash. That is why she is hiding here under another alias. I'm sure she has had a few."

"Who has a suitcase with fifty grand in it sitting in the living room?" asked Krystal.

"Jane's mob connected boyfriends? Drug dealers? Her criminal ties that bind? I don't know," I said. "But I do know that Jane gets through life by attaching herself to wealthy older men and milking them for all she can get. Jane has left a trail of old men and ex-boyfriends across the country, most of whom are minus large sums of cash and platinum credit cards. Leave it to Mom and Didi to find out. Those two are like Sherlock and Watson together, plus a pack of bloodhounds thrown in for good measure."

"Oh, baby!" exclaimed Krystal. "I knew there was something rotten there."

"Yes, oh, baby," I said. "You were right as usual. I just wonder what Jane's motives are for attaching herself to Pilar like a barnacle on a fishing fleet boat. You know it must be a scam. She is a leech and a con artist. That is an established fact. Wanted in Texas and probably also in a dozen other states for various nefarious reasons. You can bet that she plans to take Pilar to the cleaners somehow. She probably studied her mark and already has her plan mapped out."

"Honey, she sure ain't no English blueblood," said Krystal. "More like a hillbilly inbred freak who is the product of generations of kissing cousins. Are we going to turn her into the FBI?"

"No, but eventually she will end up in jail and the FBI will catch up with her. I can't believe someone like that lives here," I said.

"Hey, Tabby, I've got big news for you," said Krystal. "Creeps are everywhere. Remember Miss Marple and Saint Mary Meade. Human nature is the same everywhere. Jane Jones probably came here to hide until the heat on her latest scam died down. What better place to take candy from a baby than right here among a lot of trusting cheese heads who are not used to practicing vigilance and don't suspect people of this type of chick canes. Didn't we just start locking our doors last year?"

"Chick canes?"

"You know, tricks, scams, schemes."

"Oh, do you mean chicanery?" I asked.

"Uh, yeah. Isn't that what I said?"

"Uh, no."

"I did tell you about the flowers, didn't I?" asked Krystal.

"What flowers are those?" I asked.

"Bunches of flowers keep turning up on Pilar's bedside table, and I don't mean bouquets."

"What kind of flowers exactly?" I inquired.

"One week it's foxglove, the next week it's purple and white columbine. Two days later it's peonies, and another day it's carnations. No one knows where they come from or who puts them there. Pilar keeps asking everyone who puts the flowers by her bedside, and no one has any answers. It is like they are meant to be a statement of some kind. Gina and I kind of figured that they meant something when the hemlock appeared."

"Hemlock? As in eat this and die instantly?" I asked.

"Yeah, exactly what I mean," said Krystal.

"Curious," I said.

"More red lobsters," said Krystal.

"I think you mean red herrings," I said.

"I wonder about this Bunty babe." Krystal thought for a minute. "Yeah, that could be," she said to herself.

"What are you wondering?" I asked.

"Did I show you those three paintings that I found shoved in the grandfather clock mechanism at Pilar and Nick's house?" I looked at her askance. "Oh, I guess not. I was going to sometime. I thought you might be upset so I kind of stuffed them under my bed and forgot about them. The canvases were rolled up, like they had been cut out of a frame with a straight edge razor blade and clipped together. I took them home and put them in my room. I was cleaning at the mansion the other day and noticed that the pendulum on the grandfather clock was not moving, and the clock had stopped at 1:30 in the afternoon. So, being the mechanical person that I am, I naturally opened the clock to try and fix it." I swallowed hard.

"Did I just hear what I think I heard?" I asked. "I think I'm going into shock. Krystal, did you just say that you found three paintings rolled up and shoved into Pilar's grandfather clock? Jammed in the mechanism? That caused the clock to stop? You tried to fix the clock? You took the paintings home and put them in your room? Is that what you said?"

"Yeah, cool, right? It made me think of *The Secret of the Old Clock* by Carolyn Keene. You read that one, didn't you? I know you did. You read every Nancy Drew mystery ever written. Yes, they looked like they had been cut out of the frames with a sharp object like a razor. They might be valuable. Nick has been rampaging around the house screaming a lot lately. He is the art collector, you know. With Pilar's money, of course. He thinks he is the second coming of Picasso or Salvatore Dali or Jackson Pollock or somebody weird like that. I think that someone cut those pictures out of the frames and hid them in the clock, which caused the clock to stop. *Tempus Fugit*. That is written on the top of the clock. You know. Time flies. However, not on this clock. Time is pretty much frozen at 1:30 in the afternoon. That must be the time that the art thief stuffed the paintings into the mechanism of the clock and jammed it and it stopped. No one noticed but me."

"Naturally," I said morosely.

"I also think that Nick did not call the police to report the paintings stolen because he either got them illegally or outright stole them himself. Either that or he did some wheeling and dealing with the art, and he didn't want the police to know that he got his grubby paws on the paintings. He is super chummy with all our local artists and dealers. He thinks he knows a lot about art. Hmpf! Gina says that Nick thinks he is a real art critic. If you ask me, he couldn't tell fine art from a preschooler's finger paintings."

I felt myself about to swoon and collapse onto the bridge.

"Krystal, are you telling me that you have three stolen paintings rolled up in a tube in your room? Are you telling me that you think these three canvases are valuable paintings? That they are stolen goods taken from Nick and Pilar's house? Are you saying that these paintings have been in your room for a few days?"

"Yup."

"I am seriously going to kill you. Have you any idea what would happen if we were caught with stolen goods amounting to thousands, perhaps even millions, of dollars? Do you know what they would do to us if they found us with Nick's three stolen paintings, even if he stole them from someone else? Do you know what happens to people who harbor stolen goods, impede a grand theft investigation, and get involved with international art thieves?"

"Yup. Maybe we could ask for adjoining cells in prison. I'm afraid to tell you that with my luscious curves and Latina skin, I would look much better than you in an orange jumpsuit," she said.

"If these international art thieves or even local yokel art thieves get hold of us, we won't be wearing anything but our burial clothes. If Nick gets wind of this, we're dead. If the thief gets wind of this, we're dead. We are dead on so many levels," I said.

"Oh, Tabby, please," said Krystal. "You always make mountains out of molehills."

"Yes, because I prefer breathing to lying in an unmarked grave in the woods somewhere. What would my mother think if we disappeared? What would Stan think? What would Brook Trout think?"

"He would probably think he should get a new girlfriend who isn't involved in solving criminal activity, considering that he is a lawyer and an upstanding citizen of Sturgeon Bay, Door County, Wisconsin, USA. Aren't you going to ask me who I think stole these paintings out of the frames and stuffed them in the grandfather clock and hid them there until she can sell them on the black market?"

"She?" I asked.

"Bunty Essex Jones, also known as Jane Jones. That's what she is doing here and why she attached herself to Nick and Pilar," said Krystal. You said yourself that there must be a reasonable explanation when your mom and Didi and Charles found out what a fake and a criminal she is. Bunty isn't just hiding here in the Door."

"She is up to her old tricks," I said.

"She is not wasting any time before she pulls her next con, her next heist, her next crime spree. Bunty is after Nick's art treasures, Tabby. When she met Nick and Pilar at some rich people hang out, she was looking for someone to fleece. She smelled the money and launched herself into Pilar's confidence immediately. What a scum. I'm telling you, I'm so glad I don't have money. People with money are sitting ducks for every kind of desperate criminal mind, every kind of scam artist, and every kind of leech."

"What about Tiggy Butterfield?" I asked. "She is a consummate thief. Maybe she stole the paintings."

"No, she likes jewels. That's her gig. She doesn't do art," said Krystal. "You know, criminals like to stick to one type of crime. They get obsessed about their gig and they like to stay in their own groove. Did you ever notice that?" I stared at her aghast. "When we get home, should I show you those paintings from my room? I have them rolled up in a tube under my bed." I sighed.

"Yes, Krystal, sure. When we get home, let's see these stolen paintings," I said. "I feel quite nauseated already, so let's make it worse."

As soon as we got home from our walk, Krystal bopped off to her room as if she were getting a purse or a new dress that she had purchased that day and wanted me to look at. She came out with the tube, tossed it onto the dining room table, took off the cap, and produced three treasures for my inspection. I just about fainted when I saw what she had in that tube.

"Oh, my God! I think this one is a Winslow Homer lithograph. This one is a Hockney. Either that or it's a darn good imitation. This one is a …. I cannot believe it, but it looks awfully like a Mary Cassatt. It looks like an original. It could be worth millions. This one looks like an Andrew Wyeth. I mean, I'm not sure and I'm certainly no art expert, but it looks like an original to me, and if so it's worth megabucks. If these are originals, we are talking millions. I don't even know how many millions. I'm shaking. I feel sick. I know that some of Winslow Homer's paintings have sold for millions. Oh, Jesus. I think I'm going to faint."

"You can have that Hockney, but I like the other three. I really like that Mary Cassatt, and I like paintings and watercolors of the sea and boats and stuff like that, so I like the Andrew Wyeth and this Homer guy. I guess that is what this Homer guy did mostly, huh? Do you think I could get any more by this Winslow Homer guy? I love the

Andrew Wyeth. The colors are a little bland, but I love the rowboat. Now that is something I could hang over my couch in the living room. Do you think we could keep them and hang them over the mantel? Could we steal any more stolen paintings from Bunty? For all we know, Nick stole them or pulled a scam to get these paintings to begin with. I don't think anyone would notice if we hung them on our walls. They would probably think we bought prints at Walmart and framed them with frames from the Dollar Store." I glared at her.

"Why are you glowering at me like that?" she asked. "Isn't it true that if you want to hide something, hide it in plain sight?"

"Do you want me to pass out from fear?" I asked her vehemently. "I feel like I have the vapors, like one of those southern belles. Get me the smelling salts. If I had corsets on, they would be digging into my skin right now. I can't breathe. I seriously think I'm going to faint."

"Don't do that," said Krystal. "I'm the one who faints, remember? But only when I see a dead body."

"If we don't get rid of these things, you will be seeing both of our dead bodies as you gaze down on us from heaven! This looks like the work of a ring of international art thieves. What have you stumbled into? This is serious. What in the hell is Nick mixed up in?"

"I think he is involved in crime," said Krystal. "That is why he looks panicked and sweaty and is yelling and screaming these last few days. That is why he doesn't call the cops. He knows that the paintings he was harboring as stolen goods have now been stolen by someone else. Someone like Bunty Essex Jones. By the by, she flirts with him mercilessly and he ogles her like a hungry lion staring at a baby gazelle. She leads him around by his libido, but that isn't too difficult since he drools and lusts after every pretty girl within a ten-mile radius."

"The plot thickens," I said.

"Like a Dairy Queen Blizzard with double stuffed Oreos and M&M goodies," said Krystal. "Oh, now I'm getting hungry."

"I just hope we don't wind up dead," I said.

"Uh, yeah. Me too. I hope the FBI doesn't come after us. That would be awkward. I still want to get married and have kids. Besides that, I just started a new diet again and I really want this one to work. It's the cucumber diet. I'm eating nothing but cucumbers."

"You didn't start any new diet," I stated in an accusatory way, my eyes narrowing.

"I was going to start tomorrow. I really was. But then this came up and I got nervous, and I ate like, three chocolate bars and an éclair. I don't even really like eclairs. I really need some scones right now. Do you want to bake some, or should we go to Tasty Pastry and buy a few? I could really use a raspberry orange right now."

"Stop yammering!" I screamed. "We have to get rid of these stolen paintings!"

"Sorry. I'm just nervous. I was fine until you got me all anxious. What should we do?" asked Krystal. "I could put the paintings back into the grandfather clock, but then Bunty Essex Jones, also known as Jane Jones, would get them and make millions. I could give them back to Nick, except he would kill me. I could leave them on someone's doorstep in a baby bunting with a bottle. Or I could make an anonymous donation to the police benevolent fund with the money I could get from selling them on the black market. Is there a black market for art? Or we could turn them into the police, but then we would probably be accused of stealing, or aiding and abetting art theft, or harboring stolen goods. I guess that wouldn't be too good, would it?"

I looked down at my hands. They were trembling.

"You got us into this mess. Now you get us out," I commanded.

"Don't worry, Tabby. I'll think of something. I always do," said Krystal. "Too bad we can't call Dr. Phil and ask him what to do. He would know. Dr. Phil always knows what to do, but I can't call him. I don't have his number, and I guess I can't call Dr. Phil and ask hm what to do with millions of dollars of stolen paintings. That might be just a little awkward. I'll think of something. Just give me a little time. I'll think of something by three o'clock tomorrow. I promise I will." I gave her my coldest penetrating steely glare.

"Tick tock. Tick tock. The mouse ran up the clock. You die at three if you don't tell me what we're going to do."

"You said that like a rhyme. Is that iambic pentameter like we had in English Lit class?"

"No, that's a promise," I said. "Did you know that perfectly nice people sometimes turn into serial killers for no reason at all? I am a nice person. I am a nice person. I need to keep telling myself that." Krystal gulped.

"You look pretty mean right now, and your blue gray eyes have turned to ice," she said.

"Yes, I feel quite ruthless right now," I said. "You have landed us in it up to our necks. I repeat, you got us into this, and now you get us out!"

"If only I could talk to Dr. Phil right now," said Krystal. "What would Dr. Phil do?"

#whereisdr.phil?

Chapter Five: Scone Cold

Ah, make the most of what we yet may spend,

Before we too into the Dust descend;

Dust into Dust, and under Dust to lie,

Sans Wine, sans Song, sans Singer, and—sans End!

--From *The Rubaiyat of Omar Khayyam*, translated by Edward Fitzgerald

Alright, so Krystal couldn't come up with any great ideas by three o'clock the next afternoon, but I came up with one. I thought that we should continue to hoard the stolen paintings worth millions in a tube under Krystal's bed. Not only that, but we should also grab as many of Pilar's stolen jewels as Krystal could get her hands on if she could get them out of the clutches of Tiggy Butterfield.

I decided that we would have to act as crime stoppers. Eventually we could return the stolen articles. If not, we could just harbor them until the end of our days. Or perhaps we could claim we found them in our attic. Oh, that's right. We don't have an attic.

The first thing to do was get cell phone video of Tiggy lifting the jewels from Pilar's bedroom and stuffing them into her tennis racket. We had already talked about this. I would have to rely on Krystal and her snooping skills for that. The second thing to do was get cell phone video of Bunty Essex Jones cutting out the paintings and art from the frames or rolling up the canvases and stuffing them into the cavity and the works of the old Grandfather clock. That might be a tall order, but if anyone could do it Krystal could. She is a stealth pilot extraordinaire. For a big, strong girl, she can move with the grace of a cat, and she is sneaky as hell too.

The question was, when we had the evidence, what would we do with it? I didn't think that the FBI would look kindly on two young twenty something nurses, one of them Latina, harboring stolen paintings and stolen jewels worth millions of dollars. Although Krystal was born here and comes from generations of Hispanic Americans who fought valiantly in all the wars going back to the Revolution, when crime happens the first question that comes up is, "O.K., Latina girl, are you an illegal alien?" The second question would be, "Who is your little friend here? How would she like to spend thirty years in a twelve-by-twelve cell for grand theft, conspiracy, grand larceny, transporting stolen goods, and a host of other legal sounding charges?"

Thanks, but I think I'll pass on that one. Not only are we going to hoard the evidence and hide it in our apartment, but let's hope our Cuckoo kitty doesn't find it first. She likes to shred things and carry shiny objects around in her mouth and hide those shiny things in her little treasure trove of goodies. I even toyed with Krystal's idea of putting the art into frames purchased at Walmart and hanging them in our living room. After all, she was right. No one would suspect us of having great art in our living room, stolen or otherwise. They say that the best place to hide something is in plain sight, like in the story, *The Purloined Letter.*

"I wonder what Dr. Phil would say about your plan," commented Krystal. "I think he might say that you have criminal and antisocial tendencies. You have a criminal mind."

"I'm sure he would," I said. "In that he would agree with my know-it-all older sister Jennifer the psychologist. But let's not ask her. I'm not up for a lecture right now. Besides, we have a lot to think about."

"Are we going to dump the goods, pawn it, sell it, or just hold onto it until the heat dies down?" asked Krystal.

"Are you nuts? We're going to get Mom, Didi, and her husband Baronet Charles Huntington Gore to deal with the police and the FBI for us. They will carry a lot more clout with the authorities than you and I would. With the way that Mom and Didi have solved murders in the past, and because my mom is a lawyer, and Didi and Charles are rich, upper crust pillars of the community, it will be easy for them. When the time comes, they can say they discovered all the stolen goods through a source who remains anonymous."

"Like us?" asked Krystal.

94

"Yes, like us. They can say they found the stolen goods in the attic or the garage, or that Tiggy and Bunty planted the evidence in the garage attic to incriminate them or us or so they could steal it back later. Leave it to Didi. She is a great liar and men love her. Even at her advanced age, all she has to do is bat her long eyelashes and talk in her breathless voice and men melt, completely twitterpated. Mom can be extremely convincing too when she turns on the charm. Then there is Baronet Charles with his upper crust British accent and his dignified walrus manner. He makes an excellent impression, not to mention solid Stan, my stepfather. Leave it to Stan, Mom, Didi, and Charles. They can make sure that Tiggy Butterfield and Bunty Essex Jones are both delivered to justice and the hangman's noose." Krystal's eyes grew wide.

"Do you think they will be hanged like in the wild west?" she squeaked. I sighed.

"Krystal, please. That was just a figure of speech. I think they will both be spending major time in a high security prison. I'm sure they both have past records. I mean, we already know that Bunty Essex Jones, or more accurately, Jane Jones, is a major criminal wanted in Texas and probably in several other states. I'll bet you any money Tiggy's story is a similar one."

"How long are we going to wait before we turn them in?" asked Krystal.

"Until I think the time is right," I said. "When we have more evidence. Meanwhile, you must endeavor to get the video evidence and get those jewels out from under the snooty nose of Tiggy Butterfield. No small feat. You should also keep an eye on Bunty, a.k.a. Jane Jones, not to mention that slime Nick. He is mixed up in something smelly."

"Not a problem," said Krystal, and proceeded to file her fingernails. I must hand it to her. She has nerves of steel. I doubt that her blood pressure ever varies from the low side of normal. "I have a lot more to be upset about than that." She started to paint her nails a bilious shade of green.

"Like what? What are you upset about?" I asked. "I thought you were only going to do your nails pale pink from now on so you could look more typical, and you were going to stay away from the punk rock shades."

"I changed my mind. I decided I like puke green. It fits my mood at the moment. It's my mom," she said.

"What about her? Did you hear from her on her Italian tour? I thought that she calls you every night. What is Tammy doing? Your mom has never been a problem before. Isn't she getting along with her boyfriend Marv the mechanic? Is he mad because she went to Italy alone? Are they getting engaged?" I asked.

"God forbid. I didn't like Tammy dating Marv for all these years, but Marv is nothing compared to what she has done now. She was always a respectable widow up until now. You're right. She was never a problem before. But she never took a guided tour to Italy before. She never met and fell in love with a handsome Italian tour guide half her age before. She never threatened to elope to Venice with her tour guide and spend her honeymoon drifting around in a gondola with a hot young Italian stud muffin toy boy before. She was never a cougar before."

"What? What are you saying? Your mom, as in Tammy Maria Gigi Morales? Your mom who goes to church at St. Paul's twice a week and goes out on one chaste date a week? You have got to be kidding me," I said.

"I wish I were kidding you but I'm not. Tammy is acting like a teenager. Do you know that old song, *Tammy's in Love*? It's happened. My worst nightmare. What if Tammy comes home pregnant? What am I going to do then? If this works out, I'll have a young Romeo for a stepfather who isn't much older than I am. If it doesn't work out, I'll have a broken-hearted mother to deal with. Either way, I'm screwed. Mothers! What is this? Her second childhood? She has been reading too many Barbara Cartland novels and watching too many Hallmark movies. This is worse than when she turned forty and had that crush on Zac Efron and kept sending him embarrassing fan letters. What would my father think if he were here? It's just too terrible for words."

She sighed. I tried to hide my consternation. Krystal's mother had always been so sensible and down to earth. I could not imagine her with some young Italian Romeo.

"I wouldn't worry too much about it," I said. "Your mother is too old to get pregnant, for starters. She must be in menopause, for God's sake. How old is she? She must be at least fifty. So what if she has a middle-aged romance with Romeo the Italian tour guide? It isn't the end of the world. She will come home and forget about Romeo and probably go back to dating Marv the mechanic. Relax. She is never going to marry Marv anyway. He is always covered in grease, his hands are grimy, and he smells of oil and fast food. You know your mother is a clean freak. She is an emergency room nurse, for Pete's sake. No one can marry someone who smells like Marv. Things will all go back to normal. You'll never have to put up with a stepfather like I have. Not that Stan is difficult to put up with. Stan is elemental, like the earth, like a rock, like a large oak tree. So Tammy has a fling. So what? She is only human, you know. Cut her some slack." Krystal sighed.

"If you say so," she said. "I guess. But she better not come home pregnant. I'm not into having a little sister twenty-five years younger than I am." I could not help laughing.

"Maybe Tammy is just having a late hormonal surge before her ovaries shut down altogether. It's just a physical attraction. It's just sex." Krystal paused in painting her nails puke green and glared at me.

"Please! I don't want to talk about my mom having hormones. I don't even want to think about it! Absolutely do not say the words Tammy and sex in the same sentence!"

"You are the ultimate character! Really, Krystal, you are too much!" I exclaimed. "These vacation crushes come under the category of foreign affairs; intense, murky, confusing, complicated, and short lived. Seriously, just put it out of your mind."

"Oh, alright. If you say so. Tammy will come home and go to confession and start going to church four times a week. She will return to her boring dating life with Marv, which I'm pretty sure is celibate and involves nothing more than holding hands. I can only hope. Are we going to the Cana Island Lighthouse picnic open house and fundraiser tomorrow afternoon?"

"Why would we go there?" I inquired.

"Everyone who is anyone will be there. Gina and the entire staff have been working on the food and beverages. Pilar will take all the credit though. She and all her friends are going to be there so they can swan around playing lady of the manor. Nick is going too. Your mom, Stan, Didi, and Charles will probably be there. The whole county is probably going to be there. They are raising money to spruce up the lighthouse."

"Oh, yes, we should definitely be there," I said. Cuckoo was hungry for her treats. She rubbed against my legs and meowed pitifully. I gave her her favorite treats which she devoured in seconds.

"Mew!" said Cuckoo and proceeded to shred her latest ball of yarn all over the carpet.

I was exceedingly glad that Krystal and I did go to Bailey's Harbor to the Cana Island Lighthouse fundraiser. As it turned out, it was quite an interesting day. Everyone took the hay wagon across the causeway and enjoyed hours of sunny beatific weather munching on goodies and listening to the organizers extolling the virtues of the more than one hundred fifty-year-old lighthouse. I believe a lot of money changed hands and the wealthy dug deep into their designer pockets to give to the good cause of preservation of the old lighthouse, standing eighty-nine feet tall above the waves. Many of us took the tour, trudged up the ninety-seven steps of the spiral staircase, and listened to the history of Cana Island for something like the tenth time.

We enjoyed the view from the circular platform high above the crystal-clear waters of the eastern side of the Door looking out over Lake Michigan. We admired the staying power of those hardy lighthouse keepers who kept the lights burning for over one hundred years without modern conveniences. Krystal and I sashayed around the grounds for a few hours making small talk with everyone in the county who was there that day.

"Great party, what?" brayed Didi's husband Baronet Charles Huntington Gore. "And such a good cause! Love this old lighthouse, great establishment! Marvelous! Just marvelous!" Baronet Charles Huntington Gore looked and sounded rather like an aristocratic walrus, or at least I had always thought so. "You Americans, a clever lot, I say! Awfully good at preserving your history, although it isn't much of a history I should say. Not like Britannia, going back thousands of years. Although to be fair, we Brits didn't officially gel until something like the eleventh century, what?"

"Oh, Charles! You're so funny!" giggled Didi Spencer, my mother's best friend since kindergarten. Her melodic voice tripped up and down the scale as she talked to us and sipped her glass of wine. Didi looked just as slim and beautiful as ever. My stepfather Stan came up and stood beside me, looking glum and uncomfortable. He hated these fundraiser things. He was dressed in his good clothes which consisted of his best plaid flannel shirt, best jeans, and cowboy boots.

"I'd rather be out fishing for walleye or salmon. Maybe trout," he confided. Stan was an obsessive-compulsive fisherman. "But your mother drags me to these things."

"I know, Stan, but Mom will appreciate your efforts at socializing," I said. Stan grunted noncommittally.

"Yes, he makes huge sacrifices for me," agreed Mom as she came up on my left and gave me a conspiratorial wink.

"We might have a case for you to solve," said Krystal. I gave her a firm nudge in the ribs.

"Oh?" said my mom with interest.

"She's just joking," I said. "It's more a case of where did our little Cuckoo hide Krystal's best watch."

"Oh, yeah, my watch," said Krystal, catching herself just in time from spilling the beans. "Not the watch I have on, you know. Just to make that clear. My old watch. My good old, old watch. The keepsake I had as a kid. The one my mother gave me. Yes, that watch. Yes, the case of the missing watch."

"What's this?" asked Javier, Krystal's boyfriend. "A new case?"

"Yes, a case of measles," I said. "There has been a bad breakout from unvaccinated people suffering from measles. Just hope you don't get it. It's miserable. You should have seen the kid they brought into the clinic this week, covered in red itchy bumps." There was no kid and no measles breakout, but that was the best I could think of. That put a damper on interest in any new crime case, but Brook Trout did give me a funny sidelong look.

"Let's hope you and Krystal don't get involved in any new case," he said. "I don't like you putting yourself in danger."

Just at that moment, Claudia Cannell came striding up to me with a kitten tucked under one arm and holding the leash of a huge, old hound dog in her other hand.

"Oh, here comes trouble," breathed Krystal.

"Tabitha! I'm so glad I found you! These two are rescues and I can't find anyone, and I mean anyone to take them. Their names are Madrigal and Marmalade. They must go as a couple. They are so attached to each other. I could find someone to take the kitty, but no one will take this dear old darling drooly hound dog, and he is just so sweet!"

"No!" shouted Krystal. "We have one kitten, and we cannot take anymore."

Claudia ran on, deaf to Krystal's protestations and denials. For fully ten minutes she harangued us with the sad story of how this dear, drooly old bloodhound and this darling little angel kitten had to find a forever home together or it was curtains, yes curtains for them both. They would both have to be put down and wasn't that a shame and a crime. Yes, you bet it was.

Stan took Mom's arm and dragged her over to the craft table. He knew that she was a sucker for a sob story. Charles immediately followed suit with Didi. Krystal wandered off with Javier. That left Brook Trout and me. Claudia, sensing a willing victim in Brook, pressed her point. Fully ten more minutes of begging and pleading went on before Brook finally gave in and said he would take them both.

I think his choice was influenced by the fact that he had a few glasses of wine under his belt, and it was a sunny, mellow day without a cloud in the sky. It was the kind of day when problems seem to float away with the cottony clouds in a robin's egg blue sky, and all the world seems like one big spool of cotton candy just waiting to be eaten. The soft sound of waves lapping on the shore and the freshening breeze off the water completed the ambiance.

It was a day that lowered your blood pressure naturally and calmed the turgid soul, a day when angst was what other pathetic people clung to while you were on a natural Zen high. I could in fact feel that Brook Trout's aura today was a calm light blue with glints of rose and lavender, a state he rarely achieved in his relentless pursuit of being a legal top dog. Brook was so clueless and yet so tenaciously ambitious and driven to succeed, a quality I found endearing and exasperating at the same time.

Claudia went for the jugular and quickly handed over the reins to Brook, tucked the kitty firmly into the crook of his arm, and wrapped the leash of the bloodhound around his wrist. Brook stood there passively staring at her.

"God bless you, Brook!" was her last salvo and she was gone with the wind, probably to find more willing animal loving victims among the crowd. I gazed at Brook's new friends, Madrigal and Marmalade.

"What just happened?" he asked. "Why did I say yes?"

"What are you going to name them?" I asked. "Not Madrigal and Marmalade I hope."

"I think I'll name the kitty Misty and the dog Mossy," he said. I made noncommittal noises. I wondered how long it would be before he begged me to take them off his hands. Brook doesn't know much about taking care of animals. Just at that moment, Krystal came rushing up.

"Tabby! Tabby! Pilar just collapsed inside the lighthouse, and they have called the ambulance to take her to the hospital!"

"What?"

"Nick and Tiggy Butterfield and Bunty Essex Jones are all buzzing around her like bees around the queen, acting all panicked. Gina is looking white and scared, and all the minions are whispering about it and speculating. Everyone else is already accusing each other of giving her something she was allergic to."

"Yes, that's right," said Javier. "The funny thing is, lots of people are getting sick and saying they feel like they have to throw up."

"You didn't eat anything from the food inside the lighthouse, did you?" asked Krystal.

"No, we only had a glass of wine and those bakery cookies from Sugared Delights," I said.

"Good, because Gina thinks that everyone who ate the special scones from Pilar's house, the ones Gina made, are getting sick. She is scared she is going to be blamed. Some are running for the restroom. Others are looking green and nauseous."

"Oh, brother," I said. "So glad I didn't eat a scone. I love scones. I didn't even know there were any or I probably would have had one. Or two. Maybe three."

"Me too," said Krystal. "Maybe four, or as many as I could grab without looking like a greedy pig. In fact, I was just going to go in and see if there were any left for Javier and me. They gave Pilar her antidote."

"What antidote is that?" I asked.

"The Epi-pen Pilar always carries with her in case she should eat anything containing peanuts. They aren't sure what it was, but they suspect it was something in the scones and they had to give her the antidote. I think she will be alright because they gave her the antidote as soon as she started to feel sick, but they are taking her to the hospital to be examined anyway."

"But not everyone can be allergic to peanuts," I said. "Why would everyone else get sick? Maybe there is something else in those scones."

We all exchanged glances. Luckily, we were at the end of the afternoon. The incident with the scone, if that were indeed the culprit, put a damper on the festivities for the day. It was as if the sun went behind a cloud. The crowd quickly dispersed and melted away like cotton candy left out in the sun. That night, I consulted with Krystal. She had called Gina and gotten the scoop on Pilar and the scones.

"Guess what Gina told me."

"What did Gina tell you?" I asked.

"Never, never, never serve anything to Pilar that has peanuts in it. She is highly allergic to peanuts. Pilar carries an antidote in her purse just in case she should accidentally ingest something that has peanuts in it. Interesting, huh? You bet it is, especially considering who ordered those scones to be made and brought in today. Guess who gave Pilar her own special plate with her own special scone."

"Who?" I asked. Krystal grimaced at me.

"Who do you think? The great one himself. Nick."

"You're kidding!"

"Would I lie to you? He had them delivered to the lighthouse in a fancy woven basket with Pilar's family crest on it to make it look like she arranged for the scones to be brought into that luncheon. Incidentally, I think that family crest came straight off the Internet. There is no way that Pilar's family has some aristocratic connection in Merry Old England. No way. Pilar did not order those scones. Nick did. Gina told me that she had direct orders from Nick to have those scones delivered on time for the luncheon."

"Is Pilar home from the hospital?"

111

"Oh, yes. She is alive and well and torturing everyone. She spent the rest of the day into the evening screaming at the help, especially Gina whom she accused of trying to kill her by feeding her poison scones. Gina protested that it was Nick who doctored the scones, but strangely enough, Pilar doesn't believe her. She said that Gina put something into all the scones to make everyone sick and that was just her little Mexican joke. She accused her of having her Montezuma's revenge. She has threatened to turn her over to ICE and have her sent to a Mexican prison and all kinds of dire fates. Poor Gina spent the evening in her room crying."

"But how could Nick have put anything into the scones? Why did everyone feel the effects of those scones?" I asked. "Peanuts aren't going to make everyone sick, and besides that, who puts peanuts in scones? That's crazy."

"No one puts peanuts in scones, and Gina certainly did not. She thinks that Nasty Nick put something like laxatives or rancid butter or household cleaner in the scone batter when she had it sitting on the counter. She also thinks that Nasty Nick slipped some peanuts or peanut butter in the special scones that he had Gina prepare for Pilar. Gina saw him slinking and slithering around the kitchen. She said that Nick stole a few of the scones from the basket. She saw him do it. She is sure that Nick doctored a few of the scones and made sure that Pilar would eat the one he delivered to her."

"How could he do that, and why would he want everyone to get sick? So that he could cover up the toxic thing that he made sure Pilar would get in her specially doctored scone? Isn't that just a little crazy? What was the motive? Is she really divorcing him? Did he really try to kill her?"

"Questions, questions, my little Sherlock. Why don't you have the scone crumbs analyzed?" asked Krystal.

"I would have to have the remnants and we don't have them," I said.

"Correction. You don't have them. I do."

Here, Krystal reached behind her back and as if magically producing a rabbit from a hat, brought forward a woven basket full of scone remnants and crumbs.

"I rescued these from the general table. I also rescued Pilar's individual discarded scone from the waste basket she threw it in after she took only one bite. I saw her make a face as she bit into it, and I became very suspicious. I also rescued these crumbs."

"How did you manage that?" I asked, astounded.

"I have skills," said Krystal.

"You sure do," I agreed. "Like lock picking and body slamming criminals and taking them down, among other things."

"I hate to brag but I am good at it."

As it later turned out, Krystal did have the scones analyzed, and Gina was right. The scones were doctored with a powerful laxative so that everyone would get sick, but not lethally so. Pilar's scone, however, showed traces of peanut butter. No wonder she had made a face and thrown it away. She is allergic to peanuts and hates peanut butter. Did the perpetrator think that Pilar would eat the whole thing and get a lethal dose of peanuts before she could get the antidote? Wasn't that kind of stupid? Could it have been Nick who tried to poison Pilar? Good looking and a pretty face but not too bright. Just what is Nasty Nicky playing at?

Things were quiet for a few days. We had a short reprieve from the three-ring circus that was Pilar's household. Brook and I went on a double date with Krystal and Javier. The four of us went out to dinner at the Carrington Restaurant at the Landmark Resort and saw a play at Peninsula Players in Fish Creek. We also went on a trolley tour of ghostly Door County and took the ferry to Washington Island to see the fields of lavender.

Krystal and I took a day off and visited several local art galleries; the Lardiere Gallery & Studio in Ephraim, the Paint Box Gallery on Highway 42 in Ephraim, the Blue Dolphin House on Water Street in Ephraim, and the Edgewood Orchard Galleries in Fish Creek. Later, those few days would seem like the calm before the storm.

#NastyNickyBaby

Chapter Six: This Side of Parasites

The Moving finger writes, and having writ,

Moves on; nor all your Piety nor Wit

Shall lure it back to cancel half a Line,

Nor all your Tears wash out a Word of it,

--From *The Rubaiyat of Omar Khayyam*, translated by
Edward Fitzgerald

Saturday morning Krystal and I went on an errand
for Gina. Krystal agreed to go to the grocery store and get
Truffles' special treats and expensive gourmet dog food.
Upon our return, we waltzed into the kitchen and Gina
paid Krystal out of the household funds. On our way out
we passed by the library and just happened to overhear an
interesting conversation. Let's say it was more of an
argument. We sidled up to the library door that was open

just an inch or two, and when we realized who was talking, we listened brazenly at the door.

"Where are they?" demanded Nick.

"Where are what?" queried Bunty in a low voice. Her English accent was noticeably absent, and her voice sounded more like a Texas low country twang.

"You know what," said Nick in a gruff growl. "They weren't in the grandfather clock."

There was a pause.

"They have to be in the clock!" said Bunty. "That is where I put them. Don't be ridiculous! Are you trying to cheat me and keep everything for yourself?"

"No, but you probably are!" accused Nick. Krystal and I looked at each other and smiled.

"I swear I put them in there," said Bunty. "Do you think Pilar found them in the clock and put them into the safe? Or in the safe deposit box in the bank?"

"If you are trying to stiff me, I'll make sure you spend the rest of your days in a prison cell," promised Nick.

"I swear I'm not!" Bunty insisted.

"Am I supposed to trust the word of a criminal wanted by the FBI?" asked Nick. "If one of us is cheating, it isn't me!"

"Am I supposed to trust the word of a lying, cheating, gambling, thieving adulterer?" asked Bunty scornfully. "A gambler with a gambling habit that is so bad he needs to steal his own priceless art treasures bought for him by his own wife and sell them on the black market?" Nick chortled at her.

"Who introduced me to my life of crime, dear, dear Bunty? Who lured me into this morass of guilt and led me down the criminal garden path?" he asked.

"Don't make me laugh!" she said derisively. "You were a willing participant. You sold your soul to the devil long ago. Don't act like I'm the temptress."

"Better work on your fake English accent, dear," he said. "You're slipping into your white trash Texas twang. Get those paintings for me or you're in big trouble. If she finds those empty frames stashed away in the attic with the paintings cut out of them, both our heads will be on the chopping block. Believe me, she is without mercy. Now hurry up and get out of here before the queen walks in on us."

Krystal and I tiptoed swiftly to the front door and slipped out before Bunty's high heeled feet shod in their Manolos hit the hallway.

"Oh, brother," said Krystal. "Did you hear all that?"

"Obviously I did, Krystal, since I was standing two inches away from you," I said.

"Here is the really funny thing," said Krystal. "Bunty and Nick are collaborating in more ways than one."

"What do you mean?" I asked.

"I saw them kissing in the drawing room yesterday," she said. "It wasn't just a peck on the cheek either. It was deep throat."

"Ugh!" was my considered pronouncement on the situation.

"Yes, one minute there are co-conspirators, the next they are libido fueled hormonal animals, and the next minute they are enemies blaming each other for the theft of their stolen art. Nick has his hand on everybody's gonads I guess," mused Krystal. "Skylar is just the beginning. He has a regular harem going with Bunty and Tiggy and who knows who else? The way he was flirting with Tiggy the other day I thought he was going to start stripping his clothes off right then and there!" I laughed.

"Good thing you discovered those art treasures tucked away in the grandfather clock," I said. "Good work, Watson."

"To our mutual success, Sherlock," said Krystal. "And to their comeuppance. They are both going to get it."

"Let's see what other plots we can dig up," I said.

"As long as the plots aren't filled with decomposing bodies, I'll go along with that," said Krystal. "You know I faint when I see a dead body, especially a decomposing one." We heard footsteps behind us.

"Oh, Krystal! Wait!" Gina hurried out of the house as fast as her round and curvy body could move and waved at us. "I have something for you!"

"You already paid me for the dogfood," said Krystal.

"No, not that. Look what I found when I was helping Martha pack up some of her things and put them into her car." Gina held up a plastic zip lock bag. Inside it was a syringe. "I sneaked it out of her car and hid it to give to you and Tabby. I knew you two were asking questions about when Miss Pilar had the incident with the quinine."

"You found that in Marty's car?" asked Krystal.

"Yes, and I think that it is evidence," said Gina. "I think it is tonic water."

"But Marty is a diabetic and she has to inject herself with insulin," said Krystal. "So she would have a syringe."

"Yes, I know that, but I swear it smells like tonic water and that means it contains quinine. Martha would have good reason to have syringes and she could have used one to inject the tonic water into Pilar's food or drink. I think that this smells like tonic water. See what you think," said Gina.

Krystal took the syringe gingerly and held it up to the light.

"At first, I suspected Martha of sneaking in and emptying the syringe full of tonic water into Pilar's iced cocoa she has at ten o'clock each morning. You know that Martha still has a key to the house and could easily have entered the house whenever she wanted with no one the wiser. Then I started to think that someone else planted this syringe full of tonic water in Martha's car for me to find."

"You mean that you think someone wanted to incriminate Marty for poisoning Pilar with quinine?" I asked.

"Yes, I think so and it would not surprise me at all," said Gina. "Knowing some people around here and I am not naming any names, I think anything is possible. You girls need to know things like this if you are determined to get nosy." Krystal smelled the syringe. She pushed out a little into her palm and smelled it.

"I think you are absolutely right, Gina," said Krystal. "Thanks." Gina winked at us, put her finger to her lips indicating we had her silence, turned, and waddled back into the house. Krystal and I looked at each other.

"Maybe Nick did it and was hoping that Pilar would die of quinine poisoning," I said. "Then to throw suspicion on Marty, he could easily have planted that syringe in Marty's car. If Marty or Gina had their fingerprints on it, that would incriminate them. It had to be someone who knew that Pilar was allergic to quinine. If you inject someone with a syringe of something they are allergic to, such as penicillin or quinine, it can look just like a heart attack when it is anaphylactic shock."

"Or maybe it was Marty who had the syringe and injected Pilar's iced cocoa. She did vow revenge on Pilar. Gina and I heard her. Of course, anyone could have done it," said Krystal.

"That is just the problem. Too many people hate Pilar, and there are so many things to consider."

"Or it could be an accident," said Krystal. "Accidents happen all the time."

"They happen a little too often to Pilar to suit me," I said. We were on our way to our car when we were startled

123

by Gina. She came bounding out of the house, her round form bouncing down the walk like a soccer ball.

"Krystal! Miss Krystal! Come right away! It's Pilar again! This time she fainted right in my arms! I put her onto the couch in the library. She is seek, very seek again!"

"She is seek?" I said.

"Sick," said Krystal. "Sick as in poisoned probably. Dial 911. I'm going in."

Yes, Pilar was seek alright. She presented with a pale visage and was unable to stand. She was weak, dizzy, nauseated, and sick to her stomach. Krystal and I made her comfortable. Krystal reached into her throat and made her throw up.

Pilar spewed a lot of liquid that looked like green tea onto the Persian rug in the library. This action no doubt saved her life, not that she appreciated it. She swore a blue streak at Krystal before she passed out.

Shortly, the ambulance arrived and took Pilar to the hospital once again. This time she was so ill that she remained in the hospital for three days, at which time it was finally determined that she had accidentally ingested some form of plant poison in her tea. When we heard this, Krystal and I gave each other the look.

"You were right again, Tabby," said Krystal. "I wonder who poisoned her this time. I'll bet it was deadly nightshade. Lord knows there are enough foxglove, monkshood, and other poisonous plants and flowers in this county to kill all of us many times over. That would go along with all those mysterious clumps of flowers that someone keeps leaving on Pilar's bedside table."

"What?"

"Someone has been planting little bunches of flowers by Pilar's bed and they aren't bouquets. They are garden flowers. Gina and I suspect they are meant to be a message. I wonder who is planting those. I wonder who poisoned her this time and with what."

"Maybe it was digitalis manufactured from foxglove, as in Marty's revenge," I suggested.

"Hmmm. Someone sure likes poison, don't they?" commented Krystal. "Like Marty, for example. There are also Hadley, Bristol, and Franky to consider."

"I don't think Hadley or Franky are on the radar. Would they know about Pilar's allergies? Perhaps. Bristol Taggart is a long shot, but I think as her right-hand man, he would have known all about her allergic reactions to peanuts and quinine. After all, he had to run constantly for her food and drinks. Marty, as much as I like her and she is a sweet old lady, is also determined to get her revenge on Pilar. She told us as much. Finally, I know you don't like this idea, but who is always there at the scene doing the baking and serving when Pilar gets deathly ill? Who fixes all her food?"

"You aren't saying Gina is responsible, are you?" asked Krystal.

"I'm saying that it looks awfully suspicious. Who has access to Pilar's food, person, drink, and general welfare? You must admit, it looks awfully funny."

"I don't call it funny," said Krystal. "I can hardly believe that Gina could be the culprit. First of all, she has no motive."

"None that we know of," I said. "That doesn't mean she doesn't have one."

"I highly doubt it," said Krystal. "There are others with more obvious hatred for Pilar; Marty, Bristol, Hadley, and Franky to name a few. Let's not rule out Piper either. Then there is Sticky Icky Nicky. I wouldn't trust him as far as I could throw him. I could believe anything of him. He is a real jerk. Isn't that just like a man?" said Krystal.

"A real piece of devilish work. Something to ponder," I said.

"That's for sure."

"I don't know about that Martha connection. I just can't see Marty trying to poison Pilar with quinine. Marty is so old. Do you think that she has enough revenge passion left in her to plan and carry out a merciless attempt on Pilar's life?" I asked.

"Just because she is old doesn't mean she has no emotions left," said Krystal. "She did kill that old goat lover years ago, or at least she tried to. At any rate, he ended up dead. I know Marty is a sweetheart, but Pilar can drive anyone crazy. Marty does have insulin syringes, and anyone can buy tonic water which contains quinine. Easy enough to put quinine into cocoa."

"I think that in the end, Marty would show mercy and back off," I said. "After all, you know the classic phrase. 'The quality of mercy is not strained. It droppeth as the gentle rain from heaven upon the place beneath.'"

"Who said that? O.K., Shakespeare. I know. It's a quote from *Romeo and Juliet*, right?

"Close. Portia in *The Merchant of Venice*, Act IV, Scene I." Krystal sighed deeply.

"Oh, get out the barf bag and have mercy on me, little Miss Classical Lit. You and your literary allusions." I laughed. "I don't care what you say. I think that Marty is more of a Lady Macbeth than a Portia."

"Maybe," I said.

"One thing about working for Pilar," said Krystal. "There is never a dull moment. If it isn't someone getting poisoned and sent to the hospital emergency, it's that obnoxious little Peke shuffling up behind me and demanding another walk, another treat, and more attention."

As it so happened, the allergic reactions that sent Pilar to the hospital were just a dress rehearsal for the real thing. The very next time that Krystal and I walked up the drive to get Truffles for his daily constitutional, disaster struck.

Gina came barreling out of the house screaming, "Muerte! Muerte! Krystal! Krystal! Charlie! Charlie! It's Pilar! Oh, no! No! Madre Mia!"   #sconecolddead

Chapter Seven: Call of the Reviled

Because I could not stop for Death—

He kindly stopped for me—

The Carriage held but just Ourselves—

And Immortality.

--From *Because I could not stop for Death*, by Emily Dickinson

At this point, Gina went into hysterical screaming, but since it was all in Spanish, I didn't understand a single word.

"Are you understanding this?" I asked Krystal.

"You know I only know a few words of Spanish," said Krystal. "How would I be understanding this?" She turned to Charlie who came running when he heard Gina screaming. "What is she saying?" asked Krystal. Charlie interpreted for Gina.

"She just got a telephone call. Miss Pilar has been found in the Cana Island Lighthouse," he said. "Her body was found on the spiral staircase. She is dead. It looks like she fell down the stairs. I thought she was out of town on that business call she got the other day. What is going on? Now she turns up dead on the winding staircase in the lighthouse. How can that happen? This is terrible. Such a tragedy. We never know when we are going to leave this life. Oh, my God. I can't believe it. God have mercy on her soul."

At least someone cared about her soul. At this point, Gina started to sob and cry hysterically. Charlie put his arms around her to comfort her, but she was inconsolable.

Krystal and I adjourned to the library for a conference.

"Dead on the spiral staircase at Cana Island Lighthouse where she fell when she was working alone after hours for the 150th year celebration of the lighthouse," said Krystal. "How sad. How tragic. How unlike her. When did she ever volunteer for anything? I guess it could be. Maybe it could be. It must be. The police aren't suspecting anyone of anything."

"Call me suspicious, but that sounds fishy to me," I said. "She has three events of so-called accidental poisoning, and now she conveniently falls down the staircase at Cana Island."

"Oh, big surprise. You are always suspicious. You would suspect your own grandmother of theft if she had pennies in her penny loafers that looked a little too new and shiny. Remember when you accused me of stealing your filthy old coffee mug in college? Like I'm going to drink out of that disgusting thing. I'm surprised you didn't die of food poisoning or some deadly form of bacteria. Then there was the time you were sure your mother was stealing your diary and reading it until you found it shoved under the mattress where you hid it to begin with."

"A slim, fit woman whom everyone hates with a passion suddenly falls down a spiral staircase for no reason and dies. Doesn't it sound funny to you?" I asked.

"No, not really," answered Krystal. "Anyone can fall, especially if they take muscle relaxers every night like Pilar did, especially if they are tired and it is late at night."

"Krystal, think. All these accidental things happening to Pilar; the plant poisoning, the scooter tires sprayed with some form of cooking spray, the accidental ingestion of tonic water, and then there was the peanut laden scone. What does that all add up to?" I asked.

"It all adds up to you're not good at math," said Krystal. "Are we going to the funeral? Do I still have a job? What are we wearing?"

"Normally, I hate funerals and avoid them like the plague, but this is one funeral I am not going to miss," I said. "I'm assuming you still have a job until they say you don't. We are wearing black of course. Why do you even ask that question?"

Pilar had a lovely funeral. You would have thought she was the local saint the way her service ran, with plenty of alligator tears shed throughout. Gina, Charlie, Nick, Bunty, and even Tiggy managed a few sniffs and sobs. Piper cried inconsolably. Guilt, I thought. Bristol Taggart and Hadley Radcliffe both looked forlorn, or was it boredom? Martha pressed a handkerchief to her eyes. Was it grief, or was it allergies? Franky Perri and all his crew were there. They stonewalled it, or was that a smirk of satisfaction I saw on Franky's face?

Emotions are such a layered, twisted, complicated phenomenon, aren't they? Sometimes they are too much to deal with, so we push them down into the depths of consciousness. Later, much later, they struggle up to the surface when we least expect it. Then we cry inconsolably for no reason. Take Piper, for example. I spoke to her outside after the funeral.

"I didn't really want her to die," sobbed Piper. "Not really. Maybe I did spray her scooter tires with cooking spray. Maybe I just wanted her to fall off her scooter and scrape her perfect face and body up a little. Maybe I just wanted to bring her down a peg. I didn't really want to kill her. I would never try to kill her. Now she is dead, I can't stand it." The earnest tears made tracks on Piper's beautiful and perfectly made up Botoxed face.

"Why do you think someone killed Pilar?" asked Krystal. "She fell down the spiral steps at Cana Island Lighthouse. Nobody said anything about killing her. It wasn't murder. It was an accident. That's what the police said. It was deemed an accidental death."

"Was it?" sobbed Piper. "Was it really? I warned her about taking too much of that Tizanidine muscle relaxer she took every night in her cocoa. I warned her about trusting Nick to fix that cocoa every night. I warned her about a lot of things. I warned her about that fake Tiggy Fast Fingers Butterfield she has been hanging around with. I know that Tiggy has been stealing Pilar's jewelry. I warned her that Tiggy is a con artist. I knew it. I just knew it! I warned Pilar about barnacle Brit Bunty Essex Jones too. Her two new best friends! Huh! I was her best friend since childhood! I still loved her, even if she did take my husband from me and toss him away like her old Prada purses. I loved her even if she did cause my divorce. I've known her too long not to love that selfish, narcissistic case for the couch. I warned her about her husband who hates her, and I warned her about all the men in her life. Stupid cow should have trusted me. Everyone but me was

135

a traitor to her! One of them probably did her in! These men are all traitors!"

"Such as?" queried Krystal. "Who were all these men you warned her about?"

"Other than her wandering husband Nicky? Such as Bristol Taggart and Hadley Radcliffe, Charlie the gardener, and this new guy, Brendan O'Hara, her new publicist. Bristol and Hadley swore revenge when she dumped them. Charlie was almost forced to be her plaything and you know the resentment that causes. She was a real cougar and a predatory one. As for Brendan O'Hara, he is a first-class gigolo from the get-go, honey. He only thinks about one thing; what Brendan wants. Maybe she wasn't buying him enough Turnbull and Asser shirts, fine wines, and the best cuisine. You can bet a man is at the bottom of this. Don't ever say I didn't warn her. They didn't love her like I did!"

Piper walked away sobbing into her silk scarf, a look of abject misery on her face. Krystal turned to me in disbelief.

"She did it," I whispered. "She killed Pilar. I'll bet you she did. She just wants to throw the blame onto everyone else."

"Oh, no. You want to play Nancy Drew again? We don't even know if Pilar was murdered. Piper is a case for the couch. The doctors and the police have determined that it was death by misadventure. You are just wishing and hoping that you can have another case to solve. You and your suspicious nature. I swear if you find an enigma, a puzzle, or even a ghost of a mystery, you just have to poke your nose into it. I think you missed your calling, Miss Marple. You should have been a detective. I suppose you want me to play your Girl Friday again, your Lois Lane, Watson to your Sherlock. We will be dealing with those red lobsters or whatever they are. Not those scarlet smelt again. One fish, two fish, red fish, blue fish. Which one is the right fish?"

"I think that's red herrings, Krystal," I said. "Hopefully, we won't run into a ton of those."

"I hope not. I'm not that fond of fish. It's smelly, and those little smelts are so distracting." I sighed, turned on my heel, and ran directly into an implacable, immovable wall of a woman.

"Excuse me!" she shouted. "Do you always walk into walls and people? Who are you, anyway?"

"I'm Tabitha Nolan," I said, not without annoyance. "Just whom might you be?"

"You want to know who I am?" asked the wall woman, who had the aura of a big, gray slab of a tombstone. "I'll tell you who I am. I am Marty's daughter Valerie."

"We didn't know she had a daughter," said Krystal, her eyes agog.

"No one knew," said Valerie. "That's the whole point. Marty was just eighteen. He was an older man. He was a rich jerk who seduced my mother and dumped her. I'm the illegitimate result of that unholy union between that old philandering scum and an innocent young girl. I'm surprised you never heard the rumors."

"Oh, we heard about Martha and the older playboy who seduced her alright," said Krystal. "We just didn't know that there was a child involved."

"Yes, there was a child," said Valerie in a harsh, strangled voice. "I was the child who was taken from her young, single birth mother by the Church, by the doctors, by the nurses, by a cruel society who placed me in an orphanage in Green Bay. It was a Catholic orphanage that said I was the child of sin, the result of that mother of all mortal sins, premarital sex."

Krystal and I looked at each other.

"That's right. You know how the Catholic Church is about sex. I can see by the look in your eyes that you two are probably Catholic. But my mother was not to blame. It was that monster old man who seduced her, made her promises, and then dumped her like a hot potato. There she was, young, innocent, barely out of school, alone, poor, confused, and heartbroken, wondering what went wrong. My poor mother. She never got over it. She never even tried to meet someone else or have a normal life. She was so traumatized by the whole thing that she stayed single for the rest of her life. The orphanage kept me, always making sure that I knew I was illegitimate, the product of a bad union."

"That's terrible," I said. "My mother has told me a few things about the old days in Catholic school."

"Catholic school was nothing compared to the orphanage. At least the school children like your mother could go home to their good parents, their comfortable houses, and their nice lives. I couldn't go anywhere. Of course, the men were never to blame with the Church. It was the girls. They were sluts, whores, fallen women, not fit for decent society, shunned, ostracized, talked about, gossiped about, and blamed. That was the way things were back then, fifty years ago."

"I'm sorry," said Krystal.

"Don't be sorry. It isn't your fault. It wasn't my mother's fault. But my mother had to pay and go on paying for the rest of her life. I was eventually adopted and raised by my adoptive parents in Green Bay. When I came of age at eighteen, I set out to find my real mother, my birth mother. Martha was ecstatic when I knocked on her door. She had been wondering about me since the day they made her give me up. They made her feel like trash, and I hate them for it. I hate the Catholic Church with all my heart and soul. I hate the pig who was my father, and if he were still alive, I would kill him for what he did to my mother."

She was breathing heavily with the burden of her emotions.

"I guess that it's a good thing that he is dead then," said Krystal.

"Yes, isn't it just?" Valerie said bitterly. "He never had to face the music, did he? He just went on living his stinking, privileged life, and probably seduced lots more innocent girls."

"Probably," I said. I wasn't about to disagree with Valerie. She was a big, hulking woman with shoulders like a linebacker.

Krystal and I made agreeable noises and stood closer to each other as if to protect each other from the outpouring of vitriol emanating from Valerie's mouth and hanging in the air like a cloud. But she wasn't finished yet.

"This cow lying up there in state in her fancy gold coffin, her too. I would have killed Pilar for what she did to my mother all those years. Pilar held my existence over my mother's head and threatened her with it, almost like blackmail. Pilar constantly accused my mother of murdering the old goat when it was probably his own heart and the normal dose of digitalis that killed him. Pilar made my mother do things, cover up things, do crooked things with the numbers and the taxes. She made my mother do her bidding exactly as she wanted it done. Pilar underpaid my mother Marty and treated her like dirt."

"Dare I ask why you came to her funeral?"

"Good question. I came here to Pilar's funeral to make sure that she is truly dead. I read about Miss Fancy Pants in the papers all these fifteen years that my mother worked for her. I read about her committee work, her contributions to charity, her philanthropy. What a joke. I knew what a selfish witch she really was. Don't think I wouldn't have killed Pilar too. I gladly would have killed her for what she did to my poor mother Marty."

"Did you?" I asked and gave her a penetrating stare. "Did you kill Pilar?"

"I wish I had," she said defiantly, staring with her big, goggle eyes straight into mine. "They say it was an accident but with all the people that hated her, I doubt it. I say congratulations to whoever did the dirty deed!"

Valerie turned on her heel and stomped off towards the church hall where the luncheon would be served. We watched her walk away.

"Oh, Mommy! Wait up!" she called in a little girl's voice and rushed to Marty's side. They walked to the luncheon arm in arm.

Krystal gave me a sidelong glance which clearly said, "Wacko!"

"That one is hard as nails. She must be about fifty years old, and she still calls her mother Mommy?" asked Krystal. I raised my eyebrows and shrugged. We shuffled out of the church.

"Let's go to the luncheon and get nosy," I said.

"Don't wanna. Had enough," said Krystal. She started singing *I Wanna be Sedated* by the Ramones.

"Come on, Krystal. Do you think for one minute that Pilar fell down those spiral steps in the early evening? Think about it," I said. Krystal thought. Then her eyes opened wide.

"Do you mean you honestly think someone offed Pilar?" she asked. "As in murdered her? Marty's daughter wasn't joking about killing her or about someone else doing the dirty deed? It isn't a joke? Do you mean that you believe Piper and this Valerie woman and think someone did kill Pilar?"

"When you consider all the people who hated Pilar and consider the way she died, plus the mysterious circumstances of her death, it sure seems possible. Not only possible, but probable. The paper said that she died in a fall down the spiral staircase at Cana Island Lighthouse. That is what the police say. I happen to know there is more to it than that. There were drugs in her system. It was Tizanidine and more than a little. That's what the preliminary report said. But we must wait for the complete toxicology report and the official autopsy, and you know that can take a long time, even weeks or months."

"How did you get hold of the preliminary report?" asked Krystal.

"I have contacts," I said.

"I'll bet it's that Betty the secretary, isn't it?" asked Krystal. "She knows all the gossip about everyone and gets so nosy. She has the goods on everyone in this town and all their medical conditions. She is always willing to share. She loves to sneak in there and read the autopsy reports. I imagine she types up a lot of the reports for the record books herself."

"Alright, it was Betty," I said. "You know how she loves to gossip."

"I knew it. The paper said that the police do not suspect foul play. It said natural causes. Pilar had probably taken a tranquilizer thinking that she was going home to bed. She got drowsy and slipped and fell down the staircase and hit her head," said Krystal. "Everybody knows that she takes Tizanidine in her cocoa every night to help her calm down and relax."

"Right, and you said yourself that Nick fixes her cocoa for her every night at home. He didn't fix it for her in the Cana Island Lighthouse after hours when everyone has gone home though. So, did she take a pill there in the lighthouse? Think about it. What was she doing in the lighthouse after everyone else was gone?" I asked.

"Volunteering?" offered Krystal. "Doing extra work for the lighthouse committee?"

"You knew Pilar. Did she seem like the volunteering type? Why would she be there after everyone else had gone home? Did she seem like the kind, neighborly, concerned citizen type? Did she have any friends besides ex-friends, barnacle buddies, fake friends, hangers-on, disgruntled husbands, ex-lovers, enraged and scorned employees, lovers whom she treated like personal property, and sworn enemies?"

"Uh, no."

"I rest my case," I said. Krystal sighed.

"Here we go," she said. I looked askance at her. "You think it's murder. Here we go with those red smelts again," said Krystal and smiled. "Oh, boy. A juicy murder.

It's Sherlock and Watson to the rescue. Lead on, Lady Macbeth." I rolled my eyes.

"Krystal, please. Do not call me by the name of one of the worst and most vile villainesses in the history of literature," I said. "If you're going to quote Shakespeare, at least do it right. I think you mean, lead on Macduff."

"Oh, alright, be a stickler, little Miss English Lit. Have it your way then. Just move your bony butt and stay out of the way while I do the sleuthing. You can create a distraction while I do my best snooping. I'm getting nosy at this funeral luncheon." I smiled at her.

"As you wish," I said.

"Wait a minute. I know that Cheshire cat smile. What do you have up your sleeve that you aren't telling me?" asked Krystal.

"Oh, nothing. Shall we go? You first." I don't think Krystal realizes how easily I can get her to do what I want her to do, and I'm not going to enlighten her.

When we got to the luncheon, we mingled with the crowd. I sipped a soda and tried to sidle up to several groups of whispering mourners and listen in on their conversation.

"You know they were having marital trouble, don't you?"

"Well, I heard . . .."

"You know everyone hated her. She was so mean to the help."

"Franky Perri has an undying hatred for her. You know she sold Kerry Industries to Don Derrick. He consolidated and everyone in Kerry industries lost their jobs."

"It's all Pilar's fault, too."

"I hate to speak ill of the dead but . . .."

Bristol Taggart and Hadley Radcliffe stood in a corner commiserating with each other and sending baleful looks out into the crowd. I tiptoed up behind them.

"She dumped you. She dumped me. She dumped Martha. She was about to dump Nick too," said Hadley. "What a witch!"

"Tell me about it. At least you still have your client list. I have nothing. I'm looking at getting a corporate job with a considerable pay cut and no seniority," said Bristol. "Pilar left me high and dry after I was her closest ally and her faithful friend all those years. I hope she is burning in hell right now. I really think I will take off for parts unknown someday. I've had enough of this town. I've always wanted to see Australia."

"You and me both," said Hadley. "I think I'm going to Europe."

"Speak of the devil. Here comes Brendan O'Hara, star boy and my replacement," said Bristol. "Even he looks downcast. His cougar and the goose that laid the golden egg is dead. Whatever will he do now? Perhaps he will look for another job as a gigolo. Marketer and public relations my foot. I've read his press releases. He can barely write a simple declarative sentence. He has the vocabulary of a five-year-old. But I'm sure he has other, shall we say, talents for which he was very well paid. There were certain job requirements that came with the job if you know what I mean."

"I understand. How are you, Brendan?" asked Hadley. Hadley and Bristol each gave Brendan the frozen social smile which did not reach their eyes.

"So sad," said Brendan. "What a wonderful woman she was."

"Super," said Hadley grimly. "A saint."

"Yes, very special," choked Bristol, his lips twisting in a sardonic smile.

"I'm sure going to miss her," said Brendan.

"I'll bet you will. Won't we all?" said Hadley with emphasis.

"I don't know what we will do without her," growled Bristol through clenched teeth. Hadley turned and saw me.

"Hi, Tabitha. Nice to see you here," he said. "I decided you were right. I'm taking a vacation, a nice, long, extended vacation. I'm going to regroup, reassess, and take my time deciding what I'm going to do next with my life. My blood pressure has already improved."

"That sounds like a good idea," I said. "Where are you going on vacation?"

"I'm starting with Belize. Then I'm hopping over to Europe. I'm going to hit Amsterdam, London, Paris, Dublin, Madrid, and Munich, not necessarily in that order. I'm taking a cruise down the Danube. I want to hit all those castles and museums and steep myself in European history. I'm going to soak up everything like a sponge. After that, who knows?"

"Sounds good," I said.

"Yes, I need to disappear for a while. I need to get out of here. I have a few things on my mind I need to deal with." I wondered just how desperately Hadley needed to escape, and what was on his conscience. Was it guilt, grief, remorse, or gratitude?

Franky Perri sat at a table with all his friends. He picked up his water glass and toasted the others. "After this, we're all going out to the local bar and celebrating," he said, loudly enough to be heard halfway across the room. "Not the fancy tourist spots. One of our places where they don't darken the door with their arrogant, big city attitude!"

The others laughed and toasted him with their water glasses. Then he started to sing, "Ding, dong, the witch is dead. Which old witch? The wicked witch. Ding, dong, the wicked witch is dead!" They all laughed. Wow, what a recommendation for Pilar. I hope when I die, I evoke a little more sorrow than that.

Nick sat in a corner crying into his silk handkerchief. Can you believe that Skylar was right by his side consoling him?

"Crocodile tears if I ever saw them," I said softly to Krystal. "What an actor. He should be on the soaps." Nick broke down in jagged sobs. Both Tiggy and Bunty rushed to his side along with Skylar, their little black dresses hiking up on their thighs as they embraced him.

"The harem rushes to console the sheik. I think I'm going to toss my cookies right onto this table," said Krystal.

"No kidding. Look at Regan, Goneril, and Cordelia sucking up to King Lear. That makes me sick."

"Speaking of cookies, I hope they have some good ones for the dessert," said Krystal. "What do you think we will get to eat? Chicken casserole and scalloped potatoes? Three bean salad and baked beans with bacon?"

"Probably," I said. "Something repulsive to us vegetarians, no doubt. I hope we at least get French bread and cheese."

As it turned out, the luncheon was decent and we picked up a few tidbits of information, as we sat at the old crone table. No one knows the gossip like the old crones. They seemed to think that, just like on television, it's usually the husband.

"The police said it was an accident."

"She took too many pills and fell down the stairs at the Cana Island Lighthouse and hit her head."

"A likely story."

"I don't believe it. Somebody did her in. It's always the husband. He fits the bill."

"How many has he had affairs with?"

"How many did she have affairs with?'

153

"This whole country is going to hell in a handbasket."

"We should all be Jessica Fletchers like in *Murder, She Wrote* and investigate the case."

"I think it's a lot easier on television than it is in real life."

"I heard their marriage was on the rocks."

"Fifty percent of first marriages end in divorce. Seventy percent of second marriages. Eighty percent of third marriages. No surprise with today's morals, or shall I say lack of morals?"

"If I were young, I would never get married. I would be a nun."

"I wish mine would die. He is getting to be a real tyrant. Old men just get weirder."

"Mine started out weird and now he is senile. He used to be wild and fun. Now he is just an old man sitting in a chair. He acts like he has Alzheimer's. He can't even remember my birthday. I don't think he remembers my middle name. He doesn't even know what color my eyes are. Why can't God take him, I ask you?"

"Mine never remembered my birthday. I would circle my birthdate on the calendar and write in big red letters, this is my birthday and I like presents. Then he would say, 'I thought your birthday was September 22nd.' That was his first wife's birthday. Old maids have it best of all. They live a peaceful life without all the trouble men bring."

"My life has been a lot more peaceful since mine died. I loved him but I have to admit, life is considerably easier now. It's just me and the kids and grandkids without having to wait on him all day and night."

"So many marriages end in divorce, it isn't even worth it to get married anymore."

"That's better than ending in murder. Like this one did I'll bet."

"Oh, come now, girls. The police said it was an accident. You know those stairs at the lighthouse are winding and terrible, especially if you are tired and it's late and you are there alone. Anyone could have fallen down those stairs, and you don't need to be old to trip and fall. For Pete's sake, there are ninety-seven steps. She fell, pure and simple."

"Maybe, but you know what Miss Marple says. Always think the worst. It's probably true!" Much tittering here.

From there, Krystal and I, being nurses, were grilled on the efficacy of flu shots. There was a fierce discussion on how effective they were. Those who never got a flu shot were adamant that flu shots were totally unnecessary and didn't protect you from the worst of the bugs. Those who did get a flu shot argued just as fiercely that everyone should get a flu shot annually in the fall or suffer the dire consequences. If you die, it's your own fault.

Then we were grilled on Dr. Evans and which nurse he was after this summer to be his sailing partner on his yacht. His wife looked the other way. Maybe she didn't care. Maybe it was a relief for her. Each summer Dr. Evans chose a young nurse to be his lover for the summer. We feigned ignorance even though we knew which nurse was this year's choice. He usually picked on the nurses who weren't too choosey whose husband they spent time with. Or he picked the ones whose husbands were known to be alcoholics, workaholics, or had a wandering eye. But one thing was certain. He always picked the good-looking ones.

Krystal and I knew whom she was, but we weren't telling. Besides, why tell the crones who the nurse of the summer was when they already knew the truth or guessed it? Why do old crones somehow intuitively get right to the heart of the guilty matter?

"I'll bet it's Kelly Kramer," said Mrs. Nelson.

"I don't think so," I said. "She just got religion."

"Maybe it's Danielle Schwartz," said Mrs. Geller.

"I don't think so," I said. "She isn't pretty enough for Dr. Evans."

"Maybe it's Joanna Mueller," said Mrs. Gruber.

"I don't think so," I said. "She is a brunette and Dr. Evans always goes for blondes."

"Maybe it's Tara Hopfensperger," said Mrs. Johnson brightly. "She is a blonde and rumor has it that she gets around, if you take my meaning."

"I heard she just had a case of the clap," said Krystal. "He wouldn't pick her!" That shut them up.

After the funeral luncheon, Krystal and I strolled out of the church into the heat of a bright summer's day. The sky was a brilliant azure dotted with cottony clouds trailing fairies' gossamer wings. We walked unhurriedly to the car and speculated about what we now called The Case.

"What if Pilar was murdered?" asked Krystal. "What if the autopsy comes back with a decision of foul play? What are we going to do then?"

"Let's just assume for a minute that Pilar was indeed murdered," I said. "What are we going to do?"

"I can't believe this!" exclaimed Krystal. "Do you think Pilar was murdered? If so, how will we ever find out who did it? The suspects are already multiplying like the loaves and the fishes. There are so many people who hated her. How will we ever find the culprit?"

"It does seem like they are crawling out of the woodwork just waiting to be candidates for murderer of the year," I said. "I guess that if Pilar was indeed murdered, we are going to sift and winnow until we find the murderer."

"Sift and winnow? That sounds like panning for gold or capturing little fish in a giant net," said Krystal.

"I mean sleuth around. You know, like we did at Brook's non-wedding. We could do a little preliminary sleuthing just in case the preliminary report is wrong. You know, on the off chance that it was murder."

"Cool," said Krystal. She pulled a box of candy out of her pocket. It looked like movie candy, the kind of candy you buy in a box at the movies.

"Krystal, are you eating Dots? Dots? You don't even like those! You should not be wasting calories on Dots!"

"Sorry. Emergency candy required. Sugar high needed. Even Dots will do," said Krystal and popped about five of them into her mouth. "Besides, did you taste that cheesecake dessert? More like cardboard sugar free fake cheesecake from hell, if you ask me. Sorry if I need a little dessert, Sister Mary Tabitha. Deal with it!"

"I thought you were going on a diet again," I said.

"I'm thinking about it," said Krystal. "Do you think I should go on a diet?"

"I think you look great. You're voluptuous and beautiful. You're the one who always talks about dieting."

"Huh," said Krystal. "So, are we going to sleuth around? Who are the suspects?"

"How long do we have?" I asked. "Was it her husband Nicky baby who pushed Pilar down the stairs after he drugged her to make it look like she took too many of her muscle relaxers? Tizanidine can be a potent muscle relaxer that produces drowsiness. Add an opiate or two and Pilar is a goner. Or Nick could have put some Xanax or any other kind of sedative into Pilar's nightly cup of cocoa. That would make her drowsy too," I said.

"Pilar ends up dead, and he gets all the money. Plus, that leaves the way clear for his latest love interest, Skylar the beautiful financial advisor," said Krystal. "Now he can have Skylar plus anyone else that happens to walk by and catch his eye. He can still run around with Bunty, Tiggy, and a host of others. He is such a super slut!"

"Nick and his peripatetic love habits are quite disgusting," I said.

"Yes, he is pathetic," said Krystal.

"No, Krystal, I mean quickly moving from place to place, like a nomad, never staying in one place for long."

"Oh, right, like a rabbit. He hops from one to another. He is always on the move, isn't he?"

"Yes, from Pilar to Tiggy Butterfield to Bunty Essex Jones to Skylar to any young girl he can pick up in some bar."

"Ugh! Gross dirty old man," said Krystal.

"He is still in his thirties," I said.

"That's old," said Krystal. "And dirty."

"Yes, I think we can safely say he is gross and dirty. Between the gambling habit, the art theft or whatever game he is playing there, the promiscuity, and now evolving as one of our prime murder suspects, he is disgusting."

"The problem is, we have so many suspects," said Krystal. "I mean, if you assume that the police are wrong and Pilar's death is indeed murder, right away you can see there are a few likely candidates who had means, motive, and opportunity."

"Yes, lots. How about the old spinster Martha, Pilar's secretary who trusted Pilar to keep her long ago secret about poisoning the scum who seduced her when she was a young girl? How about Pilar holding that over her head and treating her like dirt for fifteen years and then firing her? Now that is motive. Do you think Martha could have done the nasty deed?" I asked.

"Or could it be Valerie?" said Krystal. "Martha's illegitimate daughter hated her biological father and hated Pilar with a passion for mistreating her mother Marty and firing her. Valerie seemed like she could have and would have gladly poisoned Pilar."

"Let's not forget that others also have a vendetta against Pilar. There is Franky Perri, who vowed to murder her in front of all his friends after she sold him down the river and everyone in her Kerry companies lost their jobs. There is Hadley Radcliffe, her stockbroker, who detested her for the way she treated him and vowed vengeance on her. There is Bristol Taggart, her marketer, right hand man, lover, and chief factotum of many years. He swore to get her when she dumped him for a younger, trendier man, namely Brendan O'Hara. Remember that Bristol was already apoplectic when Pilar took her gardener and pool boy Charlie as a lover. Getting dumped and replaced by Brendan O'Hara just added fuel to the fire."

"How about Piper?" asked Krystal. "She had a love hate relationship with Pilar. They sound like they were competing frenemies from childhood. She virtually admitted that she sprayed Pilar's scooter tires with cooking spray."

"I think she did," I said.

"Maybe, or maybe someone else did," said Krystal. "Who gave Pilar the quinine she was allergic to that made her collapse and again, had the potential to cause her death? We have four possible attempts on her life before her actual death. There was the peanut laced scone. There was the tea that made her weak, faint, and sick, possibly filled with some plant poison. She was in the hospital for three days with that one. There was the supposedly accidental quinine dose in the tonic water. The fourth was the scooter incident."

"Interesting," I said. "What really gets me is that it could be that more than one person was trying to murder Pilar. She had so many enemies who were anxious to deliver her karma. Then we also have Tiggy Butterfield and Bunty Essex Jones getting their claws into Pilar, or at least into her jewels and her art treasures. Who knows if they had some ulterior motive for doing her harm? This is a real enigma. It's a real conundrum."

"A what? A cunning drum?" asked Krystal.

"No, Krystal, a conundrum. A puzzle to be solved," I said.

"Right, a puzzle," agreed Krystal. "Probably, a thousand piece one. But we are up to the challenge. At least I am. I don't know about you. I think you would rather sit around reading Shakespeare and watching classic movies on the Turner Classic Movie channel." I sighed.

"Yes, I probably would enjoy that, but no rest for the weary. As the gospel says, much is asked of those to whom much is given. Think how much we have been given and how lucky we are. Now it's time for us to step up and deliver," I said.

"Much is asked of those to whom much has been given. Is that really in the gospel or are you just making that up?" asked Krystal.

"Yes, I heard that in church. I think it's a great truth, don't you?" Krystal rolled her eyes heavenward.

"If you say so, little Miss Photographic Memory," she said. "Sometimes I swear you have a photographic memory. I wish I had a photographic memory. I could have done so much better in school, especially in literature class. I could have studied a lot less, too."

"Krystal, you couldn't have studied less than you did," I corrected her. "I think you did really well for how little you studied and how cursory was your approach to reading the assigned chapters."

165

"Huh," said Krystal. "CliffsNotes saved me. That and watching the movie version."

#RebelKrystal

Chapter Eight: Scone Me!

"O I fear ye are poisoned, Lord Randall my son!
O I fear ye are poisoned, my handsome young man!"
"O yes, I am poisoned: mother, make my bed soon,
For I'm sick at the heart, and I fain wald lie down."
--from "Lord Randall" (Anonymous)

Krystal continued to work at the manse, as we now called Nick and Pilar's house. The next Saturday, I was drinking tea in the library waiting for Krystal to finish the upstairs dusting. I had agreed to help her take Truffles for his Saturday afternoon walk. Tiggy and Bunty, Tweedledum and Tweedledce, had gone out to do some shopping for Nick. The Great One was out on his customary three-hour Saturday afternoon bicycle ride. It was just Gina, Charlie, Krystal, and I at the house.

While I waited for Krystal, I decided to go to the library and read. I was deep into Chapter Three of *Far from the Madding Crowd*. Bathsheba Everdene had always been one of my favorite characters, both for her very human vanity and for her bad luck with men. At least the story ended happily for Bathsheba and Gabriel, if not for some of the other characters.

I sat back in the huge armchair in the library facing the window, completely hidden by the height and width of the chair. Thus, I was invisible to anyone having a conversation at the door of the room. That is how I happened to overhear a discussion which was a real game changer. I heard soft voices in the hallway. This is what I heard.

"Maybe Nick got rid of her. Maybe he will get rid of us too," said Charlie. "He is not the kind of enemy you want to have against you."

"Let's hope not. I need this job," said Gina. "I put up with her bossing me around, so maybe I can put up with him. I don't know who is worse, her or him. All I know is, I have to put up with it. At least you are released from being her pet Mexican at her beck and call day and night. I could not stand to know that she considered you her personal pet plaything. It made me crazy. I thank God you are free of her. We are free of her."

"We both thank God!" said Charlie fervently. "I should say five rosaries for that and thank the Virgin for releasing me."

"Did you kill her?" said Gina in a low voice. Charlie sounded appalled.

"Madre Maria! No! I swear it! I could never do something like that! God preserve us!" Gina giggled.

"I knew you never could. I was just kidding you!" she said.

"Not that I didn't think about it," said Charlie. "Don't think I wasn't tempted. Maybe you did it!" Charlie giggled. "Maybe we did it together. Confess, Mom!" More giggling. "You hated her for using me. You hated her because you could not openly be my mom. You knew she would use it as leverage against you somehow. How many times did you want to kill her?" More laughter.

"Hush! Don't let anyone hear you say that," said Gina. "No, I never would hurt her. I wanted to though. She was lucky I am a God-fearing woman. She was the only thing standing between me and ICE. No way, Jose! Now Mr. Nick is the only thing standing between me and ICE. Saints preserve us and pray for us if that useless fool gringo is the only one I am depending on."

"Hey, maybe you should get a husband. Then you don't have to worry," said Charlie. "Get one who is a citizen and gives you a green card."

"No, I don't think so," said Gina. "I haven't had a man in twenty years. I might like to have a man, but then I put up with his crap. Not worth it, amigo!" Charlie laughed. "Besides, I have you, my own handsome son to depend on. I could never admit it to her though. Then she would have had something else to hang over my head besides being illegal. It was galling to know she was using you. Don't think I didn't want to kill her for using my son. I know it wasn't your fault. I know the way she used people, threatened them, manipulated them, destroyed them. Yes, I wanted to kill her every day. But hey, who didn't want to kill her?" More laughter.

"I'm going to water the plants. Make me some flan, O.K.?"

"If you look at that loose bolt in my car, I make you flan. I make you lots of flan."

"Anything for you, Mom. See you later." I could hear Charlie's retreating footsteps. Gina sighed and headed down the hall.

So that was the lay of the land. I had wondered about that. I thought there was a resemblance between Charlie and Gina. I had thought maybe they were aunt and nephew, or cousins, or even brother and a much older sister from a large family. I never thought they were mother and son. I could see why Gina would keep that from Pilar. I could also see why it would drive Gina wild with hatred to see Pilar use Charlie the way she had.

Later, when Krystal had finished her dusting and we were walking the psycho Peke, I brought up the subject and told her what I had overheard.

171

"This changes things," I said.

"In what way?" asked Krystal. "So Gina and Charlie are mother and son. So they both had a reason to hate Pilar. Them and half the county. So what? They didn't do it."

"Maybe, or maybe not," I said. "Maybe he thinks she did it to save him from Pilar's evil clutches. Maybe she thinks that he did it to save her from Pilar's abuse. They each had means, motive, and opportunity. But my money would be on Gina. Mothers are lunatics when it comes to protecting their children. She couldn't stand watching Pilar use her one and only beloved son."

"Think so?"

"Who was there when the scones were made and delivered to the lighthouse for the fundraiser? Who knew that Pilar was allergic to peanuts and could have laced her scone with peanut butter? Who was in this kitchen making the scones? Who could have slipped quinine into Pilar's cocoa? Who was in charge of the household and knew that Pilar was allergic to quinine? Who could have put plant juice from a simple poison garden plant like foxglove or lily of the valley into Pilar's tea? Who prepared Pilar's tea? Who was right there in the kitchen every time Pilar was poisoned with something? I'll tell you who. Gina, that's who. Who could have gone into the garage and sprayed the tires of Pilar's scooter with cooking spray? Either Charlie or Gina could have done that."

"No, I think Piper did that. She admitted as much," said Krystal. "I don't think Gina would have murdered Pilar. Gina was so upset each time Pilar was poisoned, and you saw her when Pilar died. She was hysterical with grief."

"More like hysterical with guilt," I said. "Maybe she is a good actress. Gina could have slipped an overdose of Pilar's muscle relaxers into her cocoa and mixed it with something else even more deadly."

"I would hate to think so," said Krystal.

"Start thinking about it and you'll see that it is a distinct possibility," I said. "Of the two of them, Gina and Charlie, my money is on Gina. I still say that there is nothing a mother won't do for her child."

"I'm not going to think about that now. I'll think about it later," said Krystal. "I'll think about it tomorrow."

"Alright, Scarlett O'Hara, but you think about it," I said. "Let me know what you think." Krystal sighed.

"Right now, I'm thinking I wish this dog didn't poop so much," she said, "What has this thing been eating?" Truffles looked up at her and growled. I swear that dog understands English. If you ask me, Truffles takes particular pleasure in annoying his human servants.

"Can we get this walk over with and give Truffles his treats?" asked Krystal. "It's Saturday. Let's go out to Peninsula Park and climb the tower. Then we'll go miniature golfing at Pirate's Cove. After that we will stop in at Novel Bay Bookstore and pick up that new bestseller I've been wanting to read. Then we'll eat at The Inn at Cedar Crossing. Girls just wanna have fun."

"Fine with me," I said. "Whoever loses at golf buys lunch."

"That will be you for sure," said Krystal. "Your putting sucks."

"Negative. It will be you," I said. "You always overcompensate."

"Should we put a fiver on it?" asked Krystal.

"You love to throw away your money," I said. As it happened, not only did I lose a fiver, but I also had to pay for dinner.

Give me a chance and I'll attract any trouble in the atmosphere. I'm a trouble magnet. Such was the case on Sunday when Krystal and I decided to go snooping. Somehow, we ended up on Piper's tree lined street standing in front of her mansion. Our car had been parked a few blocks away.

"I don't see her car anywhere," I said.

"Let's go ring the doorbell," said Krystal. We walked up to the door and rang the bell. There was no answer. Krystal tried the door.

"The door is open. Piper hasn't even locked it. Let's go in," said Krystal.

"Should we?" I asked.

"Why not? She is clearly gone. Her car isn't here. No car in the driveway. The garage is open without a car and the door left wide open. Kind of lax about security, isn't she? Even here in God's country she should be more careful than that nowadays. Let's just snoop around a little. It isn't breaking and entering if we didn't break in. The door was open, and we thought she was here."

"Oh, alright. You first," I said.

"No, you first," said Krystal, and pushed me through the door.

"Oh, fancy! Where do these people get all their money?" asked Krystal as she looked around the place. We strolled through every room of the house. It was all neat and clean, with everything in order, thanks to Piper's maid Maria no doubt, the same Maria that Pilar fired after accusing her of theft. Maria was happy to go and work for Piper full time after that experience. We climbed the stairs and entered the five bedrooms and three bathrooms, finally ending up in Piper's bedroom. There was a small doll on the dresser.

"Krystal, did you see this?" I inquired. "Look at this! I think it's a voodoo doll. It looks like Pilar, and it has pins stuck through the head and heart. It seems like Piper was chock full of hatred for Pilar and she would stop at nothing to see her dead. She even tried voodoo spells."

"Yes, it's looks like Piper tried to kill Pilar by practicing voodoo. Does this little doll look just like Pilar or what, hey?" asked Krystal.

"The skinny blonde one with the painted face and the six-inch pins stuck in the head and heart? Yes, I would say so. It even looks snotty and stuck-up just like Pilar looked in real life."

"I've got news for Piper," said Krystal. "If voodoo could really kill you, all my ex-boyfriends would have been dead long ago. Also, that nasty boss we had at our first clinic, not to mention my high school Algebra teacher. Also, not to mention the lab teacher we had for anatomy in college. Didn't we also have her for biology lab? She really made the rounds."

"Krystal, be serious."

"I am serious. Dead serious," said Krystal. "Looks to me like Piper is a prime suspect. I think I'll put her first on my list. She is my favorite candidate for murderer of the year. That act with the crying about Pilar's death at the funeral was kind of fakey if you ask me."

Krystal strolled nonchalantly into the bath connected to Piper's bedroom and opened the medicine cabinet.

"Well, well, well. Looky what we have here!" she crowed. "Pills, pills, pills. And are those syringes I see in the corner?"

"She used to be a pharmacist, remember," I said. "God only knows what she has stashed away in here: barbiturates, cyanide, downers, uppers, quinine. She could have it all."

Krystal started to open drawers and poke around. "She is on the pill. Oh, here is a diaphragm. Guess she wants to be double sure she doesn't get pregnant."

"Don't touch anything. You're leaving your fingerprints everywhere. You didn't disturb anything, did you?" I asked.

"All left in perfect order, guv," said Krystal. "Remember, I'm used to poking around in Pilar's house and getting nosy. I'm good at this detective snooping." Suddenly we heard the roar of a car coming up the drive. Krystal looked out the window through the lace curtains.

"Oh-oh. It's Piper in her BMW. Crudley crumbs. This little Winnie the Pooh is caught with her hand in the honey jar. What are we going to do, Piglet?" We heard a car door slam. "Here she comes. Run!"

"Where the hell am I supposed to run? There is nowhere to run!" I screamed.

"Run into this closet! Hurry! Move it!" We ran into the huge walk-in closet and stowed ourselves away behind Piper's myriad dresses, suits, pants, and stacks of designer purses and shoes.

"I wish I could steal some of this stuff," said Krystal.

"Don't even think about it," I commanded. "Don't tempt yourself or me. Besides, Piper is about a size two, in case you haven't noticed."

"Sick," said Krystal. "I think she is anorexic. I'm going to pass out from fear. Oh, no. I'm getting gas. Burps coming on. Beware. You know I always get gas when I'm nervous." Krystal burped loudly.

"Stop!" I growled. "I'm going to kill you if she catches us in her closet."

"No, she is going to kill me if she catches us in her closet," said Krystal, and burped loudly again. "All this froufrou stuff is making me sneeze. Now I'm going to burp and sneeze." She sneezed loudly three times and burped again.

We heard the front door slam. I shoved my elbow in Krystal's side. She groaned.

"Ow!"

"Maybe that will help you not burp and sneeze," I whispered in a frenzy of fear.

"Has anyone ever told you that you are a ruthless, intense, controlling Scorpio?" hissed Krystal.

"Shut up!" I said between gritted teeth.

"Bossy little freak!" Krystal hissed back. We heard Piper's designer clad feet pounding up the stairs. She spoke into her cell phone.

"I didn't do it, lover! I swear! What do you think? Would I kill my childhood friend? What was my motive? Revenge for her seducing you? If I were going to kill anyone, I would have killed you, Kendall, not her, and I would have killed you right away, not months later. Ha! Ha! No, seriously. Do you really think that I am a murderess? Please. Crimes of passion are not thought out for months and then systematically put into play, darling. Crimes of jealousy and passion are done on the spur of the moment."

We held our breath as Piper entered the bedroom.

"No one has to know where I was that night. We have an airtight alibi. We were home here together all night. Remember that. It's nobody's business. I know those two little nurses are poking around asking questions. So what? If they come around here, I'll give them the stun gun. Or how about a little syringe full of insulin? Ha! Oh, relax. No one even remembers that I was a pharmacist before we were married. You know how people's memories are; short!"

Two little nurses asking questions? Stun gun? A syringe full of insulin? My heart jumped into my throat. I felt a surge of adrenalin. Fight or flight syndrome. My heart pounded so loudly I thought surely Piper must hear it. A sweat broke out all over my body and my blood seemed to turn to ice and freeze in my veins. I could feel the blood surging through my arteries and rushing at my pulse points. There was chatter from the other end of the phone. Piper laughed. I squeezed my eyes shut and held my breath. I sent up a fervent prayer and prayed far more fervently than I ever prayed in church. Piper continued to talk to Kendall.

"Tell me you didn't do it Kendall. Did you? Why would you kill her? Discarded lover's jealousy? You were surprised, weren't you? She tossed you away like she used everyone else and tossed them away, including me. Poor little you. Join the club. You weren't that much in love with her, were you? I know she was irresistible to men even though she was a completely selfish witch. I've seen it since we were kids. Men could never resist her. She was a siren, a mermaid luring sailors to their death. They had a compulsive urge to throw themselves on the rocks for her. You didn't really love her, did you? You better say no!"

I was hidden behind the door. Piper was just outside the closet and standing so close to me that I could hear a series of denials coming through the phone. I could smell her perfume. It was flowery with a hint of musk. I hoped and prayed it wouldn't cause Krystal to sneeze. Then I prayed Krystal's terror wouldn't cause her to burp. I closed my eyes and tried not to breathe.

"That is what you better say if you want me back!" said Piper into the phone. "Kendall darling, if you did do Pilar in, I don't care. I told you I didn't kill her. Don't you believe me? Oh, maybe I thought about it once or twice. Maybe I did spray a little cooking spray on her scooter tires. What if I did? That wasn't meant to kill her; only teach her a lesson. If anyone asks where I was that evening she died, just keep telling them that I was here the whole night with you. The whole night. So what? A few bloody hours unaccounted for, that's all. Nobody knows for sure if she was murdered and they're just speculating. That is just stupid gossip. It's nobody's business. You know how people talk. The official word is that her death was accidental."

More chatter from Kendall.

"I know those two little nurses are poking around. They were asking questions at Pilar's funeral luncheon, and I think they have been snooping. I'm telling you if they poke the wrong person in the beehive, they are going to get stung! Especially if they poke this queen bee! Tell me anything. Just don't tell me that you still love Pilar and will carry a torch for her as long as you live!"

I could hear him protesting his undying love.

"That's better. Let's have lunch. I'll meet you at the Inn at Cedar Crossing at one. We'll have the salmon. Your treat. No, I'm not going to the Screaming Seagull in New Belgium! How plebian! A hotdog at the Big Red Food Truck downtown by your office? Are you insane? I don't eat hotdogs from food trucks, honey. I don't care how rushed you are on this new case of yours. I don't understand why you have to go in on a Sunday to work on this stupid case. You're a partner. You sit where you want and lunch when and where you want for how long you want. I'm not eating hotdogs from food trucks. That's disgusting."

Pause for Kendall to answer.

"It's the Inn at Cedar Crossing or nothing! O.K. A half hour. I'll just throw on my gauzy blue dress. See you there. Later."

Piper rang off, tossed the phone down, and stepped forward to the closet. Krystal and I sank deeper into the depths and did not dare to breathe. I closed my eyes and prayed. I opened my left eye a slit and tried to see a gauzy blue dress. I saw it clearly in the corner. Piper threw open the door, reached out, and grabbed the dress off the hanger. Her arm was inches from my face. I could smell the perfume on her wrist which almost grazed my nose. She must work out a lot, because her arm was toned, tanned, and skinny like the rest of her.

God don't let me die. Don't let her see us. I'll do anything. I'll volunteer at the humane society for a thousand hours. Really, I will. A thousand dogs walked for a thousand hours. Please, please, please! Is my guardian angel on duty? Save me!

185

Piper must have been on automatic pilot because she barely seemed to search for the dress. She knew where everything was without registering or navigating. She slammed the closet door shut, and we could hear her quickly changing. It sounded like she grabbed the phone, and then she started to leave the room, but not before she stopped moving and started to talk to herself aloud. She paused and sniffed the air. My heart did flip flops.

"Why does it smell like candy in here?" she asked herself. "Smells like chocolate and…and something else. Is it jellybeans? Probably it was Maria. She eats candy like a kid just let into a candy store with a pocket full of money."

Oh, God! Witches can smell children and she smells us!

Piper started to hum a happy tune. Then she wailed, "Oh, this hair!" and left the bedroom.

I exhaled. I could hear water running in the adjoining bathroom. Presumably, Piper was retouching her hair and makeup. I heard what I knew to be the spray of aerosol hairspray. After a few minutes of primping, there

186

were retreating footsteps. She jogged down the stairs and ran out the door. It did not appear that she stopped to lock the door. We stayed frozen, unable to move. Seconds later, we heard her BMW roar out of the driveway.

"Tabby are you still alive?" asked Krystal in a strangled voice that did not sound like her.

"Just barely," I answered. "Almost dead from fear but still breathing."

Krystal let out a long, extended, loud burp. Then she sneezed loudly.

"Boy, I've been holding that in forever," said Krystal in her normal voice. "I thought I was going to choke on the smell of her perfume." I sighed and tried to get my blood pressure down to normal.

"Were you eating chocolate and jellybeans in the car?" I asked accusingly. "Piper must have an awfully good nose. You burped it up all over the closet. That's why she smelled it. Were you eating candy? If you did you snuck it because I didn't see you eating any candy in the car."

"Hey! A girl gets hungry, Nurse Ratchet! Who are you? The diet police? It's lunch time, O.K.? Girls just wanna have fun, O.K.?"

"Alright, let's have lunch. We'll have a salad at the diner."

"Or a burger and fries."

"Did you get a load of what Piper said? We are just two nosy little nurses playing around. I take umbrage with that," I said.

"What? You take dumb rage with what?" said Krystal.

"No, umbrage, Krystal. That means I take objection to it," I said.

"You and your mother. You should have been a lawyer just like her."

"No, I don't think so. I don't like arguing a case. I could never do it."

"Could have fooled me," said Krystal. "I think you're great at arguing a point. *Ad infinitum* if you really want to know. You're like a dog with a bone and you just

188

don't give up. I could see you in a courtroom just like your mother. They would call you the little Irish terrier. Then when you get old, you can do wills and estates like your mom does, so you don't have to go into a courtroom anymore and get your blood pressure and your pulse skyrocketing upward."

"Why are you saying these things? Don't you want me to be a nurse with you? Don't you want to be my best friend, roommate, colleague, and occasional Dr. Watson to my Sherlock Holmes? I'm hurt. I thought I was a great nurse, or at least a good one."

"That's right. Cloud the issue. Then confuse and deflect, score a point and win. I rest my case. You would make a great lawyer," said Krystal. "Rest my case. Get it?"

"Yes, I get it, Krystal," I said. "I get it."

We headed for the car. As soon as we were in the car, Krystal reached into the back seat where she kept a small cooler packed with ice, water, and snacks. She pulled out a large bag of M&Ms encased in a zip lock plastic bag and popped a few in her mouth.

"What are you doing?" I demanded. "You're going to spoil your lunch."

"Chill, Tabitha. I have been researching the latest diets. I can't decide if I want to try the Mediterranean, the Keto, the meatless vegetarian, low carb, low fat, low sodium, or just go flat-belly diet."

"Then why are you eating a bag of M&Ms?" I asked.

"This is just to tide me over while I do my research," said Krystal. "Brain work uses up a lot of calories. I need a sugar and carb boost. My brain works overtime and needs a lot of juice for the synapses to fire. We have just been through a stressful trial and some intense detective work. I need a sugar and carb boost right now. It's better than drugs, isn't it? I'm stressed out for God's sake!" I sighed.

"Put that bag back in the cooler and wait for your lunch!" I commanded.

"Yes, Mother. Yes, Sister Mary Margaret Mother Superior. When did you take your final vows? You are the bossiest little bone bag this side of Lake Michigan."

"Krystal, be serious. We have got to concentrate on this case. There are so many possibilities my head is swimming with ideas," I said.

"It's just too confusing," said Krystal. "We must pull a miracle out of the fire, or is that a chestnut out of the air? Oh, horse potatoes! Or is that horse pies?"

"I think it's called pulling a chestnut out of the fire, and I believe it's either horse apples or cow pies," I said.

"Yeah, you know. Farm poop in general. I mean, Pilar was like a fruitcake with year old fruit. She reminded me of a rabid porcupine and had the same personality. That is why she was very seriously murdered. What did men see in her besides the obvious, sex? No one could stand her X crescents."

"Do you mean her excrescence?"

"That too," said Krystal.

"But Krystal, that means abnormal warty growth, usually in the colon. Remember from anatomy class?" I asked.

"But Pilar was like a warty growth in the colon, wasn't she?"

"I, uh, I guess …," I said uncertainly.

"On top of it all, now we have got those red smelts again. Or is that haddocks?"

"Herrings?"

"That's right. Smoked herrings,"

"Red herrings?"

"That too,"

"Every darn time we try to solve a case we end up with a bunch of rose-colored sardines! Or is that perch?"

"I think it is herrings and they are red, not rose colored."

"That's just the funny thing. How can herrings be red to begin with? Fish are not red. Lobsters are red. Herrings are not red. Aren't they silver like all the other little fish?" asked Krystal.

"I believe they are silver fish about a foot long with blue metallic colors on their back. It's just an expression," I said.

"A crazy one. Why don't they say silver herring or blue herring? Why do they say red herring?" asked Krystal.

"I think that a red herring is a smoked herring that is turned red by the smoke. Thus, the expression red herring. People throw red herrings in your path to divert your attention from the real facts," I said.

"Yes, they sure are throwing a bunch of red herrings our way. We have lots of clues being tossed at us right and left that are just meant to confuse us and camouflage the real clues. And what is with this herring business anyway? Why don't they say pickled herring? Like, we are in a great big pail of pickled herring. We are in a major pickle," asked Krystal.

"I'm not sure, Krystal. Why don't you ask them?"

"Who is there to ask? It's the giant them that lurks somewhere in the sky. I mean, who do we mean when we say 'them?' Them is the great unknown, the great majority, the great unwashed crowd of yokels who decides popular opinion. You know, people in general," said Krystal.

"Yes, you are right. But how do we know what they would say? It is because we are all the they. We are all the collective consciousness, or the collective unconsciousness. We are the great archetypes."

"Speak English, would you? Yup, we're in a real mess now. A great big pile of prickly herrings. Yes, prickled herrings. And getting pricklier all the time!" exclaimed Krystal.

"You can say that again," I said. "You do mean pickled herring, right?"

"No, I mean prickled herring. Don't confuse me! Or we could say smoky herring, because the killer is throwing these herrings around trying to confuse the issue and make it all smoky so we can't see what is going on. I think smoky herrings would be a better expression," said Krystal.

"If you say so."

#Notcutoutforthis

Chapter Nine: For Whom the Cock Crows

To everything there is a season,

And a time to every purpose under the heaven:

A time to be born, and a time to die.

--*Ecclesiastes 3:1*

I could not stop thinking that Nick was a likely suspect in Pilar's death. Yet, the police had deemed her death an unlucky accident. She had prescription pills in her system, and she had fallen down the spiral steps of Cana Island Lighthouse after everyone else had gone home for the day. It was death by misadventure. Yet, I was not convinced. Krystal and I discussed what we now called the case on our way to the von Stiehl Winery in Algoma where we decided to spend our afternoon off on a wine tasting tour. But first we discussed the tourists.

"Who is that jerk behind us with the hot foot? Is he from New York City or what, hey?" asked Krystal.

"Probably from Chicago," I said.

"Ain't it, hey!" offered Krystal.

"In a hurry to get to Peninsula State Park to breathe in the beauties of nature and then hurry to the restaurant and hurry to the shopping, the winery, the gas station, and then hurry back to the condo," I said.

"In a hurry to have a stroke," said Krystal. "In a hurry to get into their grave."

"Let us just hypothesize that Nick did it," I said. "The police say it was accidental death, but let's just suppose that it wasn't. For purposes of discussion, let's entertain the theory that Nick killed Pilar. How about this? Suppose he finally succeeded in poisoning her somehow. He killed her. Then he transported her body to the lighthouse and stashed it somewhere. He said she had been called away on business out of town. Then he biked out there in the middle of the night and arranged it to look like an accidental death. He had an alibi for where he was all night long. He had an ironclad alibi. He was with Skylar, like he said at the funeral. Just suppose."

"O.K., suppose," said Krystal.

"Let's not forget that Nicky is a stellar member of the cycle club," I said. "He can bike for hours. That guy's abs and glutes and thighs would be in top shape for his age. If he were used to the route and with no traffic in the wee hours of the night, I bet he could do the route from Skylar's condo in Bailey's Harbor to the Cana Island Lighthouse almost as fast as a car. He could have been practicing his route all along. He didn't want to get cut out of Pilar's money by a divorce. He had signed a prenup. Thus, she had to die for him to get her money."

"I guess. That is, he is fit for his age. He must be thirty-five. He is old," said Krystal.

"That isn't old. All that cycling keeps him in top form," I said.

"He is ugly. I think that he looks like leftover cabbage and smells like it too," said Krystal. "I think that
198

he looks like a stay puffed mothball, like a cat who swallowed a giant hairball and can't throw it up. I don't know why women go for him. He is disgusting."

"Be that as it may, there is only one way to find out if he could have done it."

"How are we going to find out if he could have done it?" asked Krystal.

"We'll have to do it. We'll have to get on our bikes in the middle of the night and do the whole thing ourselves," I said. "The route, the causeway, the stairs, pretend to toss a sack down the stairs, and reverse the whole thing backwards. I looked it up. It is six point six miles from Skylar's condo in Bailey's Harbor to Cana Island Lighthouse via a short stint on Highway 57, County Q, then East Cana Island Road. It takes sixteen minutes one way by car."

"Are you freaking nuts?" asked Krystal. "I am not riding a bike at midnight or three a.m. on that route through forest, hill, and dale from Bailey's Harbor to Cana Island Lighthouse, not to mention a short way on Hwy 57 in the middle of the night, County Q, and East Cana Island

Road. We would have to ride through the woods and run across the causeway in at least two feet of freezing Lake Michigan water in the dark and the middle of the night, dash across the grounds, unlock the house, go through the keeper's quarters, run up the winding lighthouse stairs, and toss a dummy, or pretend to toss a dummy body down the stairs."

"So?" I mused.

"So! Yeah, so! Yeah, hey! Uffda! As my Norwegian uncle would say. Don't ask me how that tall, blond giant got into our Hispanic family. He married in, I guess. We would have to do the whole process in reverse on bikes through the woods, over the roads and the highway back to Skylar's condo in Bailey's Harbor. We would have to get the bikes stashed back into our car which would be on the side of the road somewhere and drive back to our apartment in Sturgeon Bay in the early dawn. By the way, where are we getting the keys to the lighthouse? I'm sure it is locked up as tight as a drum for the night every night."

"That is where your skills come in. Nick obviously has a set of keys to the lighthouse which he conveniently kept or stole and had a copy made. All you do is steal them off his dresser or wherever and get a copy made. Or perhaps one of your skeleton keys might work. You are good at breaking and entering, lock picking, and have various other sundry helpful skills. Maybe you don't even need the key."

"Have you lost your mind? I don't want to die. I'm not doing it. Period," said Krystal.

"Correction. You are doing it."

"You can't make me," said Krystal.

"Has anyone ever told you that you are obstinate, stubborn, and mule-headed?" I asked.

"Correction. I am bull-headed. I'm a Taurus. Remember?" asked Krystal.

"How could I possibly forget?"

"At least I'm not a Scorpio like you; intense, moody, spooky, murky, quirky, deep, and dark, with more angles than a protractor and motivations even you don't understand."

"Thanks for that compliment," I said.

"That was not a compliment," said Krystal.

"I'll take it as one anyway."

A few nights later, after considerable preparation and much discussion, we parked the car off the road near Skylar's condo at two in the morning. There was a full haloed blood moon hanging low in the sky that night. We hauled our bikes out of the rear of the SUV and quietly started down the road to the destination. Even with the full moon, we needed our bike lights and a burglar's penlight strapped to my upper arm to illuminate the darkness.

Our tires made whirring noises in the silence broken only by the sounds of crickets and rustles in the undergrowth. Suddenly a startled fox on the side of the road turned and stared at us. We saw its eyes reflected in the lights from our bikes. Two humpbacked furry creatures with long striped tails crossed in front of us, almost causing Krystal to fall off her bicycle. They were racoons hunting by the light of the huge full blood moon shining like a rose and gold doubloon.

"Just so you know," growled Krystal, "I hate your guts to the ends of time."

"Fine," I said. "Just keep pumping." The lights from our bicycles made an eerie circle of

light on the black stillness of the pine trees. Those sixteen minutes and six point six miles seemed to take forever over Highway 57, County Q, and East Cana Island Road, but finally we reached the lapping shoreline and the water of the causeway. Our bikes crunched and hissed on the gravel. I looked at the black water. Fortunately, we had worn our wet suits and old wellies to keep our feet from getting cut up on the stones.

"Let's stash the bikes here. Hurry up!" I urged. "We have to see if Nick could have done this in an hour."

Krystal balked at the edge of the water.

"Tabby, you have been drinking the psycho Kool-Aid again! I'm not going through this

freezing water without hip boots and a pony to hold onto!" insisted Krystal.

"A pony?"

"Yes, a cute sturdy little pony who loves lake water. I'm still waiting for my pony. You had a pony when we were growing up. Now I want mine."

"Correction. You are doing it without a pony. Right now! Move it! Head 'em out! Stop being a baby. You have a wetsuit on. Just pretend that you are in a classic western and we are herding the cows across the Rio Grande, or maybe a shallow little river would be better. It's not even up to your thighs. Do you want to look good on camera? Or do you want to look like a lily-livered tenderfoot? Quit whining and get with the program!" I commanded.

"No, I want to look like a sane person who just got out of hair and makeup. I'm ready for my closeup. Get my body double in here to do this wading thing for me," said Krystal.

"Sorry, that is only for the big stars, and you don't qualify. Now move it, Maureen O'Hara," I ordered. "She did her own stunts without a body double, and you will too! At my command! Go!"

"That's Miss O'Hara to you, script girl. I think you have been at the hash brownies again," said Krystal and plunged into the water ahead of me.

Several expletives deleted here as we rushed through the cold, dark water and scrambled up the banks onto the island. After all, this book is rated G for general audiences. This is a family show. No need for gratuitous sex and violence or swear words, right? Just rest assured that there were plenty of blue words flying around as we waded through two feet of freezing cold water out to Cana Island.

"Just for the record, I hate your guts!" said Krystal as we emerged onto the crunchy gravel of the island. She shook herself like a dog emerging from a bath.

"I feel like Miss Marple," I said.

"Yeah, and I'm Sam Spade," said Krystal. "Or Dick Tracy, or maybe even Philip Marlowe, Poirot, and Sherlock Holmes combined."

"O.K., move it. We are on a schedule of one hour for this whole show, remember? Hike it!" I rushed up the walkway and jogged across the grounds up to the Cana Island Lighthouse, dragging Krystal's skeleton keys from the lanyard around my neck as I ran.

"Hey! Wait up!" called Krystal. I managed to open the door to the house with Krystal's skeleton keys, although it was a little difficult. We hurried through the tiny shop, up a couple stairs, and into the living quarters and up to the second floor. From there we rushed through to the spiral staircase and started to climb to the top of the lighthouse tower. We couldn't run up because the stairs are tightly packed around the core, so we had to trudge up the stairs. Upon reaching the summit, we went out onto the outside balcony.

"Hey! Do you see that chest? Doesn't that big old wooden chest belong inside in the living quarters?" I asked. "Haven't you seen it there?:

"I don't know," said Krystal. "Does it matter?"

"It might," I said. I opened the huge old wooden chest with a mighty heave. Lo and behold, inside there were multiple plastic bags of melted ice, and the inside of the chest was wet.

"Uh-huh. See that?" I asked.

"Yup, I see that. So? Was somebody having a party up here?"

"Yeah, somebody like old Mr. Nick himself. I think he dragged this mighty old chest up the steps and out here with some extreme effort, packed it with ice, and stuffed Pilar in her body bag inside this chest overnight. Remember when she was supposed to be gone on some business trip? I think she was already dead and stuffed in this chest."

"Ick! But why?" asked Krystal.

"Because a body packed in ice will not show signs of decomposition and the time of death can be fudged. If it was Nick who killed Pilar, I think that he killed her the day before and came out here the next night and made it look like she took one too many pills and fell down the stairs the day after she supposedly came home from her business trip. Don't you see? She had to come home from the business trip and have her accidental death the next day. The whole thing took place over a two-day period."

"Why?"

"That gave him time to drive her here in his Range Rover, haul the body up the steps, plant the body in the chest filled with ice, and come back the next night on his bicycle. That way he has an ironclad alibi. He was in bed with Skylar all night, and as far as Skylar knows, he was. But if he drugged Skylar as well as Pilar, Skylar would have slept through it all. His only mistake was to leave the chest out here with the plastic bags wet with melted ice still inside." I took out my cell phone and photographed the old wooden chest and the melted ice inside.

"This is twisted," said Krystal.

"If he killed her, it is twisted," I said. "But then, Nick is a twisted character. Alright, now let's get that body in here." We pretended to get and to drag a heavy object, like a body bag inside and toss it down the stairs.

"Hey! Careful with that body!" commanded Krystal. "Even if Pilar is dead and we hated her, we should be nice to her dead body. Don't toss it so hard."

"Krystal, stop being nuts. You're talking like we really have a body. Now we rush down the stairs. Follow me and don't trip over the body."

"And you think I'm crazy?" said Krystal as rushed down the spiral staircase, again taking time around the many angles and turns so we didn't fall down the stairs and break our necks. We again darted through the living areas of the house, rushed outside, and I locked the door. We stood outside listening to the quiet and the lap of the waves on the shore.

Suddenly, Krystal toppled over. I feared that she had fainted. Sometimes, even talking about dead bodies, let alone looking at them, can make Krystal start to pass out. I ran to her and patted her face.

"Krystal! Krystal! Wake up! Please don't faint on me! I need you now! Come on! Wake up!" Krystal opened her eyes.

"Did I faint? Sometimes I faint when I think about dead bodies. Even thinking about Pilar laying on that steps makes me feel faint. Even though I am a nurse, I don't do well around dead bodies, even dead bodies that I imagine."

"Who does?" I asked.

"I mean, I didn't volunteer to have people die on me. That is why I work in a clinic. No trauma centers for me. No emergency wards. No nephrology, no coroners, and absolutely no autopsies. Thank you very much."

"How did you ever manage to dissect cats and frogs in Biology class?" I asked as I helped her to her feet. "Don't move just yet. Just stand here and take a deep breath."

"O.K. If you think back, I was conveniently sick on high school biology dissection days, or else I just had to make a long pit stop in the restroom. The day we had the cadaver in nursing school, I zoned out on pain pills, wore sunglasses, claimed to have a hangover, and closed my eyes a lot. Through the whole thing."

"Krystal, really. That is no way for a nurse to approach death."

"This nurse does not approach death at all, in any way, shape, or form. This nurse plans to be conveniently absent at her own death and funeral. I mean, why not? Elizabeth Taylor was late to her own funeral, so why can't I be too?" asked Krystal. I shook my head.

"Krystal, how are you going to help me with the occasional murder mystery if you keep fainting every time that we find a dead body or even trod a stairway where a dead body was found?"

"I'll manage. I'll think of something. I'm highly creative that way. I have excellent coping skills." I sighed. "You can take the lead with the bodies," she continued. "We all contribute our unique talents to the team. My unique talent is keeping you charging ahead, focused, and concentrating. Plus, you may have noticed that I'm excellent at research."

"Yes, I admit that you are good at research," I said.

"Also, I'm good at harmony. I'm good at making you believe in yourself. Go, Tabby, go! Forge ahead, Captain Girl!"

"I'm forging, O.K.?" I said.

"You don't mind if I just hang back and take a little breather while you forge, do you?" asked Krystal.

"Yes, I sure as hell do mind. I'm not doing this without you," I said.

"Now that makes me feel good. You do need me after all," said Krystal.

"Was there ever a time when I didn't need you?" I asked. "Do you seriously think that I would do this on my own? When have I ever not included you on an adventure? I couldn't do any of this without you. Now get ready to move. We are on a time schedule. Remember? No time for fainting. Think movement. I need you. I can't do this without you."

"No, you can't. You can't solve this. Not without my battle smarts, keen powers of observation, and superior physical prowess. Not to mention that I can crack safes, pick locks, and execute break-ins like a pro. Plus, I'm stronger than an ox. I'm ready. Now go!" commanded Krystal.

We set off in the dark across the grounds, through the tussocky grass, past the outbuildings, past the parking lot, and down the trail through the woods to the causeway.

"Good thing we thought to wear our wetsuits," I said as we again plunged into the cold water which sloshed around us up to our knees and splashed over our thighs.

"Oh, yeah. Thank God but I'm still wet," said Krystal. "Are we almost there? This is taking forever. This water is cold and there are little creatures and little fishies and minnows around me. I don't like squidgy things. This is giving me the creeps. I don't like the dark. This is scary."

"Hush! Voices carry over water," I said.

"Who will hear us? The deer? The bear? The raccoon? The red squirrel? The blue jay? The owl? The badger?" asked Krystal.

"I just hope we don't run into a bear," I said.

"God help us!" said Krystal. "Can't you move any faster?" She surged ahead and plowed through the water, easily reaching the shore ahead of me. "Where are our bikes?"

"Don't panic. They're around here somewhere," I said on a prayer. It was pitch dark and the dead of night. Not even the glowing full moon could chase away the eerie feeling of being out in the woods alone. All around us creatures rustled and slunk into and out of the hiding places that only they know about. The hedgerows and creek banks were full of furry creatures going about their routines. They went about their instinctual business in the soft black night, evading the nocturnal hunters and birds of prey, the swift attack, the brutal talons, the sharp beaks of death. I shivered.

"The woods are different at night," I said.

"Yeah, deep and black. Find my stinking bike and do it now."

"Ow!" I said as I stumbled onto a bicycle tire and went down on top of the bike, causing what I knew would be bruises by the morning light. "I think I found it, or rather my knees did." I groaned and pulled myself up.

"Oh, good," said Krystal. "Here they are at last. Come on. Jump on. Now we make tracks!" I could not speak. My knee protested mightily as we climbed onto the bikes and started pedaling in what I hoped was the right direction. I turned on the light on my handlebars. Krystal did the same.

"That's better. Get in front of me and let's go!" ordered Krystal.

We pedaled as though chased by all the hounds of hell onto the path, through the woods, and onto the roadway. The only sounds were the whirr of the tires and our deep breathing as we strove to complete our mission. We rolled down East Cana Island Road and County Q. It seemed to take forever but eventually we reached the highway, and then it was smooth sailing as we pumped up the jam down Highway 57 to Skylar's condo in Bailey's Harbor.

"Hey, Krystal, you dead yet?" I asked as we made the last turn, coasted down the road and into Skylar's driveway.

"More than dead. Double dead," gasped Krystal. "If you ever do that again, you are doing it alone. My heart gave out about three times. I can't feel it beating."

"Mine is beating, beating way too hard. I may faint."

"You can't faint. I'm the one who faints, not you."

"Oh, shut up! You're interfering with my gasping for breath. I think I'm going to puke. Is this what they do to you in the army?" I asked.

"Probably. That's why I'm never joining." Krystal groaned and looked up at the sky. I ground to a stop by dragging my feet on the blacktop and leaned over the handlebars, my chest heaving. I glanced at my watch.

"We made it," I said. "We did all that in one hour. That proves that Nick could have done it."

"Could have?" asked Krystal. "He did it. He killed her. There is no doubt in my mind."

"Good," I said. "We've proved it to ourselves. The problem is, how do we prove it to the authorities?"

"You figure it out, genius," said Krystal and moaned. "I'm too busy going into cardiac arrest."

"Hate to tell you faithful friend, but we are in Skylar's drive, and now we must ride down the road to our car, throw the bikes in the back, and drive home before you can collapse."

"Have I ever told you that I hate your guts?" asked Krystal as she turned around and started down the road to the car. I followed, my injured knee protesting painfully all the way. Finally, we reached the car.

My little car never looked so good to me. We tossed the bikes in the back. We jumped in and I started the engine, which seemed to roar into life much too loudly. I did a U turn in the middle of the highway and headed for Sturgeon Bay, back to our cozy little apartment. We drove in silence, exhausted and both thinking our own thoughts. When we arrived, I parked the car in the garage. We stumbled into our apartment, where we both collapsed onto the couches.

Cuckoo greeted us with a "Mew, mirr, meow!" It was as if she was asking us where in the world we had been in the middle of the night.

"Has anyone ever told you that you are completely psycho?" asked Krystal and sighed heavily. "The things I do for you. If I weren't so exhausted, I would go into the kitchen and eat a pint of Rocky Road ice cream right now. Maybe two. I'm just too tired to move. I don't think I have enough energy left to mastodon my food, much less digest it."

"I think the word is masticate," I said.

"What?" said Krystal.

"Masticate your food, not mastodon. You mean chew it, right?" I asked.

"If I want help from you with my word choices, I'll ask, smartass."

"Oh, O.K."

"Does Brook Trout understand just how deeply disturbed you are?"

"I hope not," I said.

"He should consult Dr. Phil before he makes any permanent arrangements."

"Such as?" I inquired.

"Such as an engagement ring or a marriage license," said Krystal.

"I should call Brook Trout and tell him about our sleuthing," I said.

"At four in the morning? I don't think so. Brook Trout is probably deep in the middle of a dream involving contract law, a bunch of stuffy old lawbooks, and a decision about what conservative gray suit he should wear to work in a few hours. I think we should make a pact that we tell absolutely nothing to Javier or to Brook about our sleuthing. You know how men are. They will want in on the fun, and we just can't have them gumming up the works before we have definitively solved the case and brought Nicky, or whoever the killer is, to justice and made him face the music."

"True," I said. "It's a deal. Pinky swear to not tell the men. Not to mention the fact that we must get up in exactly two point five hours and go to work at the clinic."

"Kindly shut up, Miss Wet Blanket," said Krystal. "You are interfering with me falling into a deep dreamless sleep on this couch. Wake me up later. Fill me with caffeine. Pick out my scrubs for me. Comb my hair for me. Put on my makeup. Fix my breakfast and don't bother me."

In two minutes, she was snoring soundly. I wonder if she heard me say, "I just hope Nicky baby wasn't at Skylar's condo tonight and just happened to look out the window in the middle of the night and see us on our bikes in Skylar's driveway."

#SherlockandfaithfulWatson

Chapter Ten: A Tale of Two Kitties

The cat went here and there
And the moon spun round like a top,
And the nearest kin of the moon,
The creeping cat, looked up.
--From *The Cat and the Moon* by William Butler Yeats

Let me tell you about our little Cuckoo. Cuckoo subscribes to the theory that you can never be too cute and furry or get too many treats and neck rubs. She is our little darling. That was why we were so surprised one day when on a playdate with Brook Trout's bloodhound Mossy and kitty Misty whom we were babysitting for the day, we discovered that Cuckoo was a thief. Cuckoo and Misty came out of the bedroom playing tag, chasing, rolling, and pouncing on a bangle bracelet. Cuckoo picked it up and carried it in her mouth.

To our surprise, we discovered that the bracelet we thought must be a cheap bangle was in fact a real diamond bracelet. We were at a complete loss as to where the bracelet came from. We called every friend who had visited us lately. We thought and thought how Cuckoo had come to be in possession of the bracelet. Finally, Krystal came up with the answer.

"I think it must have fallen into my pocket when I was dusting," she said. "Or maybe it was part of the stash that Tiggy stole from Pilar, and I stole from Tiggy."

"What? Fell into your pocket when you were dusting? First of all, you don't really dust. Secondly, things don't just fall into your pocket. You've been stealing from Tiggy?" I asked.

"Yup, I stole some of the stash that she stole from Pilar. After all, it is stolen goods. When we solve this case, I'm turning over all the stolen goods and stolen paintings to the police. But not before I get both Bunty and Tiggy arrested for conspiracy, theft, or even murder."

"What about the rest of the stash that Tiggy stole from Pilar? Would she have it all in the handles of her tennis rackets? Do you think the rackets are in the condo she rents?" I asked.

"Uh, yeah."

"Do you think we should steal those tennis rackets?"

"Uh, yeah. That would be a good idea," said Krystal. "Or better yet, we should steal the jewels out of the tennis rackets."

"That could be dicey. Where does Tiggy live?" I asked.

"The Tigster lives as a permanent resident in the Landmark Hotel Resort in Egg Harbor. She has a lease arrangement with one of the condo owners in the Flagship building," said Krystal. "It's the one on the second floor at the end of the hall. It's the one closest to the elevator."

"How do you know that?" I asked.

"I overheard her talking to Pilar about it after one of their private tennis sessions at the house," said Krystal. "Pilar was going to visit her there."

That night, guess who staked out the parking lot at the Flagship building at the Landmark in Egg Harbor after dinner. We had a clear view, aided by a host of bright stars flung across the sky as if God had played a game of jacks. They danced around a moon as glowing as a piece of pirate silver from the Spanish main. We didn't have too long to wait before we saw Tiggy go into the pool building in her swimming suit with her beach towel slung over her shoulder. I say swimming suit, but it was more like something a stripper would wear. It left nothing to the imagination.

"Great! There she goes! Let's move!" Within minutes, we were standing at the door to Tiggy's condo. Krystal slipped on her gloves and went to work with her lock pick. I stood in front of her to block the view in case anyone should walk down the hall. In thirty seconds, she had opened the door to the condo. We made a quick sweep of the condo and found Tiggy's rackets at the back of her walk-in closet. Krystal carefully extracted the putty from the end of the rackets and all the jewels from the handles of each racket. There was a total of five rackets, all with jewels packed into the handles. She then returned all the putty to the handles just as she found them and placed the rackets exactly as they were at the back of Tiggy's closet.

Krystal photographed everything with her phone to get a record of all the jewels and listed which racket the jewels were in originally. I threw all the jewels into a big plastic zip lock bag and put them into the tote I had brought along.

"Wait!" ordered Krystal. "You dropped one." She picked up a red ruby ring from the floor and dropped it into the tote. "Look at this," said Krystal. "Addresses for diamond dealers in Antwerp, art dealers in London and Paris, and their addresses and phone numbers. I should photograph this."

"Good idea," I said. "Do it quickly and let's get out of here."

We hustled out of the building and got into our car in the lot just in time. We saw Tiggy coming out of the Flagship building. Her swim took less than thirty minutes. We ducked down in the car hoping she wouldn't see us.

"Whew! That was close," I said.

"She won't be any wiser," said Krystal. "We left no fingerprints and disturbed nothing. There were no cameras anywhere. I looked. All those rackets are exactly as we

225

found them. The only way she will know anything is missing is if she goes back into the rackets just to gloat over her many-colored jewels like Smaug the dragon."

"I bet she does just that," I said. "Just like Smaug or Silas Marner."

"Who the heck is Silas Marner?" asked Krystal.

"Sophomore English class. George Elliot's *Silas Marner*. He was the broken-hearted jilted miser who had all his gold stolen by the rich neighbor and raised the little orphan girl who turned out to be his greatest treasure. Remember?"

"Vaguely. I think I watched the movie," said Krystal. "Just like I watched the movie and read the CliffsNotes for *The Scarlet Letter* and *To Kill a Mockingbird*."

"You really are hopeless," I said.

"No, I'm just efficient and practical," said Krystal. "Unlike you, dreamer. Besides, I couldn't understand that language they used. I needed an interpreter."

"Let's hope Tiggy never suspects us of stealing her stolen goods," I said.

"Uh, yeah, or we're Post Toasties," said Krystal. "I wish she wouldn't suspect me." Unfortunately, if wishes were horses, beggars would ride.

Three days after we stole the stolen jewels from Tiggy's condo at the Landmark, Millie, the old lady next door who likes to sit by the window and spy on everybody, said to Krystal and me when we came home to the apartment that evening, "Oh, I hope your cousin got hold of you at the clinic."

"Which cousin was that?" I asked. "I have a ton of cousins."

"Oh, you know, the one from Kentucky that was here visiting," said Millie. "She was so sorry she had missed you and she said she would go to the clinic and catch you there."

"Hmmmm. Nobody came to see me at the clinic," I said.

"That's funny. She said she was going directly to the clinic. I saw her going into your apartment, so I walked in after her and asked her what she was doing. You must have left the door unlocked. I thought she might be an intruder. She said that you had left the door open for her to pick up a silk blouse, but you must have forgotten because she couldn't find it where you said you would leave it for her. She looked everywhere."

"Oh, right. My cousin. Which one was that? I have so many."

"I can't remember what she said her name was, but she was athletic looking; tall and tanned, with short blonde spiky hair and big brown eyes, lots of makeup, and very white teeth. Her teeth when she smiled were so bright and white, it was almost scary. She looked a little bit predatory, kind of like a lioness."

"Oh, sure! That's right," I said, rolling my eyes at Krystal. "Good old Tig. Sure thing. She must have been looking for that blouse. You didn't happen to notice if she walked out with anything besides a blouse, did you Millie? I'm afraid good old Tig can be a wee bit of a kleptomaniac at times. She didn't have any purse or bag or backpack with her, did she? Or any bulges in her pockets?"

"Yeah, good old Tig," said Krystal. "She will lift jewelry and such if you don't keep your eye on her all the time. She will even lift clothes and shoes, or anything that takes her fancy."

"Oh, no, that skin-tight white tennis outfit she was wearing showed every curve and bone," said Millie. "There wasn't any room to hide a darn thing! She did carry a big purse though. Very attractive girl. She looks like a Vogue model. I'll bet the men really go for her in a big way."

"They sure do," I said. "Yup, they sure do. In a big, major way."

"I guess we better feed the cat, Millie," said Krystal. "Cuckoo gets impatient if we don't feed her promptly at six."

"Oh, yes, and one more thing before I go, girls," said Millie in her tinny, aged, and quavering voice. She sounded like a rusty tin can. "That is what I was trying to remember. Your cat, Cuckoo, didn't like Tig at all. In fact,

229

I stood in the doorway of the bedroom while Tig looked for the silk blouse. I thought I would keep an eye on her and have a little chat with her while she looked around your apartment because after all, I don't know her from Eve. The thing is, Cuckoo gave her a real nasty scratch when Tig was looking through your closet and dresser drawers. It was almost as if Cuckoo didn't like her pawing through your things. Cuckoo is almost like a watchdog." I looked at Krystal and she at me.

"Golly, gee," said Krystal. "Good for Cuckoo. That Tig can get a little presumptuous at times, can't she Tabby? You better have a talk with her about going through people's things when they aren't home. It's a good thing you followed her into the apartment and then into the bedroom, Millie. I'm glad you got nosy and investigated what Tig was up to."

"I don't think it was nosy," said Millie, slightly insulted. "I just try to help out is all."

"I sure am glad you did, Millie. Yup, I sure am," I said. "Thanks for that. You can help any time you want. I'm glad you keep an eye on things around here."

Just at that moment, Cuckoo came out of the bedroom with a shiny object in her mouth, dropped it at my feet, and said, "Mew, mew, mew!" I looked down. There was a red ruby ring the size of an olive at my feet. The gold of the setting shone in the light coming in from the window. It was the one that I had dropped in Tig's condo and Krystal threw into the tote. I guess I should have found a better hiding place for all the jewels than my navy-blue cloth tote which I had shoved under my bed. That bag can hold a lot of stuff.

"Wow! Look at that!" said Millie. "Did your boyfriend give you that ring, Tabby? You better hold onto that one! That Brook is a real keeper!"

"Oh, that old thing," I said. "That's just a fake. Someday Brook will buy me a real one." I scooped up the ring and shoved it into my pocket. "Cuckoo, you naughty little kitty. You should stop getting into my jewelry box and playing with my costume jewelry. She just loves anything bright and shiny. It's hard to keep it away from her." I gave Millie my social smile. "Thanks for dropping by and telling us about Tig, Millie. I'll be sure to get in touch with her real soon and get her that silk blouse that she wanted to borrow."

"Yeah, thanks, Millie," said Krystal.

"Anytime girls," said Millie as she turned to leave. "If you want me to water your plants if you're going to be gone just let me know. I'll be happy to oblige. I can feed Cuckoo too if you want me to when you are gone." I rolled my eyes at Krystal behind Millie's back.

"Super! Thanks, Millie," said Krystal. We watched Millie go out the door.

"Good hiding place, dork!" said Krystal. "What amazes me is that Tig didn't find all our stash under the bed. She could have grabbed the jewelry and all the paintings in their cardboard tubes too. Here, give me that ring. I'll find a better place for it." I dug in my pocket and gave Krystal the ring.

"I don't know. It appears that all Pilar's stolen jewels turned out to be safer under my bed than they were anywhere else. I wonder if Tig is sure that we were the ones who stole the stolen jewels from her tennis rackets, or if she was just fishing."

"Huh!" said Krystal. "I say just fishing. She has no evidence. I'm a great thief. I may have missed my calling."

#crownjewels

Chapter Eleven: Secret Scone

By the pricking of my thumbs something wicked this way comes.

--From *Macbeth*, by William Shakespeare

I was out on my bike in the park early the next morning enjoying the sunshine and admiring the trees in the height of their summer glory. The wind through the poplar trees evoked angels, spirits, dreams, and visions. It's odd that the humble poplar tree gives some of the prettiest music when the wind blows through the trees and turns the silver backed leaves to a hymn of praise equal to anything sung in church.

The moon was a silvery disc which had not yet set below the horizon and the sun rose in the east through a fog of low-lying morning mist. A flock of geese flew overhead, their wings a quiet whisper on the wind. The dappled rays of early morning sunshine peeked among the limbs of the trees. A long line of sugar maples stretched the length of the park, standing like sentinels in the glow of the rising sun. I squinted into the bright light of the just risen sun and breathed deeply of the smell of freshly mown grass.

Suddenly someone rode up on my left side and gave me a vicious shove which knocked me off my bicycle onto the gravel path. I crashed down hard on the gravel and didn't see who it was. They were gone in a rush of wind while I lay on the gravel moaning in pain. Thank God I didn't hit my head, but every other part of my right side was scraped and bloody. I dragged myself to my feet slowly and gingerly, gasping with pain.

My right shoulder, right hip, and right leg showed lacerations and contusions. I probably would have to dig the gravel out of the wounds. Great! So much for exercise in an empty park at six a.m. Who was that jerk on the bike who had deliberately shoved me as hard as he could? Or was it she? I had a vague vision of a slim black clad athletic type on a pricey bicycle, but with the sun shining directly into my eyes and with the speed and viciousness of the way they had pushed me and rushed away, it was hard to tell. All I recalled clearly was a muscled calf and expensive athletic shoes.

The next question I asked myself was why would someone come after me and try to render me out of commission or worse, dead? The only thing I could think of was that someone was trying to warn me to stop asking questions about Pilar's death. Since I had no enemies that I knew of, that seemed to be the only reasonable answer.

Not only was I scraped up and bloody, but my bicycle had suffered a few dents. I limped all the way home dragging my bike with me. I felt woozy and sick but there was nothing to it but to keep going. I hoped I wouldn't faint before I got home to a hot shower, bandages, ice packs, and got some pain pills down my throat.

I tried doing some addition, subtraction, and some fractions in my head on the way home to prove to myself that I didn't have a concussion. That seemed mildly difficult, so I tried to remember the capitals of all fifty states. That was more difficult. I tried reciting the Henry Wadsworth Longfellow poem they made us memorize in fifth grade. All I could remember was, "Under the spreading chestnut tree the village smithy stands," and then something about arms like iron bands. Maybe I had hit my head after all. Maybe I was in shock. Ice pack to the head also, I noted.

Krystal, ever sympathetic, clarified things for me when I arrived home.

"Are you freaking nuts? Why didn't you call me? You have your cell phone! You're filthy, bloody, scraped up, and limping. You are going to the doctor for x-rays!"

"No."

"What do you mean, no? You're going!"

"No. I'm going to work."

"The hell you are! You are going in for x-rays!"

"No, I'm not. Beat me. Stick bamboo shoots under my fingernails. Pull my hair out. See if I'll go."

Nurses are notoriously reluctant to get x-rays, CT scans, therapy, and operations. I compromised. I let Krystal nurse me before she went into work, and I stayed home from work and watched television with my body covered in ice packs. I dosed myself with pain pills and zoned out on the Hallmark channel all day long.

When Krystal got home with takeout, I ate a lot of it, for me. Then I dozed on the couch while Krystal fussed over me and yelled at me for not going to the doctor. She is such a good nurse.

The next day I determined that I should go to work, even though I looked terrible and felt worse. I thought it would do me good to do normal things like work. I peered into the mirror. After a considerable amount of time trying to do my makeup, I gave up.

"How are you doing?" asked Krystal. "You look like death warmed over."

"Oh, a little pale today but I primped enough for one day. After all, it's not like I'm going to visit the Pope or something," I said. "Maybe I'll leave the eyelashes off. I don't think that I have the strength to do lashes today."

"You are too pale, white Irish frog belly pale. Put some darker makeup on," said Krystal.

"Yes, permanently tanned one. Whatever you say." I applied more makeup.

"How do I look now?" I asked.

"You still look sickly white," said Krystal.

"I guess my scintillating personality and incredible charm will just have to make up for my sickly whiteness today. Besides, it's only work. I'll have to think of something to tell Brook Trout. I'll say I ran over a curb and fell off the bike. I think I can get him to believe that. How about this deal, huh? Who would do this to me? Something is rotten in the State of Denmark, Krystal," I said.

"Yeah, and in South America, India, Canada, Europe, Russia, the Mideast, Korea, Africa, the USA, and China too. It's called mankind. Or shall we say unkind?

Let's just say man. This world would be a nice place if it weren't for men."

Life went on as normal for a few days. On Saturday I joined Krystal at Pilar's house after she was finished cleaning, and we took the psycho Pekinese for a walk. We were just bringing Truffles around the corner of the house at the conclusion of our walk when something came crashing down from the second story balcony and shattered into bits on the concrete right in front of us, nearly missing Krystal's head. We both jumped a foot. Krystal screamed. Truffles started barking and growling as if all the hounds of hell were upon us. It turned out to be a heavy plaster statue bust of Venus.

Krystal let fly with a stream of cuss words. "Are you freaking kidding me?" she said. She threw Truffles' leash at me and went bounding into the house. In seconds she was upstairs leaning over the balcony.

"See anything?" I inquired.

"No, but I have my suspicions," she said.

Gina came bustling out of the house. "What in the world has happened, Miss Krystal?" she called. Charlie came running from the garden.

"Are you alright, Miss Krystal?" he asked. "What happened?"

"That's what we would like to know!" Krystal answered from the balcony. "Someone just tried to kill us, and that was no accident."

I immediately went into the house and determined who was there. All the usual suspects appeared. Bunty, Tiggy, and Nick all lounged around looking like their usual suspicious selfish selves. Ugh! It could be any one of these drips, I thought.

I noted that Nick was lying on the leather couch in the library. He sported a heather colored soft woven mohair sweater. Yes, it was an unnaturally cool morning for a summer day and all the windows were open to the breeze, but really? I gave him a squinty stare. He did not look up from his iced cappuccino. Did this guy think he was a Hollywood producer or something? Barf. Krystal joined me in the kitchen.

I told her that I had seen Bunty and Tiggy in the drawing room comparing notes and one upping each other on their Coach purses, Prada bags, and Manolo heels. Gag.

"They looked for all the world as though they had been there for hours, just as Nick looked like he had been lying on the couch for days. Right. I say one of them was the culprit. By the way, Gina was in the immediate area too, and I haven't totally crossed her off my suspect list either. That plaster bust crashing down on us was no accident. That thing was heavy. It didn't just fall off the balcony. That stupid Nick. It was probably him," I said. "It wouldn't surprise me. Or it could be Tiggy or Bunty. Those two are both shady characters."

"I don't know what these women see in Nick," said Krystal. "Sure, he is good looking for his age, but he is such a wuss, such a snotty, privileged twit. I wouldn't take his scrawny ripped and rippled muscled bod if you handed it to me. I think that he looks like leftover cabbage and smells like it too. He looks like a stay puffed mothball, like a cat who swallowed a giant hairball and can't throw it up. I wouldn't take him on a silver platter, dirty old man."

"Me neither," I said. "I like Brook Trout. He is solid, dependable, and clueless. He's such a sweetheart."

"He's not sexy though, not like my Javier," she said proudly. Such a guapo diablo.

"Handsome devil? I have to admit that Javier has definite SA," I said. "Brook is a bit bland. I admit it, but I like it that way."

"Javier is definitely muy caliente," said Krystal. "Super hot! Not like that former boyfriend of mine. You remember Carlos."

"Unfortunately, yes I do," I said.

"He was good enough for a lengthy one-night stand and that is really all that it was in the end. No regrets. He was a loser anyway. I can do better, much better. In fact, when I met Javier at Brook Trout's non-wedding to Horrible Holly in Egg Harbor, I think I hit the jackpot. He is so sweet and wonderful. I think I love him."

"Does this mean that you will soon be leaving me to get married? Is that why you're saving up for that condo?" I asked archly. Krystal looked alarmed.

"Let's not get carried away with any Disney movie conclusions just yet," she said. "I want to enjoy the courtship with Javier before we plan the walk down the aisle."

"Like in the classic movie *Flower Drum Song*? I enjoy being a girl?"

"You betcha! A nice, long courtship and then a lifetime of bliss."

"Right! Same for me with my Brook Trout. Do you think that our children will grow up together and be best friends?" I sighed.

"I think we should get married first," said Krystal, ever the practical one. Suddenly, my mind popped back to reality.

"By the way, where is Truffles?" I asked.

"Oh, boy. I forgot about him. I think he probably wandered off and is digging in Charlie's garden again," said Krystal. "Better run and get him before he destroys all the bleeding hearts and cockle shells. Charlie gets upset if he even suspects that Truffles has been in the garden."

We ran towards the garden. Truffles was indeed in the garden. He had already destroyed the cockle shells, trampled down the bleeding hearts, and was chewing on a broken piece of plaster.

"Oh, dear. It looks like Truffles found a piece of Venus de Milo's private parts. Too bad he doesn't choke on all the garbage he eats," sighed Krystal as she grabbed the leash. Truffles wasn't happy about being dragged out of the garden and into the house, but he was somewhat mollified when he got his favorite treats.

That very same Saturday night, the four of us, Brook, Krystal, Javier, and myself went out on a double date at the Carrington Pub & Grill in the Landmark Resort in Egg Harbor. It has a panoramic view of the bay of Green Bay. The four of us were out for a special dinner to celebrate Javier's twenty-fifth birthday. We were sitting at the bar having a drink and waiting for our table. Krystal and I explained to Javier and Brook about my scrapes and scratches, but I don't think they really bought our story about me running up a curb with the bike.

We saw Tiggy Butterfield sitting at a table alone in the opposite corner of the darkened bar staring daggers at us.

"Who is that?" asked Javier. "She sure is glaring at you two. Do you know her?"

"Yes and no," said Krystal. "She is a so-called friend of Nick and Pilar Lightfoot, or was anyway. We suspect her of being a major criminal and a few other things."

Tiggy picked that moment to walk over to our corner at the end of the bar.

"I'm getting tired of looking at you two. I'm tired of you two poking around and putting your noses where they don't belong. I want you to stay away from me wherever I am," she jeered. She drew closer to us, uncomfortably close.

Completely unprovoked, Tiggy suddenly threw her drink right in my face. The alcohol sprayed all over my new lapis lazuli colored silk dress that cost me a bundle I couldn't afford. I almost cried but I stopped myself and put on my stoic face. Immediately, Brook, Javier, and Krystal all jumped out of their chairs and grabbed Tiggy by the throat, the arm, and the shoulders, respectively.

Collectively, they slammed her against the wall. She bounced off the painted silver wall and sprang back into Brook's face. She threw a punch at him which he easily blocked and twisted her arm up her back a little harder than was necessary. She screamed and swore at him.

"No! Stop!" I commanded. "That is just what she wants you to do. Don't you see? She wants to have us all arrested for assault while she claims that it was unprovoked. Don't touch her. She isn't worth it." James the bartender rushed over.

"Call 911 and have these people arrested!" demanded Tiggy. "They just threw me against the wall and twisted my arm for no reason." She rubbed her shoulder ruefully.

"Not likely, honey," said James. "I saw what happened. You accosted them, threw your drink at Tabitha, ruined her dress, and provoked the whole incident. Get out! We don't want your kind around here!" Thank you, James!

"I'll put my fist through your Botoxed face if you ever, ever, ever do that again!" swore Krystal. "Get out of here you cheap piece of flim-flam scamming trash! We all know what you have been up to, and you are going to get yours, little Miss Ruby Red Jewel! Did you ever hear of karma, Miss Sticky Fingers Butterfingers?"

I grabbed a bunch of napkins and attempted to blot my dress.

"Plucked any jewels from the crown lately, Tiggy?" I asked with an edge in my voice. "What are you doing here in God's country anyway? Who are you? Where are you from? Not anywhere near here by the sound of your voice. You don't belong here with decent people. One thing is for sure; you are not whom you say you are."

"She's a hillbilly from the hills of Tennessee," said Brook. "Or maybe she was a poor ghetto child, the daughter of a pimp and a prostitute, or maybe she is a stray from the streets of Los Angeles. The way she acts, talks, and sounds, she could be any one of those."

"Maybe she is the spawn of Satan," said Javier. He turned on Tiggy and loomed over her. "Get out of here now and leave us alone, pretentious white trash! Shouldn't you be trawling the bars for some young guy so you can be a gross old cougar?"

Tiggy stared daggers at all of us, turned on her heel, and stalked out slowly, her short black cocktail dress swinging with the rhythm of her hips, her diamonds shining in the reflected light of the chandeliers, her short, spiky blonde hair gleaming in the bar lights.

"She looks like an expensive call girl," said Krystal.

"What does an expensive call girl look like, Krystal?" I asked.

"Like any cloned Hollywood actress ho," said Krystal. "Aren't they all the same? Let's go to the restroom and try to fix your dress."

After Krystal and I fixed my dress, Brook and Javier got nosy about what was going on at the Lightfoot mansion, but we got very tightlipped about it.

"I've heard rumors," said Brook. "I really don't want you girls spending time at that house. Something strange is going on there and I don't want you involved Tabby."

"Yeah, you don't need to work as a maid, Krystal," said Javier. "You don't need a second job. You work enough long hours as a nurse. I don't like what I hear about that Nick, and remember, Pilar Lightfoot ended up dead. She is dead and he is a playboy. Add that one up. She ran around with anything in pants, and he has the morals of a weasel. Now she is dead."

"They say it was an accident," said Brook.

"Yes, that's what they say," said Javier. "But I know Gina and Charlie, and they have their suspicions. Where does this Tiggy come in? Is she a criminal? A thief?" I shrugged.

"Who knows?" I said.

Krystal looked away and played opossum. I pretended to fuss with my dress. There was no way we were getting into this conversation. I wasn't about to be drawn into a speculation about Pilar's death. The whole thing was far too tangled a plot, and besides, this was supposed to be a birthday celebration.

"So, Javier," I said. "Maybe you would like to tell me what your intentions are regarding my best friend, Krystal Morales. Exactly." I knew that would get everyone's attention. Javier stared at me like a deer in the headlights. I laughed "Just teasing you. Or maybe not." Fortunately, we were able to close the door on the Pilar discussion, and the talk turned to lighter subjects. The rest of the evening passed without incident.

Early Sunday morning, Krystal had the bright idea of breaking into the locked art treasure room at the top of Pilar's house on the fourth floor and photographing all the art that Pilar and Nick owned. Krystal wanted a record of all of it just in case Bunty and Nick planned any more art thefts. There was a code to get into the locked room which Krystal cracked in about five minutes. Gina offered to be our lookout while Krystal and I sweated it out in the hallway for those five minutes hoping we could avoid the eagle eye of dear, sweet Nick. We didn't know where he was.

"Don't worry, girls," said Gina. "Mr. Nick was out late last night. He is sleeping peacefully in the carriage house bedroom over the garage. That was where he slept when he had been out carousing all night. If he came into her bedroom late and drunk, Miss Pilar would scream bloody murder. He got into the habit of staying in the carriage house, and you know, old habits are hard to break."

Gina wasn't worried but I was. Good old Nick could still come striding down the hallway at any moment. After all, it was his house and his art treasure room that we were breaking into. I urged Krystal to hurry. Krystal turned off the cameras above the art treasure door by pressing a few buttons.

"How in the world did you know how to do that?" I asked.

"I told you. I have skills," said Krystal.

"I should say so," I said. "I hope you never decide to join the criminal classes. You would be darn hard to catch."

It took Krystal a few minutes to crack the triple lock on the door, but she managed. Once in, it was a simple matter for her to break into the safe and photograph all of Pilar's jewels that were still in there and hadn't been stolen by Tiggy. Krystal photographed them with a real camera, not her phone, for future reference.

We then moved onto the art, which hung on the walls as in a gallery. We poked into personal papers in the wall safe which Krystal cracked in about two minutes. What did we find there? We discovered Nick's birth certificate. Apparently, he had been born and raised in Paris, France. Thus, his slightly French accent which Krystal thought was fake.

"He is a real Frenchie, and you know how they are!" exclaimed Krystal. "Boy does this explain a lot! His real name is Nicholas Jean LaChapelle. I should have known he would turn out to be a Frenchie! You know what that means. Immoral!"

"Yes, in his case at least. How about amoral?" I asked. "Hurry up and photograph everything. Do you have pictures of all the art on the walls? Just in case more art should disappear out of the frames, we have proof that it hung in this personal gallery."

"What's the hurry?" asked Krystal as she clicked away with the camera.

"Just a feeling," I said. "Call it intuition." There was a knock on the door. We both jumped about a foot and stared at each other.

"Girls! Miss Krystal!" cried Gina. "Lock the door! Mr. Nick is coming! Hide!" We heard her footsteps scurrying away down the hall. Krystal's eyes grew wide. We froze, and then we ran in circles chasing each other in a panic.

At last, Krystal flew to the door, locked it, yanked my arm, and pulled me into a closet. The closet turned out to be a huge walk-in closet containing multiple paintings on easels covered in large white cloths. There was a gigantic table in the corner of the closet which held several clean folded drop-cloths.

Krystal grabbed one of the drop-cloths which was as big as a sheet. She unfurled it, whipped it over the table like a sheet over a bed, grabbed my arm, and crawled under the table with me in tow. Then she pulled the drop-cloth to the floor on three sides to hide us completely. The fourth side was against the wall and could not be seen. We huddled in terror under the table as we heard the door open with a key. We held our breath.

It was Nick. I could tell by his footsteps. I squeezed my eyes shut tight and prayed he would not open the walk-in closet and approach the table. He groaned and yawned loudly. He was probably tired from his night out. It appeared that he was there to check on things, as we heard him go around the room methodically opening each safe and then closing it again. I heard him utter one whispered, "Damn!" presumably because the safe did not immediately yield to his touch, or maybe he had forgotten the combination. I heard the soft click of jeweled stones. The closet door opened with a slight creak. He came in. I started to sweat. Then the footsteps paused directly in front of our table. He was so near that I could smell his cologne.

Oh, Holy Mary Mother of God, help me, a poor sinner. Through a small slit in the corner of the cloth, I could see Nick's soft gray suede slippers hesitate. I pressed my lips together, scrunched my eyes closed, held my breath, and prayed.

"Why is this cloth on the table like this?" he asked himself aloud. I heard him run his hand over the cloth. Maybe he was going to take it off the table and rearrange things. Be still my heart. We were sitting ducks.

"Mr. Nick! Mr. Nick!" yelled Gina through the closed door. "I've got an emergency! Truffles fell into the pool and Charlie is trying to resuscitate him! Please, Mr. Nick! Now!"

"Oh, for God's sake," said Nick. "Can't these people stop bothering me with trifles?" After a few seconds of hesitation, Nick moved towards the door, characteristically dragging his feet over the thick pile of the carpet. Thank God he was gone. I heard the key turn in the lock. I exhaled.

"Blessed angels save us!" breathed Krystal and let out a long, slow, deep burp.

"Would you stop?" I hissed.

"Can't help it," she said, and burped again. "It's fear burps. I'll die if I can't let out these burps. He would have killed us. I mean fatal. I'm sweating. I think I'm going to faint."

"I'll kill you if you keep it up," I said. She took an Almond Joy candy bar out of her pocket, ripped it open, and shoved it in her mouth.

"I am going to kill you!" I said through clenched teeth. "I hate coconut and I hate the smell of those stinking Almond Joy candy bars!"

"Then have one of these," she said. She reached into her pocket again and handed me a Kit-Kat bar. "Break me off a piece of that Kit-Kat bar!" she sung.

"Oh, keep your candy. If I ate anything right now, I would throw up. I don't know why I put up with you! I want a divorce!" I said and crawled out from under the table. We heard footsteps again.

"Oh, no! Not again! Get back under the table!" I whispered. It was Gina again.

"Miss Krystal!" we heard Gina say through the locked door. "It's O.K. You can come out now. Mr. Nick went away in the car. He was in a big hurry." We hopped to the door and opened it. "It's O.K.," said Gina. "Mr. Nick went away. He took that necklace of Miss Pilar's with him. I think that he is going to sell it back to the

257

jewelry store for cash. You know he has a gambling habit."

"Thank God it's you," said Krystal fervently. "I was getting scrunched up under that table, not to mention filled with fear gas."

"She is driving me crazy with those fear burps," I said. "Get me out of here!"

"Turn around. Do you see that priest's outfit hanging there? Why do you think that Mr. Nick has a priest's uniform hanging here?" asked Gina. "It isn't Halloween, and he doesn't know any priests." I looked and sure enough, there was a priest's garb hanging in the closet. Why?

"Your guess is as good as mine," said Krystal. "Nick is one twisted individual."

"One more mystery," I said.

"As long as you two are here, could you walk Truffles?" said Gina. "He gets so crabby when he doesn't get his walks. He needs a walk after the pool." I looked at Krystal and rolled my eyes.

"Did the poor dog get resuscitated?" asked Krystal.

"Oh, yes. Mr. Nick was very irritated with me for calling him to the pool for Truffles. Charlie thought the dog was drowning, but Truffles just wanted to take a swim. It turns out that Truffles snorts when he is swimming and we thought he was a goner. He was only expressing his happiness."

"Too bad he wasn't a goner!" I said. "I guess we will have to walk the little bugger. Between walking Truffles and walking Brook's dog Mossy, I'm getting more than my share of walking." After breathing a sigh of relief that Nick hadn't found and killed us, Krystal and I retired to the kitchen before walking Truffles and Gina hustled off to the laundry room.

In the kitchen, we found a tempting icy cold vanilla milkshake and two scrumptious scones on the counter with a note from Gina for Krystal. "Krystal, please enjoy! From Gina." Krystal grabbed the milkshake.

"Hits the spot!" she said and put it to her mouth. Something told me to take that shake away. I wrestled it away from Krystal and insisted on smelling it before she took a sip. I was right to do so, and boy, was I glad I did. It had the smell of bitter almonds. Cyanide! Krystal grabbed it back from me, but I dashed it from her hands just as she was about to take a big gulp. It spilled out onto the floor.

"What did you do that for?" screeched Krystal. "I'm not on a diet yet!"

"Krystal, don't you smell it? It's the smell of bitter almonds! Someone left that for you to drink and laced it with cyanide!"

"I don't smell anything! You're crazy! You are a weird girl!"

"No, I'm not! Sodium cyanide is easy to purchase and turns into hydrogen cyanide when mixed with liquid. Cyanide is very soluble in water, and just a few drops of concentrated cyanide mixed with a liquid can kill you. You can buy bitter almonds which contain cyanide. Not everyone can smell it, but I can. Why do you think they call me the nose? If you smash them up and add them to a drink it can kill you. But the easier way would be to obtain the concentrated powder and mix it with a few drops of any liquid and put it into the milkshake or the scone batter. Would you listen? Just stop."

"Alright, watchdog with the nose. I'm listening. Just relax."

"I'm not going to relax! Someone wants you dead, not to mention me also. They did push me off my bike, you know. Someone is onto us. Someone knows we are asking questions, namely the same someone who pushed me off my bike. It's the same someone who pushed the plaster bust off the second story portico and tried to kill you when we were walking Truffles. Now we know that was no accident. It's the same someone who tried to poison Pilar with peanuts, with quinine, with plant derived poison in her tea, and perhaps the same someone who arranged an accident for her on her scooter. There is a murderer on the loose and no one is safe!"

"I can at least eat one of the scones," said Krystal and reached for one.

"No, you don't!" I commanded and grabbed them both.

"You don't have to be such a pig," said Krystal. "I would have shared one with you."

"You are not eating anything that comes from this kitchen," I said. "These scones and the remnants of that milkshake are both going to be analyzed, and I'll bet you anything that the scones are laced with cyanide as well as the milkshake."

"Alright, be a little Debbie Downer," harumphed Krystal. "I'm hungry for scones!"

"I'll buy you two delicious scones at Tasty Pastry. Sound good?"

"Sounds great. Let's go," said Krystal. Truffles the Peke shuffled into the kitchen, looked up at us, and growled for his walk.

"Maybe not," said Krystal and grimaced. "Truffles wants his walk. I could feed him the cyanide scones. What do you think? Should I poison him with cyanide? We could conduct an experiment." Truffles growled and barked. "Oh, alright, psycho Pekinese who likes to try to drown himself in the pool," said Krystal dejectedly. "Get your stupid leash." This set off a volley of growls and

262

barks from Truffles. "And a treat," sighed Krystal. Truffles whined and yipped.

"He is no dummy," I said as I slipped the scones into a bag and poured out the milkshake, saving some of it in a small container. I slipped that into the bag also. "He only works for treats."

#truffleslovestreats

Chapter Twelve: Far from the Maddening Shroud

I'll no say, men are villains a':

The real, harden'd wicked.

Wha hae nae check but human law,

Are to a few restricked;

But, och! Mankind are unco weak

An 'little to be trusted;

If Self the wavering balance shake,

It's rarely right adjusted!

---From *Letter to a Young Friend*, Robert Burns

"There is something odd going on with Truffles," said Krystal. "You know that Pilar had him neutered and he had Torbutrol for the pain. It is only given to cats and dogs, but it is a drug and a serious one."

"So what?" I asked. "Gina is giving it to him, right?"

"The Torbutrol disappeared, and no one can find it, so Gina gave Truffles some brandy. Now he loves brandy and wants it every night before he goes to sleep."

"Interesting," I said. "Truffles is getting addicted to his nightcap. Who would steal a dog's painkillers?"

"Someone who likes pain pills and will take a dog's medicine?" offered Krystal. "Pretty desperate. Or someone who likes to hoard drugs just in case they can be used to off an enemy?"

While we walked the psycho Peke, we speculated on who could have tried to poison Krystal with cyanide. That should also tell us who was the perpetrator of all this mischief.

"Marty vowed revenge on Pilar," I said. "Marty is old, crafty, and smart. Marty might and probably did poison her old lover with an overdose of Digitalis when she was only eighteen years old. Pilar held it over her head all those years and threatened to betray her confidence.

Then Pilar fired her. I would say that was a motive to kill Pilar, wouldn't you?"

"Marty was serious about getting Pilar," agreed Krystal. "But I don't know about murder. They say if you commit one murder it gets easier to commit another one. She supposedly killed that old goat years ago so maybe that made it easier for her to kill Pilar."

"They say? Who are they?" I asked.

"Oh, you know. Poirot, Miss Marple, Agatha Christie. The usual."

"But Marty has an alibi. She was in church that Saturday evening praying at the time Pilar died," I said. "She always stays for the whole service, and she even stays afterward to kneel and pray."

"Oh, right. Prove it. How many times did I tell my mother I was in church or at the library when I wasn't?" asked Krystal. "Nobody can corroborate that. There are no videos of church, and if you go to church a lot like she does, people could say that she was in church because they are used to seeing her there in the same pew every

Saturday night, Sunday morning, and holy day. Who will contradict the word of a nice old lady like Marty? No one."

"You know something? You're right. Church isn't much of an alibi, is it? But would Marty try to poison you with cyanide? Would she shove me off my bicycle? Would she try to bean you with a plaster bust from the second floor?" I asked.

"I don't think so, but there are people in this house who would do any one of those things," said Krystal.

"Such as Nick, Tiggy, and Bunty?" I asked. "My head is swimming with all these suspects. I was so sure it was Nick, but then I start thinking about all the others and I'm confused."

"Affirmative. I concur, counselor. How about Piper as Pilar's killer?" asked Krystal. "I vote for Piper. Piper worked as a pharmacist before she married her rich husband, Kendall. Rumor has it that she once told Kendall that if he ever left her, she would poison him with strychnine. She told him that at a dinner party in front of twelve people."

"She did?" I inquired. "Who told you that? That could be hearsay."

"Please, Tabitha. When you hear all the first-class gossip in this town, you know what is true and what is malicious speculation. I know it's true because I have sources. I am a discerning gossip. I know what goes on around here. Believe me. Then there is the evidence of the voodoo doll we found in Piper's house."

"That is not evidence," I said.

"No, but it's pretty darn good speculation. Who could have poisoned Pilar with peanuts and with quinine, her two allergic agents? Who could have made that tea we suspected was made with lily of the valley? Who has both foxglove and lily of the valley growing in her own garden and encircling the borders of the gardens of her house? Who could have brewed Pilar up a tea derived from either or both of those highly poisonous plants? Piper, that's who. Who knows a woman better than her lifelong childhood friend?"

"No one," I said. "Not even her own mother."

"Piper knew Pilar inside out and just how to get to her. She knew her habits. She knew what Pilar was allergic to. Then there was the scooter incident. Charlie the gardener said that he saw Piper hanging around the garage the day before the scooter tires were allegedly sprayed with cooking spray. The cyanide incident in Gina's kitchen seems to clinch the answer. Piper was a pharmacist before she married her wealthy lawyer husband and upper-class scion of a rich family. She could have gotten hold of cyanide. Then there was the bicycle incident. Piper is very fit. She could have cycled up behind you and shoved you off your bike. Piper could have attempted to topple that plaster cast onto my head from the second story. I'll bet you anything Piper has a key to Pilar's house. She knows her way around that house as if it were her own. She could have entered the house, done the deed, and slipped out without anyone being the wiser, just like a ghost who comes and goes. All these incidents could easily have been the work of Piper. Piper could have done any of those things."

"Yes, but Piper has a watertight alibi for the Saturday evening of Pilar's death. She was in bed with her estranged husband," I said.

"Oh, please," said Krystal. "Going to bed with the ex-husband and using him as an alibi is the oldest trick in the book! So, they ate dinner together. She seduced him after dinner, and they were in bed all evening. Give me the proof. There was no one there with them. Besides, you heard her say to Kendall on the phone when we were hiding in the closet that he was her alibi for that night. She alluded to the fact that she wasn't there with him every minute of the night."

"Oh, that's right," I agreed. "That was strange, wasn't it? She was apparently gone for a while."

"It sounds like she was gone for an hour or two and she isn't saying where she was. At the same time, she was telling Kendall she didn't murder Pilar, she was also telling him to keep saying that she never left him alone. Did she mention where she had gone? No. Doesn't that sound fishy to you? She is guilty of something. She told him not to tell anyone."

"That's right. She did say she was gone for a while. I almost forgot about that because I was so scared out of my mind that she would discover us in the closet."

"Maybe Piper's husband feels guilty for going to bed with Pilar," said Krystal. "Maybe Kendall is still in love with Piper and wants her back, so he is going to go along with the game. He will give her the alibi. You bet. Piper was a pharmacist before she married him. She knows all about poisons and how to use them to maximum advantage. She could have drugged Pilar. She could have made Pilar overdose and fall down that winding staircase. She is no dummy."

"True," I said.

"She could have met Pilar at the lighthouse on some pretense late in the evening and stuck her with a syringe of something to make her quiet and inert. She could have ground up an opiate overdose and shoved it into Pilar's veins. The opiate overdose would have sealed Pilar's fate. One little overdose and good-bye old friend."

"So what is the motive?" I asked.

"Revenge, just like the other motives from our many suspects. Pilar slept with and seduced Piper's husband which no doubt led to their divorce."

"Oh, right. Good thinking," I said. Our psycho Peke promptly pooped, snuffled, and scratched up mounds of the neighbor's turf. "You clean it up," I said.

"No, you," said Krystal.

"No, you," I said. Krystal sighed. "Why do I always have to clean up the poop?"

"Because you are the one getting paid to do it," I grinned. "Besides, I clean up the litter box and do more than my share of the cleaning and dusting at the apartment because you have a tendency to break things."

"That's why when I am told by Gina to dust the fine china, crystal, and valuables, I only pretend to dust it. Sometimes I run the duster over everything lightly, but I don't ever pick it up and clean it with a cloth. I don't want to have to pay for Pilar's Waterford and Lalique treasures."

"That would take more than you make," I said.

"O.K., entertain this thought," said Krystal as she scooped up the poop. "What do you think of Bristol Taggart the former marketer, right hand man, and lover as the culprit?"

"Why him?" I asked. "You just jumped from Piper to Bristol. You just made a great case for Piper. You made her sound like Lady Macbeth. Now you've focused on Bristol. Why?"

"Think about it. Pilar dumped Bristol ignominiously after all those years. Fifteen to be exact. He was enraged and wanted revenge. We both heard him at Minty's screaming at her and saw him dump his milkshake on her head. We heard what he said to her, and it wasn't pretty. Bristol has a wicked temper. He could have planted the peanuts in the scone after it was delivered to the lighthouse. He was there at the fundraiser, along with all the usual suspects."

"You think so?"

"Yuppers! Bristol knew about Pilar's allergy to quinine and to peanuts because he was constantly running for her drinks and her lunches. He had to have known. He can make a tea filled with lily of the valley as well as anyone. It isn't that hard to do. He could have snuck into the open garage and sprayed the scooter tires, as he owns motorcycles. He would be aware that spraying the tires is highly dangerous. He could have killed Piper and left her body in the lighthouse."

"Yes, my dear friend. You are so right," I said. "I think we might have to face the fact that one or two of the attempts on Pilar's life might have been made by a second candidate. Perhaps more than one of our suspects was trying to kill her. Maybe Bristol was involved after all."

"Also, he bought a one-way ticket to Australia and is leaving everything behind to go be a sheep farmer in the outback. He was talking about it at the funeral. Remember? He is running away today. Get it? He is going halfway around the world and never coming back. Gina told me. She knows everything. She knows when the foxglove blooms on the hillside. She knows where all the bodies are buried. She knows what gel Nicky puts in his hair. She knows their shoe sizes, for Pete's sake. Gina knows almost as much as God."

"What?" I screamed. "Why didn't you tell me this? Come on! Dump this little doggy-doo. We have to get to Bristol before he leaves for Australia. Seriously, Krystal. Really? Today? Why didn't you tell me about this before?"

"Because you didn't ask," said Krystal, stating the obvious. I marveled at her composure. Like I said, Krystal's blood pressure never goes above the low side of normal.

We rushed Truffles through the rest of the walk, took him into the kitchen, and gave him several good treats. Then we hiked it out to the car and buzzed down to Green Bay to the airport as fast as we possibly could, pushing the speed limit all the way. We were just in time to confront Bristol as he walked in the sliding glass doors of the airport lobby.

"Bristol! Bristol!" we called. He didn't look happy to see us.

As it turned out, Bristol did have an alibi for the night of Pilar's murder. When we confronted him, he blustered, blathered, hemmed, and hawed.

Finally, he said, "You two are barking up the wrong tree. I was picked up for drunk driving the night Pilar was murdered. Why don't you ask our Eeyore look-alike copper over there in New Belgium? That ridiculous excuse for a policeman, Sgt. Frances LeCaptain, picked me up for drunk driving and threw me into one of the two jail cells in New Belgium to make me sleep it off. Incompetent clod! I wasn't even that drunk! He said he wasn't going to officially charge me, and he would just let me sleep it off in the cell. Thus, it never got into the paper, and no one knew. He apparently forgot the breathalyzer that evening. Good old Eyeore the incompetent copper gives me an airtight alibi."

"Will Sergeant Frances LeCaptain corroborate your statement?" inquired Krystal.

"He sure will. I guess you two girls are disappointed. But there you go. It was fortunate I was picked up for drunkenness because it proves I'm innocent. Now I'm off to Australia to carve out a new life for myself as a sheep farmer in the outback. Every time I survey my land and animals, I will savor and enjoy the lonely peace and quiet. I will feel glad that I'm there and not here in

God's country U.S.A. with all of you mental cases. This place is getting too crowded and full of tourists anyway. It started out as a God's country retreat, and it's turned into Grand Central Station from May to November. Not my scene. Too many people. Too many tourists. The ratio of bad people to good people is on the rise. Not my cup of tea. Not that I'm sorry Pilar is dead. I was addicted to her but now I'm over it. The world is a better place without that female Benedict Arnold! I'm glad Pilar is dead and congratulations to whoever did the dirty deed!"

We stared at him speechlessly.

"Now if you don't mind, ladies, I have a plane to catch! Have a nice life!" said Bristol and bustled towards the security gate.

"We'll be checking that alibi with Sgt. LeCaptain!" called out Krystal. "I will be calling him!" I sighed.

"Be my guest!" yelled Bristol.

"So much for that tidy theory," I said. "Back to the drawing board. Is there anyone else we can bug, follow, spy on, or question today?" I asked as we walked back to our car parked in the lot. Krystal's brow furrowed with the effort of thinking over all the people we had encountered since she began working at Pilar's house.

"How about Marty? I just feel that there is something there we have overlooked. I think that she knows more than she is letting on," said Krystal.

"Alright," I said. "Let's go ask Marty some questions."

Marty's house was a small white clapboard house set back in a deep lot with a large garden. We parked the car in the gravel driveway and walked up to the door. Krystal knocked. No answer. Krystal tried the door. It opened easily.

"The door is open," said Krystal. "Should we go in?"

"No, you shouldn't!" said a deep, stentorian voice behind us. We both jumped about a foot in the air, swiveled, and turned to face the angry visage of Valerie, Martha's daughter. I never realized how big, masculine, and intimidating Valerie was, or how scary looking. "Just what in the hell are you two doing here?" she demanded.

Valerie had an armful of books with her. Perhaps because she was so upset with us, she dropped the books at our feet. She bent to pick them up while we struggled to come up with a reasonable answer to her question.

"Uh, we, uh, j-j-j-just wanted to talk to Martha," Krystal finally managed to choke out.

"Oh, yeah? Well, you can't talk to her. My mother is in the hospital where this town and everybody in it has managed to put her!" said Valerie. "She is having chest pains and arrythmia. She was in church the whole evening that Pilar died, and I was with her, so we both have an alibi. Please note and write that down. Poor Mom. Now she is almost dead from stress, and she is suffering in the hospital. Not that it is any of your business!"

"Oh, I'm sorry," said Krystal.

"I'll bet you are! Now get lost!" said Valerie. "Don't come back here looking for my mother or me. We don't want you bugging us anymore! Or else I promise you that you will be sorry!"

Krystal and I sidled around Valerie and complied. We weren't about to argue with this one. No way. Hairy, scary, and quite contrary. We crab-walked toward the car, looking over our shoulder frequently to make sure that Stella the Fella wasn't after us. We gained the car and hopped in. I had trouble fitting the key into the ignition because my hands were shaking so hard. When the engine roared into life, I stomped on the gas, and we made tracks out of there. I looked at my hands trembling on the wheel.

"Jesus, Mary and Joseph!" exclaimed Krystal. "Get me the hell out of here!"

"Krystal, I think we have suspect number seven," I said.

"Only seven? It feels like two hundred," said Krystal. "That is one scary babe!"

"Where was Valerie the night Pilar was murdered, I wonder?" I speculated. "Do you think that she was with Marty at church that evening?"

"I don't know. I doubt it. She doesn't seem like the churchgoing type. Where was Valerie? Why don't you go back and ask her? Just don't take me with you," said Krystal fervently. "By the way, did you note what kind of flowers Marty had growing in that big garden on the side of the house?"

"No, did you?" I asked.

"I did. She has all kinds of old-fashioned old lady plants in that garden, peonies, pansies, columbines, lavender, sage, narcissus, hollyhocks, bleeding hearts, and geraniums. But here is the interesting thing. She has lily of the valley and some very healthy-looking foxglove. Foxglove as in digitalis. Digitalis derived from foxglove is exactly what Marty allegedly used to poison and murder her old goat lover when she was only eighteen. I'm sure that Valerie is aware that there are foxglove and lily of the valley growing right in her mother's own garden. Dig it? Score!"

"You're right! Not only that, but did you see the titles of the books Marty dropped?" I asked.

"Uh, no."

"The Study of Botany," I said. "A Primer of Poisons, and The Practice of Witchcraft."

"So she likes boring books?" asked Krystal.

"Yes, books in which she can study which plants are poisonous. Poisonous as in foxglove, poisonous as in lily of the valley, poisonous as in Digitalis. Poisonous as in her garden."

"In other words, Marty could have carried out that unsuccessful attempt on Pilar's life which put Pilar in the hospital for three days with a hefty dose of Digitalis in her veins. Likewise for Valerie. Like mother, like daughter. Maybe Marty and Valerie have worked together on project Pilar. Just how poisonous are these plants? In fact, I'm going to research that right now."

Krystal started applying her digits on the net and in a very few minutes, she had come up with info about lily of the valley. She read from the text.

"Uh-huh! A flower of the asparagus family. Native to South America and other cool climes the world over. Blooms in the early spring. Noted at least fifteen times in the Bible. A sign of purity and Easter. A member of the deadly nightshade family. Highly poisonous if ingested. Just like foxglove, lily of the valley is poisonous in every part of the plant, leaves, stems, and flowers. In fact, it was once considered the tool of witches. Lily of the valley can be fatal if ingested, especially to children. The method of action is through cardiac glycosides, which create an effect much like exposure to that of Digitalis, found in foxglove. There are at least 42 cardiac glycosides in lily of the valley. The plant is classified as a one on the poison scale, which means it has major toxicity that can lead to death. Oh, boy!"

"Now we have three people with foxglove and lily of the valley in their very own garden, Marty, Valerie, and Piper. My oh my oh my," I said. "We might as well add a third person to our list of poisoners, namely Valerie."

"Oh, boy! More of those silverfish everywhere!" exclaimed Krystal. "If it isn't the mother, it could darn well be the daughter. Why else would she be so defensive and mean to us? She knows that we are poking around in the case, and she doesn't like it one little bit. Maybe she is the one who is trying to kill us."

"Or maybe it's Piper. Remember, Piper also has all those poisonous plants in her garden."

"Hey! That could be where Piper was on the night that Pilar died," I said. "When Piper was out for those few hours and she wanted to make sure that Kendall would back her up and say that they were together all night and she never left his side, she could have been up to some mischief. I'll bet that is where she was."

"Where?"

"She could have been out late stalking Pilar with a syringe filled with Digitalis or lily of the valley venom. After all, she too has those plants aplenty in her very own yard. With her knowledge of pharmacy, it wouldn't be that difficult to manufacture some poison and stick it into Pilar's veins."

"You're right," said Krystal. "More of those red lobsters jumping about everywhere. I'm starting to see red lobsters dancing in my sleep, clicking their little clackers and dancing the samba, the rhumba, or the salsa. Can't stand those red lobsters, or are those red halibuts? I can just see those little buggers swimming around too, right next to the dancing red lobsters."

"Red herrings?" I offered.

"Those too," said Krystal. "Speaking of salsa, would you like to go out for chips and salsa followed by a taco or two? I'm getting awful hungry."

"Sure, but first home," I said. When we got home, I went directly to the landline phone and called the hospital. We had contacts on the admitting desk there.

"Hey, Carol, this is Tabitha Nolan. I'm here at home with Krystal and we are wondering if our elderly friend Martha Gilson was admitted with arrhythmia and chest pain today. She would have been brought in by her daughter Valerie a few hours ago. Female, Caucasian, late sixties, brown hair turning gray, faded blue eyes, slender, beaten down by life, deferential manner, quiet, unassuming. Was she admitted for observation?"

"You know I'm not officially supposed to tell you that," said Carol.

"Yes, I know, but maybe unofficially you could," I said. "Maybe you could just say something like, 'Merry Christmas in July.' Or maybe you could say, 'My cousin looks like Teddy Roosevelt.'"

"My cousin looks like Cousin It, actually. But I think I could just say Merry Christmas in July," said Carol. "Or maybe I could say stress and anxiety are a killer and overnight observation is the answer. Someone is going home tomorrow provided everything checks out. I could say her domineering daughter brought her in and left not long ago. She scares me. She looms over one like Lurch. I think she has too much androgen, or is that testosterone? I don't know. I couldn't say. But I could say that daughter will be picking her up tomorrow. Or I could say nothing at all. Maybe I will say nothing at all. I should say nothing at all. I haven't said anything, have I?"

"No, I don't think you have said anything," I said. "I'm sure I didn't hear you say anything. In fact, you are annoyingly silent today because I can't hear a word you say. I must be going deaf."

"You are hard of hearing. You better get checked out. Bye," said Carol and hung up.

"I still don't think we can entirely rule out Martha or her daughter Valerie," I said. "They may have been in church the night Pilar was killed, but how to prove it?" Krystal gazed upwards and sighed.

"Yup, we're in a real mess now. A great big pile of prickly herrings. Yes, prickled herrings. And getting pricklier all the time!" said Krystal. "So many suspects. So little time."

"You can say that again," I said. "You do mean pickled herring, right?"

"No, I mean prickled herring. Don't confuse me! Or we could say smoky herring, because the killer is throwing these herrings around trying to confuse the issue and make it all smoky so we can't see what is going on. I think smoky herrings would be a better expression," said Krystal.

"If you say so. I acquiesce."

"It's about time, know-it-all," said Krystal. "Can we take a break from sleuthing now? I'm still hungry and I hear that salsa calling my name."

"Whatever you want," I said. "Let's go."

Our break from sleuthing was destined to be a short one. Bunty Essex Jones appeared on our doorstep that very night and threatened us with mayhem if we didn't stand down, quit poking around, stop asking questions, and mind our own business. I thought of the cardboard tubes under Krystal's bed that contained the rolled-up canvases of precious art worth perhaps millions of dollars. If Bunty only knew that we stole her stolen art pieces which she had hidden in the grandfather clock. How the fur would fly then!

She wanted to come into the house, but luckily, Krystal kept her out on the porch.

But it was when Bunty got right up into my face with a gold handled letter opener and threatened to cut out my beautiful blue eyes that Krystal started to go berserk. She grabbed Bunty by the throat and squeezed.

"That's it!" declared Krystal. "I've had enough of you and your phony accent to last me three lifetimes. Get out!" she said through clenched teeth. "Next time I see you on our doorstep, I'm dialing 911. That will be after I put my Glock in your face! Now go and don't come back!"

Unbeknown to us, our little Cuckoo had been watching the whole incident from inside the screen door. I don't know what possessed our sweet little Cuckoo, but she had enough too. Cuckoo flew round and round like a gyre in ever widening circles, running in concentric circles like a mad thing. I had seen dogs do this. I called it cracker dog. But I had never seen a cat do it. She ran like one possessed, little kitty teeth gleaming and eyes glowing, until she jumped right up on Bunty's face and gave her a good scratching. Oops! Too bad I don't believe in declawing kitties. So sorry. Not.

Bunty swatted her down, but Cuckoo wasn't having it. She sprang past Krystal and with one leap, she was on Bunty again. With a scream of a meow, she twisted her body and with both front feet, she gave Bunty's face a good clawing. Bunty jumped back about two feet and screamed. Her face showed red with blood where Cuckoo had dug in her claws.

"That thing should be put down!" cried Bunty. "What are you two, witches or something? Nick is right about you two. He said you are both witches!" She let out another scream of anger and frustration and then she ran.

"Gee," I said. "Funny how she dropped her phony aristocratic English accent and reverted to her white trash Texas twang as soon as Cuckoo attacked her. It's a good thing I don't believe in declawing cats."

"A darn good thing," agreed Krystal and closed the door. "Bunty is going to have a few scars for a while. Good kitty, Cuckoo! How would you like a real big treat? I'm telling you, Tabitha, we must solve this case. Now I'm even more determined to do it. We solve this case, and the world is our clam. Happy as a clam. Or is that our crab? Our lobster? Our scallop? Our snail?" mused Krystal.

"You mean the world is our oyster?" I asked.

"That too. You know, one of those smelly things with a shell," said Krystal. "All of that smelly seafood stuff. Just give me a burger any day, or if I eat fish, it must be a perch dinner from the Screaming Seagull in New Belgium. Friday night fish there is the best. I could go for a perch dinner right now. Come on, Cuckoo. Time for your treat!"

#watchcatcuckoostrikesagain

Chapter Thirteen: In Search of Lost Crime

The best laid plans of mice o' men gang aft agley

An' lea's us nought but grief and pain for promised joy!

--From *To a Mouse*, by Robert Burns

The next Sunday dawned bright, clear, and breezy, a perfect summer's day of shimmering water, luscious rich green fields, and silvery sky. The air was laced with the scent of apple and cherry blossoms and fragrant lavender. My phone rang.

"Oh, dang," I said. "It's Valerie. I wonder what she wants."

"She wants you to take care of Marty until her caregiver gets there later this afternoon," said Krystal.

"Marty is so bad now she can barely move or speak. She should be in the nursing home, but Valerie insists that her mother should be taken care of at home. She is sinking fast, poor unfortunate thing. She won't last long. She goes in and out of consciousness. They have the visiting nurse there constantly and hospice care too. Val can't take care of Marty around the clock. After all, she does have to work. She supplements her bank teller job with working at the AmericInn as a maid, so she works a lot of hours. It's Sunday and I bet one of the caregivers is absent today."

"Don't be silly," I said. "Valerie can't possibly want me to take care of her mother." It turned out that is exactly what Valerie wanted. I answered the phone. "Hi, Valerie."

"Hi, Tabitha. You're a nurse, right? Can you come over for a few hours? I absolutely have to work today. Martha wants you. She keeps talking in this guttural growl nobody but me can understand. If you come over and read to her that's all she wants."

"She wants me?" I asked.

"Yeah, who knows why. She asked for you specifically. She likes you, I guess. No accounting for taste."

"Gee, thanks for the compliment," I said. Valerie ignored me.

"I have been reading two books to her constantly. She only wants the same two books. One is *The Last Tycoon* and the other one is *The Great Gatsby*, both by that F. Scott Fitzgerald guy. You know, the roaring twenties, the lost generation, Paris, the Algonquin, Hemingway, Fitzgerald; all that stuff that English majors love."

"Yeah, I'm familiar with that," I said.

"Marty was a diehard English major. She taught English and Language Arts at the Catholic school for years after she put herself through college, but they paid her so little that she found she could make more money by being a legal assistant and an office manager. Then finally she ended up as Pilar's assistant, secretary, and gal Friday. It's harder to get jobs after you turn fifty so Marty had to take a job with the witch in the end."

"Poor her," I said.

"Yeah, no kidding. Marty keeps trying to tell me something, but I cannot understand her. I believe that my poor mother had a slight stroke, so I have a personal caregiver coming in every day. I can't nurse her the way that she should be and give her the care that she needs now. I refuse to put her in the nursing home so she will stay in her own home with me until the end. I'm leaving now for my weekend job at the AmericInn. You know I moonlight there as a maid and as a waitress for their luncheons, especially on weekends. So can you come over and sit with her for an hour or two until the caregiver comes over?"

"I suppose I can," I said reluctantly.

"Hurry up. I'm leaving right now, and she can't be left alone. I have to go. Later." Marty rang off. Such beautiful manners. She must have gone to charm school.

"Looks like I'm going to babysit Marty," I said.

"Better you than me," said Krystal. "I'll be watching *The Ghost and Mrs. Muir* on TCM, eating raspberry scones, and playing with Cuckoo."

"TCM? Raspberry scones? Gene Tierney? Mrs. Muir? Darn! Wish I could stay," I said.

"Well, you can't so you better go."

"Heartless," I pronounced, and started to get ready. By the time I reached Marty's, Valerie had gone to her job. The door was open. On the way in the door, I saw a little piece of soft heather colored woven cloth caught on the peonies near the front door. Absentmindedly, I picked it off the peony plant and put it in my pocket.

Once inside, I walked directly upstairs to Marty's bedroom. The house was old and shabby, but clean. Marty greeted me with a wan, twisted smile. The poor old thing was lying in bed with her hand on her books. I smiled at her.

"Hi, Marty. Valerie said you wanted me to read *The Great Gatsby*. Right?" Marty blinked. That served as her yes. She really should be in the nursing home, but she lived in fear of nursing homes and Valerie refused to put her in one. We all knew she wasn't long for this world.

I smiled in what I hoped was an amiable way and started to read Chapter One of *The Great Gatsby*. I read along until Martha's breathing became rhythmic and steady. She closed her eyes and seemed to drift so I stopped reading. Immediately, she started to make growling noises that meant continue. I read on. She put her hand on the other book, *The Last Tycoon,* and somehow tucked it under her arm as if she didn't want to let it go.

"*The Last Tycoon?*" I laughed. "Isn't that what Pilar always called Nasty Nick?" I asked. Marty made eager noises in her throat and seemed to get excited. Then her breathing accelerated and suddenly stopped. She started to cough and choke. She couldn't catch her breath. I realized she might be having cardiac arrest. I ran into the living room where I had left my purse, grabbed my phone, and dialed 911.

When I had the ambulance dispatched, I ran back into the bedroom, only to find that Marty had stopped breathing. I felt for a pulse and found nothing. Immediately, I began to apply CPR to Marty's now inert body. I noted that *The Last Tycoon* was still tucked firmly under arm, and with her left hand, she seemed to be pointing to a phrase on the page of *The Great Gatsby*, but the significance of those clues did not hit me until later.

"Oh, God, please!" I cried on a rising note of panic. "Please don't take her! Don't take her on my watch!" I continued to give her CPR without success. Within minutes the ambulance personnel arrived and took over, giving her CPR, oxygen, and used the defibrillator. They worked on her for five minutes with no response before transporting her to the hospital, still working on her the entire time. Poor Marty. Tears welled up in my eyes. Pilar's rejection of her was the final straw that drove her poor old body over the edge. I had seen it so many times. Stress was a deadly killer.

I just happened to glance at Marty's bedside table. There was a small slim ancient looking volume there with some of the pages marked. It was called *The Language of Flowers*. Just out of curiosity, I picked it up. Understanding dawned when I saw that some of the flower names were circled and checked. I read that hemlock means you will be the death of me. Foxglove stands for insincerity; carnations mean alas for my poor heart. Purple columbine stands for resolution, white columbine for folly, and finally, peonies stand for shame.

Marty was the only person I knew with a truly old-fashioned garden featuring hollyhocks, sunflowers, pansies, peonies, lavender, sage, marigold, narcissus, columbine, iris, day lilies, lily of the valley, starflower, sedum, barberry, and an abundance of roses. She even cultivated an area of milkweed to attract the Monarch butterflies and stocked butterfly bushes in profusion. There was even a hemlock tree near the road.

I realized that all those flowers with the names circled in Marty's little bedside book grew abundantly in Marty's old-fashioned garden, and that she had cut each of them and placed them at Pilar's bedside, each one of them as a message. Even after she was fired by Pilar, she still had a key to the house, and she still had access.

"That clears up one mystery," I said to myself.

I called the visiting nurse caregiver service and told them not to send their employee to the house. Then I called Valerie at the inn and told her that Marty had been transported to the hospital with what appeared to be cardiac arrest and it wasn't looking good. She said she would leave immediately and go to the hospital. I disconnected, tucked the phone into my purse, and suddenly, it was as if I were struck by lightning.

Quickly, I searched Marty's room before anyone else could get into the house. I looked in the dresser drawers and even under the mattress. I found just what I expected to find; a vial of hydrocodone, a vial of tizanidine, and two syringes. Gingerly, I picked them up with a Kleenex and put them all into a plastic baggie which I put carefully into my purse so that they wouldn't have my fingerprints on them. Nor would I destroy any fingerprints that were on them.

On the floor, I found another syringe. I had a good idea what was in that syringe. I believed that it was Truffles' missing Torbutrol, the painkiller used for dogs and cats. I added that syringe to my evidence bag. Then I dialed my cell phone with shaking hands.

"Krystal! Evidence! Coming home! Get ready!" I barked into the phone.

"What?" she asked, stupefied.

"You heard me!" I screamed. "Now! Oh, forget it! I'm coming home!" I ran for the car, my head throbbing with the knowledge. *I know. I know. Now I know. Get Krystal. Get Krystal.*

I ran into the apartment screaming. "Krystal! Krystal! Now!" Krystal came running out of the kitchen holding a half-eaten raspberry scone.

"What! What!"

"Car! Now! It's Nick! I know it! This time I have the proof!"

Krystal threw the half-eaten scone on the kitchen table. "I'm getting my lock picks and duct tape. Get back in the car."

"Get my little tape recorder for me too!" I called to Krystal. Within a minute, Krystal was in the car with me, along with Cuckoo, Misty, and Mossy. She handed me my little tape recorder and I slipped it into my pocket. I peeled out of the parking lot of the apartment building with tires squealing and we made tracks\ to Pilar and Nick's house. Suddenly I heard the protesting mews, meows, and mirrs of the kitties, Misty, and Cuckoo. Mossy gave a grumble from the back seat.

"Sorry creatures, but we're in a hurry!" I said and stomped on the accelerator all the way to Pilar and Nick's mansion. Upon arrival, we slammed into the circular drive, jumped out of the car, and ran into the house.

"Gina!" I called. Gina came jogging out of the kitchen, her round face curious. "Gina, where is Nick?" I demanded.

"Mr. Nick went out on his bicycle just as usual," she said. "Is he in trouble?"

"You bet he is in trouble. He is in more trouble than he has ever been in his life!" said Krystal. "Where is that depraved creep?"

"He usually goes out to Potawatomie State Park for his bicycle ride," said Gina. "Are you going after Mr. Nick?"

"You bet we are!" said Krystal. Gina smiled and gave Krystal a high five.

"You go girl!" said Gina. "But if you are going after him then you should take Charlie with you. He is very powerful. He is outside trimming the hedges. I'll call him."

"Thanks, but we are doing this ourselves," Krystal flung over her shoulder as we ran out the door. I peeled out of the circular drive, and we made tracks to Potawatomie State Park. We drove up and down the roads, peering through the trees and gazing into the dappled sunshine, scanning the light and shadows for Nick on his bicycle.

"Nick always wears a yellow and gold helmet and a fancy black spandex outfit with a fanny pack. He rides a fancy bicycle," said Krystal.

"Of course," I said. "Look! There he is!" I stomped on the accelerator and almost ran Nick over in my zealous effort to make him pull over and stop. I swerved to the side of the road and stopped the car. We jumped out and pursued him hotly on foot. Krystal, always faster than me, got to him before I did. She reached out and yanked him off his bicycle by the helmet. She grabbed one arm, and I grabbed the other. Together, we got him halfway down to the ground.

He seemed to know why we had assaulted him. Somehow, he unzipped his fanny pack and grabbed something out of it. Before I knew what he was doing, he had angled a syringe at me and plunged the needle into my forearm.

#dodgeittabby!

Chapter Fourteen: The Scone Also Rises

If you can keep your head when all about you

Are losing theirs and blaming it on you....

--From *If*, by Rudyard Kipling

"No!" screamed Krystal. Just in time she body slammed Nick to the ground, yanked the syringe out of my arm before Nick managed to depress it, and kicked away the syringe, saving me from being stuck with a vial of what might be insulin, or something equally insidious. Krystal jumped on Nick's back and wrenched both his arms behind his back. Fit as he was, he was no match for Krystal.

"Let's just take that syringe and put it in this little plastic baggie in my purse," I said. "Lord only knows what he has in there. Insulin maybe. A full syringe of that can kill anyone even if they aren't a diabetic." I picked up the syringe gingerly, covered it in plastic, and put it in the small purse I wore slung over my shoulder.

"Maybe we should give him 4CCs of hydrochloride to knock him out and then give him an overdose of something to dispatch him right now," said Krystal. "How about shooting him up with whatever is in that syringe? After all the evil he has done, shouldn't he have something evil done to him?"

"Tempting," I said. "But I think he needs to stand trial for his crimes."

"You always want to spoil all the fun," said Krystal. Nick struggled and bristled.

"What are you two doing following me?" said Nick. "Couldn't you take a hint? Who do you think pushed you off your bike, Tabitha? Who do you think tumbled that plaster cast off the second- floor landing and aimed for your head, Krystal? I missed, more's the pity. Who do you think planted the delicious milkshake and scones with the note from Gina for you, Krystal? Who do you think laced that shake and the scones with cyanide? I was sure you would drink the milkshake down, eat the scones, and die right there in the kitchen. Or better yet, take it all home and die somewhere other than my kitchen. My bad luck that you didn't. Couldn't you take a hint and leave me alone? You two nosy broads are really starting to bug me. How dare you follow me around and harass me?"

"How dare we?" I asked, looking down at him lying on the ground with Krystal sitting on his back. "Maybe it's because you killed your wife. Pilar was a pain in the butt and lots of people hated her guts. They probably all wanted her dead, but you stood to gain the most by her death. If she divorced you, you would get nothing because of the prenup. Why walk away without a dime when you could have it all? As the surviving spouse you get the whole empire and your freedom too. So much better than being tossed out without a dime."

"Greedy guts!" said Krystal and yanked Nick's arms tighter behind his back. "First you tried to kill Pilar by serving her peanut laced scones especially designed for her at the Cana Island Lighthouse fundraiser. That didn't work because it tasted awful, and she spit it out. She got her antidote in time. You tried to poison her again with quinine, which she is allergic to. That was a good try because only a few people know about her allergy to quinine. She might have dropped dead. You planted a syringe full of quinine in Marty's car, didn't you? You thought you could incriminate poor old Marty."

"I did nothing of the sort. You two pretend detectives playing at being Nancy Drew are ridiculous. I never gave Pilar any peanuts or any quinine."

"Like hell you didn't," I said. "But neither worked, so it was back to the drawing board. Then you got a great idea. You poisoned Pilar with an overdose of ground up Tizanidine, which is a muscle relaxer. You also gave her an opioid, something like hydrocodone. She has prescriptions for both. One night, maybe she got confused and took them together. She was so tired and uptight from running her empire that she miscalculated and overdosed. At least that is what you wanted everyone to think."

"You're crazy. You are imagining things," said Nick.

"Pilar took that Tizanidine muscle relaxer in her cocoa every night. Who prepared that for her every night? You did. Gina fixed her iced chocolate at ten in the morning every day. You could easily have snuck in and doctored that with some tonic water, causing her near demise from her quinine allergy that morning. But Gina was there to rush her to the clinic, wasn't she? Too bad for you. And it was you that fixed Pilar that special tea laced with plant poison, something like lily of the valley or foxglove. Piper sprayed her scooter tires with cooking oil, but it was you that planned the three unsuccessful poisonings before the real thing."

"Yeah!" chimed in Krystal. "You jerk!"

"But you didn't give up your evil plan so easily," I continued. "You had another plan in mind. There was the final poisoning. You tampered with Pilar's evening cocoa which you fixed yourself. We got that from Gina so don't lie about it. It was so easy to slip some barbies and some extra Tizanidine into that cocoa. Maybe some sweet little barbiturate like Hydrocodone, Butalbital, or Oxycodone. You gave her an overdose."

"No!" said Nick.

"Yes! Then you put her body into your Land Rover Range Rover and drove to the Cana Island Lighthouse after dark. This was one time when you didn't want to drive your very recognizable classic Porsche 911. The causeway was no problem for you. Since your upscale Land Rover can manage two feet of flood water. It was easy. You drove right up to the lighthouse late at night when everyone was gone. The lighthouse closes promptly at five o'clock seven days a week. You knew you would not be interrupted by anyone. You used the skeleton keys that you had made when you stole the keys to the lighthouse from Bobbie or Vivica or someone on the fundraiser committee."

"Sucker!" exclaimed Krystal.

"First you had to ingratiate yourself with the ladies by being on the committee and being so cozy with them. But that wasn't difficult for you because you are such a charm boy and so devastating to women. How many do you keep on the string at once? Four? Five? Skylar, Tiggy,

Bunty, and a few strays here and there plus the older volunteer ladies you always flirt with. They just love you. You turn that charm on and off like a faucet, don't you?"

"You don't know what you are talking about," said Nick.

"Wrong, babe," said Krystal. "She does know exactly what she is talking about."

"You carried Pilar's dead body up the ninety-seven steps of the spiral staircase," I continued "Again, easy for you because you are constantly working out. With those muscles of yours, not difficult. You hid the body in the Cana Island Lighthouse at the top level, or maybe even out on the platform so the body would not start to decompose. But my guess is that possibly, you hid the body in the big wooden chest in the topmost room and dragged it up the stairs and arranged it to look like she had fallen."

"Preposterous!" exclaimed Nick.

"Think so? No one would find Pilar there in that wooden chest the next day. No one looks in that chest. It was business as usual in the lighthouse until everyone went home at five none the wiser. You acted like Pilar was out of town on business. No one doubted that. She was called somewhere for a business emergency. That was a plausible reason for her temporary absence. That night you finalized your evil plan. You biked out to Cana Island in the middle of the night."

"Wrong!" said Nick.

"Right!" said Krystal.

"You left Skylar sleeping in her condo. Maybe you slipped her something to knock her out. You biked back to the lighthouse in the middle of the night, waded across the causeway and jogged to the lighthouse, unlocked the door again using your skeleton key copy."

"You are insane!"

"You probably had donned a wetsuit and footwear just for that little job. You ran up the stairs. Then you dragged Pilar out from the hiding place where you had hidden her body. You then arranged the body on the stairs to make it look like she had accidentally overdosed on her downers when she was there tending to some final task after hours when everyone had gone home. How easy to make it look like she overdosed and fell down the stairs."

"All lies!" said Nick.

"Not! Truth! Then you ran hell bent for leather down the stairs and outside, locked the door, ran across the grounds, sloshed back across the causeway, jumped on your bike, and pedaled like hell back to Skylar's condo in

Bailey's Harbor. We know because we traced your steps at two in the morning to find out if you could do it all in an hour and get back to Skylar's condo by three in the morning on your bike. We proved it could be done. What did you do, drug Skylar with some of the Tizanidine so she wouldn't wake up while you set the scene and completed your dirty work?"

"You're all wet," snarled Nick.

"Not!" said Krystal.

"You left Skylar sleeping peacefully. After your escapade in the wee hours at Cana Island Lighthouse, you quickly returned to Skylar's condo. There, instead of going back to bed, you prepared to drive to Milwaukee. You must have a fool proof alibi which Skylar would corroborate."

"You are an idiot!" said Nick. Krystal gave him a good kick.

"Shut up and listen to Tabby! You're the idiot!" she said.

"You were in bed with her all night, until you got a call early in the morning and had to rush down to Milwaukee to talk to your banker. This was an in-person kind of crisis which you could not resolve over the phone. You called Skylar on the road at seven, telling her that you left her sleeping between five and six a.m."

"You can't prove that!"

"Yes, we can. Your cell phone records will prove that, and Skylar swears that you were with her from the early evening on and all night. Thus, your foolproof alibi. However, you neglected one minor detail. There was no call from your banker to summon you for an emergency meeting at Chase Manhattan Bank in Milwaukee, was there? Your cell phone records will prove that. You did, indeed, go to Milwaukee and visit your banker at Chase Bank to establish your whereabouts that morning. You have proof of your parking receipt, no doubt, and the cameras in the bank will certainly show you coming in and leaving later, as you were sure to be seen on camera. Did you smile your pretty, charming smile for the cameras?"

"I didn't do it! I have an alibi!" yelled Nick. "I was with Skylar the evening before and all night! Skylar has sworn to it, and that day I was in Milwaukee with my banker at Chase Manhattan National Bank!"

"Like hell. We know you did it," said Krystal. "That banker didn't call you and he won't commit perjury for you, dummy! There are those phone records to prove it, or rather the lack of them. You did it! You're caught dead to rights! Dead bang on!"

"Then you did a truly despicable thing," I continued. "You set up Marty to take the fall. You planted the evidence in her bedroom. How do I know? I found a bit of your heather-colored woven sweater clinging to the peony plant at Marty's front door. That bit of cloth was unique, and I distinctly remember seeing you wearing that sweater on a cool morning when you were lying on your couch having your cappuccino."

"Proves nothing!"

"Proves you were there and left a bit of yourself. Poor Marty had heart problems and then a stroke. She could barely move, and she couldn't speak well enough to be understood. You waited until Valerie went off to work. You slipped in the open door before the caregiver arrived.

You forced Martha's hand onto the pill bottles and the syringe to leave fingerprints. Then you tucked them away into the drawers and under the mattress. You set Martha up to take the fall for you. You thought she was dying anyway, so why shouldn't she take the blame? Then you injected her with the Torbutrol that you stole which was supposed to be used for Truffles' painkiller. You made sure that Marty would die. She couldn't speak and could hardly move, and was probably only hours from death, but you wanted to make sure she wouldn't talk. She couldn't accuse you without a voice, could she? What you did when you forced her old fingers onto those syringes and pill bottles to leave her fingerprints on them and then hid the syringes and pill bottles in her room to incriminate her for your crimes probably brought on her final cardiac arrest. How convenient for you, despicable scum!"

"That's all a load of bull!" yelled Nick. Krystal shoved Nick's face into the dirt.

"Shut up and listen, freak!" screamed Krystal.

"But Marty wasn't quite done for yet. While I was reading to her before she died, she pointed to one name in *The Great Gatsby*, yours! She pointed to the name Nick, the narrator of the novel. She had enough strength to tuck F. Scott Fitzgerald's novel *The Last Tycoon* under her arm. Wasn't that what Pilar used to call you? The Last Tycoon. Ha! That was why Martha wanted us to read Fitzgerald's novels. She couldn't speak and she could barely move, but she was determined to get you. Marty won at last!"

"All lies!" screamed Nick.

"You're toast, stupid. Tabitha figured it out down to the last detail! You're guilty and you have a snowball's chance in hell. Admit it! You did it!" yelled Krystal and yanked Nick's arms.

"Ow! What if I did? Prove it," said Nick. His chin jutted out and his gray eyes turned to ice. "Not one person will believe you. I'm too smart for all of you. I did it. Big deal. I'm not sorry. Pilar deserved to die. I wasn't about to go penniless after all those years of putting up with her and her ego. Drag me in if you can. You'll never get anyone to believe it. It's my word against yours. Who would believe you two losers instead of me? It's ridiculous. I'm a big man in this town. You're nothing! Two little nurses? Don't make me laugh! You losers!"

"Not exactly," I said. "I think you're the loser. You stole your own art in cahoots with Bunty Essex Jones, alias plain Jane Jones from Texas. No matter how hard she tries she can't cover up that little southern twang which creeps into her imitation English aristocratic accent. You needed the cash from the stolen art to pay off your enormous gambling debts. The art was insured so Pilar would get reimbursed. You would collect from your snooty European art theft ring with Bunty working the con for you and splitting the loot."

"That I would partner with that little nobody. What a joke!"

"What was the matter? Were the casino's cleanup men coming after you? Pressuring you? Threatening you? You were going to fence those priceless art treasures Bunty stole for you through some European art theft ring, weren't you? That alone will send you to jail for a few decades, plus your murder rap. Premeditated in the first degree. Not good, Nicky baby. Dirtball."

"You can't prove any of that," groaned Nick.

"Wrong. We have the proof, and we will produce it in good time. All in good time, dirtball. Then there is Bunty. She came here to pull a scam, but you saw through that. Instead of turning her in, you were in cahoots with her. You always look for the main chance, don't you Nicky baby?"

"You know nothing about me," said Nick.

"Not only that, but you wanted to be cut in on the deal to save your butt and pay off your gambling debts. You included Bunty in your harem, maybe to gain more control over her. You used her like you use everyone. You used Skylar too for your alibi. You cheated on Pilar with everything you could grab from eighteen to eighty, including Bunty and Tiggy."

"No!"

"Yes! Then you murdered your wife. She was a royal pain, but murder? A drastic solution to a mundane problem which should have been solved with a divorce. You could not divorce her or have her divorce you because there was a prenuptial agreement, and you would get nothing in a divorce. So, you murdered her instead, old greedy guts. Greed is one of the deadly sins, and murder is the king of deadly mortal sins. Cheater, liar, gambler, thief, murderer, loser. That's you, you corrupted bag of mortal dust, you whoreson knave, you bloody vermin, you satyr's tail."

"Yeah! You greedy guts S.O.B.!" said Krystal.

"You know, Nasty Nick, sometimes you just have to look at cute little sparrows or a video clip of funny cats and kittens so you can stop feeling like killing someone who desperately deserves it," I said. "Like you for example. I hear the devil calling you, Nick. You better go! To jail, that is!"

"You two nosy rosies will never convince the police of that wild story," he sneered.

"Won't we?" said Krystal. "Tabby is wired. She has this whole thing on tape. Your denials won't stand up in court when they play the tape for the jury. Besides that, I went snooping in Charlie the gardener's tool and pool house. Guess what I found? I found a black leather bag stashed underneath the big bags of wood chips. It was a big bag. The kind you can stash a body in. I wonder how much of Pilar's DNA and hair and skin cells they will find in that bag. Your DNA and fingerprints will be all over that bag, Mr. Cool. That's called evidence, as if we needed any more proof that you are a stinking murderer. As if this tape-recorded message of your confession won't be enough. Show him, Tabby."

I took the tiny tape recorder out of my pocket and held it up to Nick's face so he could see it. I gave him my best charming smile.

"Looks like your goose is cooked, Nicky baby," I said. "I guess you're going to miss your luxury lifestyle in prison. Maybe they will give you the best cell and send in the call girls for you. Think so? I guess we two losers are smarter than you, Mr. Cool genius rich guy. I hope you like wearing orange. I guess you won't be needing your fancy cars and designer clothes in prison."

"Yeah, Mr. Dumpling Dick," said Krystal. "That's right Mr. Scraggyface, Mr. Wrinkle Butt, Mr. Arrogant Potato Head, Mr. Poopy Pie."

"Poopy Pie?" I said.

"Yes! He is a Poopy Pie!" insisted Krystal.

Nick blanched. First, he turned white, then red, and finally purple with rage and started swearing at us. Many expletives deleted here as he let loose with some extremely vulgar swear words, nasty little man.

"You two stupid idiots!" he yelled.

"I don't like your insults!" Krystal said. "You better shut it now! Right now!"

"You shut it, Fatso!" choked Nick.

"I am not fat," said Krystal. "I'm big and tall. I have big bones."

"No, you're just fat," said Nick in a voice filled with venom. Big mistake. Krystal slammed her entire body weight on him and wrenched his arms tighter behind his back.

"Do you think so?" she asked. "Are you sure?" Nick let out a moan of pain.

"I would say she is just real strong," I added. "Wouldn't you agree? I would say that she is statuesque. I would say that she is a statuesque brunette with a commanding presence." Krystal glowed.

"Gee thanks Tabby. That is one of the nicest things you ever said about me."

"Wouldn't you agree, Nick?" I asked.

Nick groaned, gasped, and lay still.

"I thought you would agree," I said. "Do you know who she is?"

"I know who she is," Nick choked out. "She is our latest maid. Krystal," said Nicky baby in a strangled voice.

He looked up at me from the ground and squinted at me. He frowned.

"I thought she was an illegal who could barely speak English. As for you, little weirdo, you are the faithful friend. I suppose you two are the ones who stole my priceless art treasures from the grandfather clock. Bunty tried to find them in your hovel of a living space, but she failed. Stupid cow, just like all women. How could you two idiot nobodies get the better of me?" he choked out. I looked at Krystal and chuckled.

"Did you hear that, Krystal? He thinks that we are idiot nobodies. 'Ah'd love ta kiss ya but ah just washed mah hay-ah," I said. "Or maybe, 'Fasten your seatbelts, it's going to be a bumpy night,' might be a better quote."

"O.K., Bette Davis," said Krystal. "How about this arrogant twit? What a narcissist! I listened to Dr. Phil's podcast on narcissists. Too bad Dr. Phil couldn't be here to hear this," said Krystal. "What would he think of Nick and Pilar and all these warped personalities?" I laughed.

"What would he think of Nick and this entire cast of Shakespearian characters, complete with evil schemers, thieves, conspirators, murderers, manipulators, victims, fawning parasites, and devilishly clever opportunists? Just another day in Hollywood? Probably. In fact, I think that Dr. Phil would have a field day with his narcissism studies if he went to Hollywood. He could study personality disorders forever and podcast every day."

#DrPhilwhereareyou?

Chapter Fifteen: Sconed to Death

And therefore, never send for to know for whom the bell tolls,

It tolls for thee.

--From *For Whom the Bell Tolls*, by John Donne, published within *Devotions Upon Emergent Occasions*

The next part of our adventure is inexplicable. Somehow, even though Krystal was sitting on The Deuce, the Old Nicholas, the Devil Incarnate, he somehow twisted and turned like a shiny new slinky, like a greased pig, like a slithering snake, and managed to get away, get up, and run. Krystal flopped down on the ground in frustration while I stood there with cement feet wondering what happened.

"I swear nothing could surprise me more in my entire life or ever will until they wrap me in my winding sheet and put the pennies on my eyes," I said.

"What?" asked Krystal, looking up at me through slit eyes, her face a grimace of anger and disbelief.

"Until I'm dead," I said.

"Oh," said Krystal and let out a string of her own special brand of cuss words which I won't bother explaining. Suffice it to say that incongruously, even though she doesn't know hardly any Spanish, she knows lots of Spanish cuss words.

"If I ever get my hands on that son of a gun, I'm going to twist him into a pretzel, especially his parts," she said.

"Which parts are those?" I asked.

"Never mind, Sister Tabitha of the Little Sisters of the Blessed Virgin. Just move your butt and help me out of this dirt." I complied with her wishes.

Then I saw that he who shall not be named had left his windbreaker behind in the fracas. Somehow Krystal had ripped it off his body in her last desperate attempt to hold him down.

Suddenly, a cell phone rang. It was Nick's. Krystal reached into the depths of the windbreaker pocket. The ring tone sounded. Krystal swiped right and answered it. She put on the speaker phone.

"Yeah," she answered in a low guttural tone, trying to imitate Nick's voice.

"Nicki! Diana here. You sound froggy. I hope you're not getting a cold. Ready honey?" There was a slight pause while Krystal figured out what to say.

"Yeah!"

"Good. I'll pick you up at the house in one hour, hon. Be on time! I have the tickets and our suitcases all packed. Everything is ready. Don't forget the cash. I hope it all fits in the leather briefcase I bought for you, angel. Money smells so much better in a Marks and Spencer case."

"You are going to marry me, aren't you Nicky? You promised," said Diana.

"Uh...," said Krystal. "Yeah, I think so."

"Think so? No, you know so! I didn't go through all this to come away with nothing, darling. Ha! I can't believe we pulled it off! Just think! We'll be airborne in a few hours. St. Thomas here we come! From there it's on to Madagascar and points unknown! I'm so excited! We'll be so happy! Just the two of us without the old witch to drag us down! With all that lovely money. See you in an hour sweetie! Look for the Jaguar darling. Love you!"

"Love you!" growled Krystal and hung up. "Who the hell is Diana?" she asked me in her own voice.

"How should I know?" I asked. "It sounds like this Diana is another mistress. A young, enthusiastic one too from the sound of it."

"I'll bet this Diana is the first lady partner in crime," said Krystal. "If she is picking Nick up at home in an hour and they are off to the Green Bay airport for destination St. Thomas and from there to parts unknown, they must be on the run with a lot of loot and ill-gotten goods."

"Such as cash from jewelry and paintings, with future plans to collect on Pilar's estate, assets, and life insurance?" I inquired.

"We can just about be sure of that," said Krystal. "Isn't that just like a man? Scum!"

"I'm surmising that Nick was just using Skylar, Tiggy, and Bunty," I said. "I'll bet Nick double crossed all of them and chose this Diana as the number one girl. I'll lay odds that this Diana is a society girl with a trust fund and a rich daddy. She is a newer, younger, trophy version of Pilar. Maybe she and Nick planned to murder Pilar together. Now they are set to collect, disappear, and enjoy life on easy street spending millions of their ill-gotten gains in exotic ports of call."

"Is there no end to his evil?" asked Krystal, disgusted. "Nick was just taking his daily bicycle ride to throw Gina and everyone else off the scent. He had this planned all along. Then he planned to head home, grab his suitcase of money, jump in the Jag with Diana, whoever she is, abscond to destinations unknown, and goodbye forever to Door County, USA."

"What are we going to do now?" I asked. "Do you think he will try to get all the way to Sturgeon Bay and get home on foot? He doesn't have his cell so he can't call Diana or anyone else to pick him up. He knows Diana is due to pick him up at home at a certain time and I'm sure he realizes the time is getting close."

"I'm sure he will. He is the type who will stick to the plan. Wait. Unless he plans to double cross this one also. Maybe he plans to take all the money for himself and disappear without Diana. Or maybe he will murder her too, after he has everything he wants. Maybe he even arranged it so Diana will be proven guilty of murder and take the rap. After all, he tried to incriminate Marty." I thought about it a minute.

"I'll bet you're right," I said. "I think we should assume the worst about him. He has already double-crossed four women and murdered one. Why not double-cross another one, evade her, blame her for his wife's death, and start his new life all alone where he has all the money and no clinging female? There is only one way to find out where he is."

"How are we going to do that?" asked Krystal. "He could be half-way home or a mile away in any direction by now as fast as he is. I know that sucker can run like the wind. I guess we will just have to get in the car and cruise to his house or wander around in this park looking for his ugly carcass."

"Set the dogs on him," I said.

"Tabby, this isn't a movie set in an English castle. We don't have dogs to set on him." I laughed.

"No, but we have one good, old hound dog named Mossy."

"Don't make me laugh! Mossy couldn't track down Icky Nicky Sticky," said Krystal. I grabbed Nick's windbreaker and jogged the short distance back to the car where we had left Mossy in the back seat. True to form, good old Mossy was asleep on the warm back seat, snoring softly in the dappled rays of the golden sun slanting through the trees.

Cuckoo and Misty played together in the front seat, batting dust motes and rolling around on the soft lining of the car. I opened the car door. The kitties sat up and greeted me with, "Mew! Mirr! Meow! Where have you been, human servant? Time to take us home for snackies and treaties! Meow!"

"Hey! Mossy!" I goaded the dog a little with my outstretched hand and rubbed Nick's windbreaker over his nose. "Seek and find, Mossy old boy old boyo! Find Waldo!" I commanded. Krystal snorted.

"Tabby, if you think that old shelter hound was trained to find lost and runaway people or escaped criminals, you are nuts. That dog is a lazy, retired old fire and hearth layabout who has seen better days. You haven't the slightest idea how to make a bloodhound set out on a search and destroy mission. Don't make me laugh! Tabitha Nolan, you have been at the hash brownies again! Have you been smoking wacky weed, my idealistic little daydreamer?"

Mossy surprised us, the kittens, and probably himself when he rolled over, sat up, stuck his nose in the windbreaker, snorted, choked, barked, and leapt out of the open door. He ran around in widening circles for a few minutes getting the scent. Then he took off like a bat out of hell. We gave a cheer and jumped in the car.

I started the ignition. Krystal and the kitties sat staring straight ahead in the passenger seat while I scrunched over the steering wheel and we rolled down the road after Mossy at a slow pace, gathering speed as he picked up a stronger scent. No one was more astounded than I was as good old Mossy chugged steadily along like an old steam engine.

We rolled out of Potawatomie State Park and a considerable way down the service road. We were almost to Highway 42 in no time. We got some strange looks from the occasional car full of people who passed us by. Not to mention the fact that we got a few evil eyes from those who thought that we were exercising our old hound dog by making him trot down the road while we sat in the comfort of our car urging him on with cries of "Go, Mossy, go!" It scared me how fast the old hound dog was travelling. I hoped he wouldn't have a heart attack before this was over.

We reached Highway 42 and suddenly, the trail went cold. Mossy ran around in circles, his nose to the ground, searching in vain for the scent. I stopped the car. Krystal got out, grabbed Mossy, and led him by the collar back to the car. There was a change in the atmosphere. The air seemed charged and there was a rising wind. I sniffed the breeze. We definitely had rain on the way. I looked up. The billowing storm clouds gathered out on the lake to the east. The wind came in from the northeast. We were in for some weather. Mossy got into the car reluctantly.

"Good job, old boy! Now come on. We don't want you to get run over by some idiot tourist speeding down the highway!" said Krystal.

"Good boy, Mossy!" I said as Mossy folded up his limbs on the back seat of the car, where he lay panting, drooling, and looking proud and pleased with himself.

"I'll bet you any money that scum sucking pig hitched a ride on Highway 42," said Krystal. "He is sitting in comfort in the back seat of some car, enjoying his getaway and laughing his head off at us." I gunned it all the way into Sturgeon Bay and squealed into the circular drive of Nick and Pilar's palatial home. Krystal jumped out and ran up the drive.

"Gina!" she screamed. "Gina!" Gina came hustling out the front door.

"Yes, Miss Krystal," said Gina. "What is it?"

"Where is that bastard?" yelled Krystal. "Did he come home?"

"No!" said Gina. "He never came home. I don't know where that sick gringo got to. I just hope I never see him again!" At that moment, my phone rang. I picked it up. It was my mother, of all people.

"Not now, Mom!" I yelled into the phone. "I'm on a manhunt."

"I thought you and Brook Trout were an item," said Mom. "You don't have to go into bars hunting for men. It's almost six o'clock on a Saturday night. You should be at church, not sitting in some bar picking up men."

"Mom! You don't understand! I'm not looking for a man! I'm looking for Nick."

"Oh, well, I'll let you go then. Who is Nick, anyway? I hope he isn't some new guy. I like Brook Trout. The reason I called was, Father Dunn just called me. Some guy just got dropped off out of a car and ran into St. Paul's church here in New Belgium."

"What?" My mom ignored me and kept talking.

"It's almost time for mass at six o'clock and he is running through the church like a madman. Some of the young, athletic men are trying to catch him but he is eluding them. He is disturbing everyone. They are afraid he is some crazy lunatic. He ran into the confessional and grabbed some leather briefcase he had apparently hidden in there somehow. Who would hide something in a confessional and why? He could be an insane dangerous criminal."

"What?" I screamed.

"Yes, well Father Dunn called me because, naturally when there is trouble in New Belgium, I'm usually at the bottom of it. He thought I might know what is going on. I got in the car and went to church immediately to see if I could figure it out. Didi is with me."

"Hi, Tabby!" called Didi's voice. "Isn't this exciting? Maybe your mom and I can get in on a case."

"Mom!" I screamed into the phone. "Don't do anything until I get there!" I hung up. "Krystal! Nick is in St. Paul's church in New Belgium. He must have hitched a ride there!" I called. She ran to the car and flung herself into the front seat, scaring the kitties half to death in the process.

"He hid his briefcase of money in the confessional at St. Paul's, probably because he knew that no one would ever look for it there. It's the safest place in town. Remember how Gina wondered why Mr. Nick had a priest's outfit hanging in his closet? I'll bet you anything that he planned to escape disguised as a priest, but you and I foiled his plan. I'll bet you that if we look under that kneeler in the confessional or hidden away somewhere in there, we will find a rolled up priest's costume. That was his disguise. Who would question a priest traveling with a briefcase? You were right. He was going to double-cross that Diana girl. He ran in there, grabbed the money, and now he is running around in panic in church scaring everyone out of their wits. Some of the men are trying to catch him and have so far failed. We have to get there in time before he does anything crazy! Let's go" I screamed.

"What the hell are you waiting for? Drive!" screamed Krystal. I drove totally Nascar all the way to New Belgium, tore through the streets, squealed the tires around the corners, peeled into the front apron of the driveway of the church, and slammed the car into park. We left the car blocking the way up onto the steps of St. Paul's and jumped out.

Mossy gamely jumped out, picked up Nick's scent and up the steps of St. Paul's we all ran. Sirens started to wail as several police apparently decided to pursue those two crazy girls in that late model Ford. There must have been a lot of phone calls from helpful citizens who should all mind their own blasted business.

Father Dunn stood shaking his head on the steps of St. Paul's with Mom, Didi, and numerous astounded parishioners behind them.

"Nobody draws trouble like a Nolan," said Father Dunn sadly. "Tabitha, what is going on? Are you trying to be like your mother?"

"I resent that remark," said my mother stoutly. "Kids! I should have been a nun. My biggest worry would be finding my sandals in time to get to Vespers."

"Me too," chimed in Didi. "I should have been a nun with you, Rhi. We could be like Audrey Hepburn in *The Nun's Story*. So romantic and tragic. So just what is going on, Tabby?"

"Tell you later!" I yelled. Krystal and I followed Mossy into church where he ran around madly trying to get Nick's scent and finding it everywhere. We ran in circles pursuing Mossy. All the people in church waiting for the six o'clock mass to start stared at us in shock with open mouths. The choirboys in their black smocks with the

349

white surplices stared. The organist stared. The deacon holding the big crucifix stared. The police who had caught up with us on the steps stared. Everyone stared, but Krystal, undaunted as usual, said, "Chill, people! We are after a killer!"

Some of the old ladies screamed. One of them fainted onto the pew. Mossy finally picked up the solid scent. He started up the bell tower.

"No!" called Father Dunn. "Don't go up the church belfry! The bells are due to sound in seconds! If he went up there stop him! Stop!" As one accord, we all looked at the steps which ascended to the bell tower. Krystal grabbed Mossy's collar and tugged with all her might to keep Mossy from running up the stairs in pursuit of Nick.

"He ran up there!" yelled little Kelly Logan. "That crazy man ran up there, Father!" A look of dismay and shock came over Father Dunn's face. We all looked from

Father's face to the top of the bell tower, peering and angling our necks to try and see the top.

"Come down immediately!" ordered Father Dunn. We heard footsteps running up the steps. "Stop!" Nick ignored Father Dunn and kept on going, scurrying up the stairs to the bell tower. "I say come down now!" yelled Father Dunn. He put his hand on the railing and said one more time, "Stop! I order you to come down immediately! The sound of those bells can kill a man! Your eardrums will burst! You will pass out and die." But it was too late for any more warnings. Nick was not listening, and he did not intend to start listening and come down from the bell tower. At exactly five minutes to six o'clock the bells calling everyone to mass began to toll and clang. Nick, arrogant to the last, refused to believe that they tolled for him.

#theytollforthee

Chapter Sixteen: For Whom the Knell Trolls

Oh, the bells, bells, bells!
What a tale their terror tells of Despair!
How they clang, and clash, and roar! What a horror they outpour
On the bosom of the palpitating air!

--From *The Bells*, by Edgar Allen Poe

The clanging of the bells finally ceased. With a sense of dread at what we were going to find, Krystal and I followed Father Dunn up the stairs to the belfry.

"I'm afraid this could be fatal," said Father Dunn. "People just don't understand. They have no respect for danger. If only he had listened. High intensity sounds above 150 decibels can burst your eardrums, while sounds above 185 decibels can impact your inner organs and cause death. Be prepared for the worst when we get up there."

Mom and Didi blocked the way so curious parishioners could not follow us up the stairs. At that moment, the wicked storm that had been holding off blew up just as we found Nick's body in the bell tower. The rain began to blow into the open bell tower borne upon strong winds. The thunder and lightning roared and crackled, and the very air seemed electric.

A spectacular flash of lightning lit up the belfry with an orange glow, and in that glow, we plainly saw Nick's dead body.

Just as Father Dunn had predicted, Nick had died from the sound of the bells. A loud bellow of thunder was followed by a frightening crack of lightning which raised the hair on my head and lit up Nick's corpse as it lay on the cement platform of the belfry. Apparently, at the last he realized the danger he was in and attempted to escape but his fate was sealed. Beside him was his briefcase full of money, the money that he had schemed, lied, killed, and died for.

Krystal took one look at Nick's sad, crumpled up body and promptly fainted.

"Great!" I exclaimed. "Now I have a dead body to contend with as well as Krystal's fainting habit."

"Krystal!" I said as I shook her shoulders and patted her face. "Wake up! Don't lie here when we need you! Wake up!" She opened her eyes and fluttered her eyelashes.

"Did I faint?" she asked.

"Yes, you did. Knock it off! We are going to have to answer a lot of questions from the police and it will probably take all night!"

"In that case, I think I'll just lie here," said Krystal. "You go talk for me." She closed her eyes.

"No, you don't!" I commanded and prodded her unmercifully until she recovered.

Eventually, Father Dunn got the other priest, Father Kelly, to say the mass that the people were waiting for downstairs. Father Kelly bravely plowed ahead with the service while the ambulance people and the police dealt with Nick's body. Many people craned their necks to try to see what was going on in the belfry, but like a good priest, Father Kelly sternly told them to stop ogling and pay attention to the service.

While the parishioners prayed for Nick's soul like good Catholics, Krystal and I cast a cold eye on his remains. Nick got no sympathy from either of us, and not much from Father Dunn.

"Poor lost soul," said Father Dunn. "I guess the hammer of God simply caught up with him in the end and justice was done."

"You can say that again," said Krystal.

"If Nicky baby ever went to church, he might have realized that a church belfry was a confounded stupid place to hide," I said. "He runs all the way to New Belgium, grabs his money stash from the confessional where he had hidden it, and climbs the tower into the belfry. Like we weren't going to know where he had gone in our own little hometown. Like Rhiannon and Didi wouldn't be there to help us, plus the expert help of Mossy the bloodhound. We could have tracked him down blindfolded."

"Dumb ignorant pagan," said Krystal. "That's what he gets for never going to church. If he had been at church when the bells rang and clanged to wake the dead and call everybody to church, he would have realized how loud they were. The clang of the church bells can be heard all over town. No wonder Father Dunn is so proud of his new bells. They can be heard five miles away."

"Or ten," I said.

"Or more," said Father Dunn. "I made sure that we have only the best. I wanted everyone in this town to hear the church bells and get to church on time."

"I think you succeeded," I said.

"God bless you and those bells, Father Dunn," said Krystal.

"Oh! I forgot! Krystal! Diana is waiting at the airport for you know who. She probably went to pick him up and when he wasn't there, she went on to the airport to meet him there. We must tell the police immediately so they can intercept her there! She is an accessory to murder!"

Later, much later, Krystal and I finished explaining to the police at great length what had occurred. Two of them were dispatched to the Green Bay airport to catch up with Diana and arrest her on suspicion of being an accessory to murder. We explained to the others how we had determined that Nick had means, motive, and opportunity to murder Pilar. We told them how he had planted fake evidence to incriminate Marty, and how he had almost certainly helped her along to her death by injecting her with Torbutrol.

We explained how Marty had tried to tell me that Nick was the killer as she died. We told them how we had done the bicycle fun run on that night we had repeated Nick's set up to make it appear that Pilar had overdosed and fallen down the spiral staircase at Cana Island Lighthouse. We told them about the chest which we thought had held her body, and the body bag Krystal found in the tool shed. Lastly, we produced the admission of Nick's guilt that we taped in Potawatomie State Park. I produced the tape from my pocket. Then we produced the priest's uniform from the confessional, the outfit that Nick planned to wear to make his solo escape after he had dumped Diana. The police were astounded, to say the least.

Krystal's phone rang.

"I have to answer this," she said. "It's my mom. She is running around Italy with some stud muffin. It's her hot Latin blood that makes her do these crazy things. Hello? Mom? You're coming home? Alone? He turned out to be a real jerk? A runaround playboy flirt, huh? Big surprise. I could have told you about those Italians, but you never listen to me. You never want to see another man as long as you live? Especially an Italian one? Great. I'll pick you up at the airport. Yes, I'll be there on time. No, I won't forget. What have I been up to? Oh, nothing much. Tabby is always getting into mischief, so I have my hands full just keeping her out of trouble. She is fine. I'm fine. Javier is fine. Work is fine. Cuckoo is fine. Everything is fine. Yup, see you then." Krystal hung up and sighed. Then she smiled at me. "O.K., I'm done now. Need food. Need it now. I'm outta here."

#gimmefoodnow

Chapter Seventeen: The Hound and the Fury

The wind was a torrent of darkness among the gusty
trees.
The moon was a ghostly galleon tossed upon cloudy
seas.
The road was a ribbon of moonlight over the purple
moor,
As the highwayman came riding, riding, riding,
The highwayman came riding, up to the old inn door.

--From *The Highwayman*, by Alfred Noyes

After Krystal and I finished talking at great length to

the police, to Mom, Didi, Stan, and to Didi's husband

Baronet Charles, we needed a relief moment from too

much humanity and adrenalin pumping excitement. First,

we made an emergency drive-through food forage trip. We

got burgers and fries for Krystal, a milkshake and fries for me, and treats for Mossy, Misty, and Cuckoo who had waited patiently for us through the entire brouhaha.

Then we took a drive out Highway 57 to Whitefish Dunes State Park, parked the car on a little-known lookout, and gazed out over Lake Michigan. We both sighed with relief at escaping humanity and savored the quiet.

We watched the storm roll out over Lake Michigan on black, billowing clouds which burst with rain, thunder, and lightning. The animals all crashed on the back seat, too tired to be afraid of the storm. The storm blew back to the east out over the lake, but the wind remained, moaning and groaning, whipping around us.

The lonely calling and screaming of the seagulls were as drowned men's souls crying out from the submerged skeletons of their shipwrecked boats. The souls of the dead seemed tossed about on the wild waves and lingered in the blown spume and spray which created whitecapped crested mares' tales on the lake.

We listened in silence to the rhythmic boom and crash of the thunderous waves in the hollows of the cliffs below which sounded like the trumpet on the last day calling the souls to the last judgment. I could almost feel the echo of those rhythmic pounding waves in the beating of my heart. Krystal and I both sighed with contentment. We both love a good storm.

"So glad that's over," sighed Krystal. "Don't want to do that again until the next solar eclipse. Feels so good to get back to normal."

"Ditto," I said. "All we have to do now is go to the police with all the evidence on Bunty Essex Jones, that is, Plain Jane, and on Tiggy Butterfield."

"Ugh!" said Krystal. "Forgot about those two dizzy losers! I'm too tired. Can that wait for tomorrow?"

"I suppose," I said uncertainly. "As long as they don't scarper before tomorrow."

"Are you kidding?" said Krystal. "My guess is that they already know about Nick's death, and they are both at the house right now stealing everything they can get their hands on. I bet they both figure that they will grab what they can before they move on." I considered this.

"I'll bet you're right," I said. "Poor Gina is probably trying to keep everything locked down and get those two brazen hussies and bold opportunists out of the house."

"Mew! Meow! Mirr!" said Cuckoo and Misty. Mossy chimed in with a "Woof!"

"Time to go home and feed our furry friends. What an exhausting day, Watson."

"I'm ready for my bubble bath," said Krystal. "Turn the horses for home, Sherlock."

Bright and early the next day, Krystal and I went to the police with the story of the jewelry and the art theft. Just for good measure, we took Javier, Brook, Stan, Mom, Didi, and Baronet Charles along with us so they could hear the whole story for the first time. We also produced the cell phone video evidence of the stolen paintings, the empty frames hidden away in the attic, the stolen jewelry, plus the photos that Krystal took in the vault upstairs. Then we explained Nick's involvement with both Tiggy and Bunty.

The police were astounded, to say the least. They called the FBI. Apparently, Bunty Essex Jones and Tiggy Butterfield were wanted felons and the FBI welcomed our stellar detective work. It was quite gratifying to see Javier and Brook Trout's jaws drop as they listened to the whole involved story, especially when we included the tale of Nick and his guilt which was woven throughout the extended tale. The police were immediately dispatched to bring in Tiggy and Bunty. They had already apprehended Diana at the airport the evening before and arrested her.

"Don't worry, girls. We'll bring in Tiggy Butterfield and Jane Jones," said one of the officers. "Thanks for your help in proving their guilt."

"We can bring them in for you," offered Krystal. "We're good at this stuff."

"No!" A chorus of voices chimed in on that no. And so ended our involvement in bringing justice to our little corner of God's country. Darn good work if you ask me.

Later that day, we went to pick up Krystal's mom at the airport in Green Bay. Tammy chattered non-stop about her trip, about Italy, about the Sistine Chapel, the Pieta, the Pope, the Basilica, the art, the statues, the fountains, and about the stud muffin. In the end, she dumped him.

"It would never have worked anyway. He smelled of garlic and I hate garlic. I'm over him. So over him already. No big deal. What have you two been up to?" she asked. "You're always up to something."

"Oh, nothing much," said Krystal. "You know. Same old, same old."

In an odd twist, an art specialist was later called in to certify that the stolen paintings were originals and verify their worth. The art dealer confirmed that they were all forgeries. Krystal and I were gratified to learn that Pilar and Nick had bought forgeries and insured them for millions. Since Pilar and Nick were both deceased and the art canvases were forgeries, the paintings were deemed worthless, and the insurance company would not pay the estate.

Bunty was arrested for theft, conspiracy, fraud, and a long string of crimes in several states. The same was true for Tiggy. Both Bunty and Tiggy, as wanted felons, were arrested, tried, and prosecuted, largely due to the gumshoe work of yours truly and my trusty BFF, Krystal Morales.

After the case was settled, Krystal asked her friends at the police department if she could have the paintings since they were worthless. She stuck them in frames from Walmart, just as she said she would, and hung them in the living room of our apartment as souvenirs of our latest caper. When Tiggy and Bunty were arrested, she also begged her friends at the police department to let her take a selfie with Tiggy and one with Bunty as souvenirs. That Krystal is the ab-fab best, isn't she?

The pictures were made possible because Krystal's friends on the police force held up the prisoners, Tiggy and Bunty, and made them face the camera while Krystal took the selfie. Tiggy and Bunty are both scowling and looking into the camera with gritted teeth and snarling lips, but Krystal is smiling broadly. Krystal had the pictures printed, framed, and hung on the wall of her bedroom. She calls it her most wanted list. What a total character.

"Don't I look like I just got out of hair and makeup Tabby?" asked Krystal one day as she gazed at the portraits. "I look a little bit like Jennifer Lopez, don't I?"

"Yeah, except you're a lot taller, younger, and better looking," I said. "Plus that, you are all natural, not plastic from the knees up. Plus that, you aren't a ho who tries to look eternally young and dance on stripper poles in her movies to prove how sexy she still is even though she is over fifty. Also, you're much more statuesque than Jennifer. I would say you are as statuesque as Maureen O'Hara. You're the Latina Maureen O'Hara, and just as tough as she was. And just as photogenic. The camera loves you." Krystal's face glowed with pride.

"Gee, really? Thanks, BFF. I guess all's well that ends well, huh Sherlock?"

"You bet, Watson, and to celebrate, I think we should have some delicious fresh baked raspberry scones."

"Did you make them?" asked Krystal.

"What is that note of dismay creeping into your voice? Are you kidding? I bought them at the Tasty Pastry."

"Oh, good," said Krystal. "I'll have one, maybe two. Hey, what do you think Dr. Phil would have to say about us?"

"I think he would say we are two spectacular human beings, and we should appear on his show," I said.

"Cool! I hope I get to do my own hair and makeup. I'm ready for my closeup, Dr. Phil!"

"Krystal, what is that ruby red rock on your finger? Is that the ruby that Tiggy stole from Pilar, and we stole from Tig? Is that the one that fell out of the tote full of jewels Cuckoo found under my bed? The one she had in her mouth and was playing with when Millie was here? You said you would find a safe place for it. Apparently, you didn't turn it into the police with all the other jewels as evidence."

"Gee, it must have slipped my mind," said Krystal. "Don't give me that look. I deserve a little something for all you put me through. Pilar's jewels will sit in an evidence locker and then go to her estate and be given to some ancient aunt, hairy cousin, or teenage snit. I deserve some small reward for all my strenuous efforts. You and your red halibuts, haddocks, herrings, and smelts. I wanted a little something red of my own, and ruby red is my favorite color. So there. Huh!"

What can I say, gentle reader? After all, Krystal is the world's best BFF and my kindred spirit. That's it for this case. Hope you had fun. We sure did!

Yours truly,

Krystal Morales and Tabitha Nolan

#casewrappedup

Gentle Reader,

And now I shall leave each lady to say and believe whatever she pleases, for the time has come for me to bring all words to an end and offer my humble thanks to Him who assisted me in my protracted labour and conveyed me to the goal I desired. May His grace and peace, sweet ladies, remain with you always, and if by chance these stories should bring you any profit, remember me.

---From *The DeCameron*, by Giovanni Boccaccio

Chapter Titles:

Do those chapter titles sound familiar? Go to the head of the class if you recognized the play on words in these chapter titles.

Tale of Two Kitties (Tale of Two Cities) Charles Dickens

The Scone Also Rises (The Sun Also Rises) Ernest Hemingway

Scone with the Wind (Gone with the Wind) Margaret Mitchell

For Whom the Cock Crows *and* For Whom the Knell Trolls (For Whom the Bell Tolls) Ernest Hemingway

The Beautiful and Groomed (The Beautiful and Damned) F. Scott Fitzgerald

The Great Patsy (The Great Gatsby) F. Scott Fitzgerald

This Side of Parasites (This Side of Paradise) F. Scott Fitzgerald

A Broom of One's Own (A Room of One's Own) Virginia Wolff

Far from the Maddening Shroud (Far from the Madding Crowd) Thomas Hardy

The Hound and the Fury (The Sound and the Fury) William Faulkner

As I Lay Crying (As I Lay Dying) William Faulkner

In Search of Lost Crime (In Search of Lost Time) Marcel Proust

Call of the Reviled (Call of the Wild) Jack London

Scone Cold, Clotted Cream, Sconed to Death, Scone Me, and Secret Scone are the exceptions.

Recipes:

It wouldn't be any fun if there weren't a few recipes to try! Try these cherry pie, scone, cookie, candy, and salad recipes. Super yum! You won't spend hours in the kitchen with these easy desserts! You know me. I'm not sweating over a hot stove!

Scones and Clotted Cream (Yum Yum!)

Clotted cream is also called Cornish Cream or Devonshire Cream, with recipes dating from the sixteenth century. Clotted cream is difficult to find in America but easy to make (unless you are me.) It is ab-fab delicious and worth the wait. Incidentally, clotted, for us Americans calls to mind horrible pictures of clotted blood or other gross images, but it basically means settled, so call it that if it makes you feel better. It takes a lot of cream to make a small amount, so be patient! (Also, something I'm not good at.)

Clotted cream and English scones

Prep Time: 20 minutes

Cook Time: 10 hours

INGREDIENTS:

Clotted cream

- 4 cups heavy cream (1 quart) No substitutes!

English Scones

- 2 cups all-purpose flour
- ½ cup granulated white sugar
- 1 tbsp vanilla
- 1 tbsp almond extract - optional
- 1 tbsp baking powder
- 1/4 tsp salt
- 4 tbsp butter, diced -- works much better if butter is very cold!
- 1 large egg, beaten (or use a liquid such as Great Egg-Spectations)
- 5 tbsp milk
- 5 tbsp heavy whipping cream (no substitutes!)
- 1 large egg, beaten to glaze the tops of the scones (or use liquid egg substitute)

You will need:

For Cream: a double boiler or heatproof bowl and saucepan, pan of ice water.

For Scones: mixing bowl, baking sheet, butter, or parchment for the baking sheet, rolling pin, biscuit cutter, or water glass

Instructions to make Clotted Cream:

Forget those recipes that call for you to leave your oven on for twelve hours. Seriously? Just do it this way. In a double boiler over medium heat bring the cream to 175 degrees. If you don't have a double boiler place a heatproof bowl over a saucepan of water. Stir a little so that the cream heats evenly. Once you reach 175, bring up the temperature—180 to 200 degrees. Keep that temp for about 45 minutes to an hour. At this point the cream will take on a cracked, yellow skin. Next, remove the bowl or top of your double boiler and settle in a pan of ice water to cool quickly. Cover with plastic wrap and stow in the fridge overnight. Then carefully skim the clotted cream off the top with a shallow spoon and layer it into a bowl. It will keep for about a week in your fridge. Use the rest of the cream as you would regular cream (it will be thinner than heavy cream but can still be added to beverages). Serve your clotted cream with strawberries or jam on a scone, or a slice of cherry pie.

Instructions to make English scones:

Preheat the oven to 425 degrees. Prepare a baking sheet with butter or parchment paper. Sift the flour, sugar, baking powder and salt together and then work in the diced cold butter. Make a well in the middle and then add the egg, almond, vanilla, heavy cream, and milk. Mix to form a soft dough.

Turn the dough out onto a floured surface and then knead quickly until the dough comes together. Roll out the dough to an inch thick. Cut it into rounds with a biscuit cutter or waterglass. Move to the baking sheet and brush the tops with the beaten egg. Bake for 8 minutes or until golden.

Do you prefer pie to scones? Then read on:

Ab-Fab Best Cherry Pie:

This is what you will need:

- 1 (15 ounce) package double crust ready-to-use pie crust

- 3 cups cherries

- ¾ cup white sugar

- 3 tablespoons cornstarch

- ¼ teaspoon almond extract

2 tablespoons cold salted butter, cut into bits

Preheat oven to 400 degrees F (200 degrees C). Line a baking sheet with aluminum foil. Place bottom pie crust into a 9-inch pie pan; made pricks along the bottom with a fork.

Bake in the preheated oven until pie crust is lightly browned, about 8 minutes. Remove crust from oven and cool for 5 minutes.

Combine cherries, sugar, cornstarch, and almond extract together in a bowl. Pour cherry mixture into the prepared pie pan. Dot with butter. Cover with top crusts, crimp the edges to seal, and cut vents into the top with a sharp knife. Place the pie on a foil-covered baking sheet.

Bake in the preheated oven for 30 minutes. If it is browning too fast cover the pie with an aluminum foil tent. Continue baking until crust is golden brown and filling is bubbly, 10 to 20 minutes. Place on a wire rack to cool, about 15 minutes. Do you want the nutrition facts? Hell, no you don't. It's too good to think about calories. You know you don't care anyway.

Here is a bonus recipe for those of you who don't like to turn on the oven when it's hot outside.

Pistachio cream pie (no bake easy version)

Ingredients

- 1 package (8 ounces) cream cheese, softened
- 1 cup milk
- 1 package (3.4 ounces) instant pistachio pudding mix
- 1 can (8 ounces) crushed pineapple, drained
- 1 graham cracker crust (9 inches)
- 2 cups whipped topping

In a small bowl, beat the cream cheese, milk and pudding mix until smooth. Fold in pineapple. Spoon into crust. Spread with whipped topping and refrigerate. Told you it was easy, didn't I?

No Bake Chocolate Peanut Butter Pretzel Cookies
Easy to make and easy to eat!
PREP TIME 10 mins
COOK TIME 5 mins
TOTAL TIME 15 mins
SERVINGS 2 dozen cookies

Ingredients:

- 1/2 cup unsalted butter
- 1/2 cup milk
- 2 cups granulated sugar
- 1/4 cup unsweetened cocoa
- 1/2 cup creamy peanut butter
- 1 teaspoon vanilla extract
- 2 1/2 cups old fashioned oats

- 1 cup chopped pretzels
- 1/4 teaspoon sea salt

Instructions:

In a medium saucepan, melt butter over medium-high heat. Add milk, sugar, and cocoa and stir to combine while bringing to a boil. Boil for 1-2 minutes, stirring occasionally. Remove pan from heat. Add peanut butter and vanilla. Stir until smooth. Stir in oats, chopped pretzels, and sea salt.

Drop mixture by the spoon full onto waxed paper and let cool completely. Cookies will set up and harden when they cool. Store in an air-tight container on the counter for up to a week.

Watergate Salad So Easy to Make!

3.4 ounce package instant pistachio pudding mix

20 ounce can crushed pineapple not drained

2 cups mini marshmallows

1/2 cup pecans chopped

8 ounce container Cool Whip thawed

Mix together the dry pudding mix, crushed pineapple, mini marshmallows, and chopped pecans.

Next, fold in the thawed Cool Whip until well combined. Chill the Watergate salad until you're ready to serve.

Deep Dish Cherry Pie

- 2 cups frozen tart cherries
- 1 cup granulated sugar
- 3 tablespoons cornstarch
- 1/2 teaspoon almond extract
- Pastry for two-crust, nine-inch pie (deep dish)
- 2 tablespoons butter or margarine

Combine frozen cherries, granulated sugar, corn starch, and almond extract in a large mixing bowl; mix well. Let stand 15 minutes. Line a nine-inch pie plate with pastry; fill with cherry mixture. Dot with butter. Adjust top crust, cutting slits for steam to escape, or cut top crust into strips and make a lattice-top pie. Bake in a preheated 400-degree oven 50 to 55 minutes, or until crust is golden brown and filling is bubbly. Makes 8 servings.

Traditional Door County Cherry Pie

Filling:

- 2 1/2 cups frozen (thawed) tart cherries
- 3 Tb. tapioca
- 1 cup sugar

Crust:

- 2 sticks margarine
- 2 cups flour
- ¼ cup cold water
- Dash of salt

Mix cherries, sugar, and tapioca in bowl. Set aside while preparing crust. Put flour and margarine in a mixing bowl. Blend margarine and flour until creamy. Add water, toss lightly with fork until moist. Form the dough into 2 equal sized firm balls. Sprinkle flour on surface, roll out one piece of dough to about 1/8 inch thick and place in pie pan. Pour in cherry mixture and roll out other dough ball to 1/8 inch and place on top of filling. Pinch the edges of crusts together to seal. Lightly moisten top crust and sprinkle with sugar. Bake at 425 degrees for 15 minutes. Reduce heat to 350 degrees and bake an additional 40-45 min. or until golden brown. Makes a nine-inch pie.

White Chocolate Cherry Scones

You know you want to try this one!

- 1 stick butter cut into small pieces and kept very cold
- 1/2 cup. sugar
- 1 egg
- 1 Tb. baking powder
- 1/2 tsp. baking soda

- 1/2 cup. heavy cream (no substitutes)
- 2 cup flour
- 1/2 cup white chocolate chips)
- 1 tsp.
- 1 1/2 cup frozen cherries

Preheat oven to 350 degrees. Combine flour, sugar, baking powder and soda. Mix the cut and cold butter in with fingers. Whisk together egg, cream, and vanilla. Stir into batter with fork until clumps form. Add cherries and chocolate. Scoop ten clumps of batter into lightly greased muffin pan. Brush with milk and sprinkle with confectioner's sugar. Bake 15-18 minutes. Cool. Makes 10.

About Cana Island Lighthouse:

Explore Door County's most celebrated lighthouse in the county that has more lighthouses than any other United States county, boasting150 years of standing watch on the shore of Lake Michigan in 2019. More photographed than any other of the eleven historic lighthouses in Door County, Cana Island gives the visitor a chance to see highlights of its long history for a $12 fee for adults. Ride a hay wagon over the causeway to explore the island, including the 89-foot-tall tower, the original home of the lighthouse keeper and his family, and the oil house where fuel for the light was stored. The highlight of any Cana Island visit is climbing the 97 steps of the 89 foot tower's spiral staircase to reach the gallery deck. The outside deck delivers a sweeping view of Lake Michigan and the Door County peninsula. While the ascent is fun for visitors, imagine the lighthouse keeper's job as he trudged up and down the steps each night, carrying heated lard to keep the light burning!

Visitors:
Please be aware that due to high lake levels, water now regularly flows over the causeway to Cana Island. There is a free tractor and hay wagon ride to shuttle you to the island. If you do choose to walk across, come prepared with boots or other footwear that can withstand the water and protect your feet. Open May through October, seven days a week, 10 a.m.-5 p.m. The last hay wagon ride departs from the parking lot at 4:15 p.m. The last tower climb starts at 4:30 p.m. Check the Cana Island Lighthouse

Facebook page for daily updates and information on weather related closures.

The Cana Island lighthouse is a lighthouse located north of Baileys Harbor in Door County, Wisconsin. Along with the Baileys Harbor Range Lights, the lighthouse was built to replace the Baileys Harbor Lighthouse in 1869 and was first lit in 1870. The highlight of a visit to the Cana Island Lighthouse is climbing the tower's spiral staircase — all 97 steps — to the deck, where spectacular views of Lake Michigan and the Door Peninsula await. Visitors also can tour areas including the keeper's quarters, last occupied in 1995.

Address: 8800 E Cana Island Rd, Baileys Harbor, WI 54202
Height: 89'
Opened: 1869
Closes at 5PM

Made in the USA
Monee, IL
18 November 2022

17988417R00225